Types of Love

Danila Pitts

Copyright © 2023 by Danila Pitts

All rights reserved.

No portion of this book may be reproduced in any form without written permission from the publisher or author, except as permitted by U.S. copyright law.

Contents

Prologue	1
Chapter 1	4
Chapter 2	10
Chapter 3	20
Chapter 4	30
Chapter 5	40
Chapter 6	50
Chapter 7	61
Chapter 8	70
Chapter 9	79
Chapter 10	91
Chapter 11	102
Chapter 12	112

Chapter 13	122
Chapter 14	134
Chapter 15	146
Chapter 16	158
Chapter 17	168
Chapter 18	176
Chapter 19	190
Chapter 20	201
Chapter 21	210
Chapter 22	217
Chapter 23	223
Chapter 24	227
Chapter 25	234
Chapter 26	241
Chapter 27	251
Chapter 28	262
Chapter 29	273
Chapter 30	284
Chapter 31	295
Chapter 32	303
Chapter 33	313

Chapter 34	324
Chapter 35	337
Chapter 36	347
Chapter 37	359
Epilogue	369

Prologue

That constant noise of construction irked me as a kid. Who would want to build a house this far out in the country anyway? When my momma and daddy told me that we're getting new neighbors I didn't believe them at first. But then the bulldozers came. Trees disappeared, concrete was laid, a house was being built.

I didn't know much about building houses but I knew that it was a long process. I couldn't stand the noise. I was thankful for softball practice in the evening time. That seemed to be the time when the noise kicked up to its loudest. "Momma I have a migraine." I said.

She stopped chopping vegetables and looked at me. "Chelsea, you're only eleven. How do you know you have a migraine?" She asked. I shrugged. "I don't know actually. I just know that those noisy bulldozers and construction workers are really loud." I told her. She chuckled. "Ok, sweet pea, go get ready for softball." She said. I bolted out of the kitchen up the stairs to my room.

Our house was pretty big. I know I'm only eleven but I can describe it really good. Our house is a modern country style two story house. It sits on many acres of land and has a long dirt driveway. I love it here. Oh and I also have a calf that I'm raising along with a husky. The husky's name is Beau and my calf's name is Lily. She's a sweet calf.

I pulled on my softball pants and shirt. I put my sneakers on and placed my cleats inside of my bat bag. I ran downstairs to meet my momma. We hopped into her pickup and we drove into town.

Six years later"Ugh, why did you have to move here of all places six years ago?!" I shouted at him. He just smirked like he always did. I rolled my eyes.

"Why? You must don't like me anymore or something? Because you say that every time. " He said. He says that every time.

"How can I still like you when you're always tormenting me in some way?" I asked. This boy would drive me up a wall someday. It all started with that stupid house that was built across the street six years ago. Yeah, they had their space. A long driveway with a house far back. But their son. Their son. This boy has gotten on my nerves since the first day he moved. I don't understand because their other boys don't do that. Just him. But it's always him.

"But you know what? That's ok. Once I graduate I'm leaving here. I'm getting out of here, away from you!" I yelled. His smirk fell.

Chapter 1

I stormed off after yelling at him. That was a week ago. Good thing graduation was in one week. That night drew the line. A guy I really liked broke things off after running into him at the baseball field. The him I'm referring to is Levi. One of the sons of the people who moved in six years ago. Levi was a pain ever since I met him. He was and still is obnoxious.

This was the third time this has happened to me. The one date was the longest relationship I had all thanks to Levi. Most guys break it off after an hour of exchanging numbers. I don't know what he says or does but this was the last straw. Levi gets on my nerves. Last year we both established that we really liked each other. That was no secret but somehow, Levi always found a way to make me angry. So around

Fall last year, I decided to get over him. I guess he didn't like that because every time I was able to catch a guy, he ran him off.

All the time we bicker and argue. He finds it funny while I find it time consuming. But then again, my feelings are still there. So recently, I've decided to rid myself of Levi Anderson for a while. And college was going to help that.

I showered then got ready for bed. I closed my eyes to try and get sleep. Fifteen minutes of no sleep later I heard handle of my balcony door opening.

I sat up and turned the light on. Levi walked in and sat in my beanbag chair. I sighed and turned my light off. "I don't want to be bothered by you." I said and closed my eyes. I heard him get up. His footsteps getting closer and closer. The light was turned on once again. "You just can't ignore me. You didn't mean what you said either." He said.

I opened my eyes and looked at him. "I actually did, Levi." I said.

"Maybe you should think about your decision before you do anything rash." He said.

"Levi, what am I going to stay around for? I got accepted in Florida on a sports scholarship and that's where in going. Sure I have one here but I'm going to Florida. The sooner I leave, the sooner I can get away from here." I said.

"When you say from here you mean from me." He said.

"I'm glad you can read between the lines." I told him. He sat on my bed and grabbed my hand. "What am I gonna do?" He asked softly. I held his hand and sighed. "I don't know. You'll live without me." I said. He leaned in and hugged me. Levi and I had these moments often, and that was when we weren't fighting. It was very rare. This wasn't the first time.

The next morning I got up for school. I guess Levi had let himself out. Or so I thought. As I was walking to my bathroom, I saw a movement in my bed. I tip toes over to the bed and slowly lifted the covers. Levi was under them sleeping peacefully. "Levi!" I screamed. He jumped and fell out of the bed. I laughed and he glared at me.

"What, Chelsea?"

"Why are you here? I thought you left?" I said. He shrugged. "I planned on staying here last night anyway." He said. I rolled my eyes and walked into the bathroom with my stuff. When I came out, Levi was getting dressed. "Ew, you could've walked into my closet and got dressed." I said. He looked at me.

"And you can go change." He said sternly. I rolled my eyes. "What I have on is perfectly fine." I said. I had on some skinny jeans that defined my butt more, a cute shirt, and converse. I skipped out on the boots today. "You're asking for it." He muttered. What?

"Are you working tonight?" He asked. I nodded as I put on a little mascara. "Ok good, I'm expecting a discount when I come with the team tonight." He said and I rolled my eyes. "I'll give a discount to Jake, but not you." I said. His jaw clenched. Jake was his best friend.

"Try it and see what happens." He said. I stepped closer and folded my arms. "Is that a threat?" I asked. He stepped closer and grabbed my waist. "You better believe it." He said to me. I rolled my eyes and backed away from him. "I don't like you." I said. He smirked. "I know, but I like you." He said and kissed my forehead. I wiped my forehead and scowled.

I grabbed my keys and proceeded downstairs to leave for school. He was hot on my heels. I hopped into my truck and I heard the passenger door open. "I don't want you riding with me." I said.

"Well, too bad babe because my truck is unavailable at the moment." He said. I rolled my eyes. "What happened to your truck this time?" I asked as I drove. "Lets just say that I ran into some trouble two nights ago." He said. I sighed. "And now you expect me to cover for you." I said.

"Sort of." He said. I tapped the steering wheel to the music. "Too bad I'm not going to." I said.

"Really? Come on, Chelsea. In my defense I was hurting." He said. I gave him the side eye. "Hurting? Who hurt you, Levi?" I asked.

"You, with your 'I gonna leave' nonsense." He said. I glanced at him and was staring out the window. "Well I am leaving but you shouldn't be upset about it." I said. When we got to school I parked and got out. Levi came and wrapped an arm around me. I rolled my eyes and he just smirked. He walked me to my locker and kissed my forehead. "Don't wipe it off." He said. I nodded and he turned to leave.

I reached my hand up and wiped it right off. Levi turned and jogged back to me. He trapped me between him and my locker. He leaned in and it seemed as if he was going to kiss my lips. He leaned in closer and kissed the corner of my lips. He looked me in the eye. "Now that one better not be wiped off." He said, kissed my forehead one more time and walked off.

Levi Anderson, the guy who could make me want to hurt him and kiss him at the same time.

Chapter 2

Levi Chelsea is something else. I just really hope that her wanting to leave is a phase. She means more to me than anything else. I looked down the hallway to find my friends. I saw them and caught up to them. "Levi!" Jake shouted.

"What's up Jake." I said as I neared him. Jake was a close friend. He was the first guy I met when I moved here. "So where we meeting up after the game?" He asked.

"Chelsea's job." I said. He nodded. "Ooh! She promised me a discount." He said. I shook my head. "That discount is going to me." I said.

He laughed. "So I assume that she is talking to you again." He said.

I shrugged. "It's complicated. But I went to her room last night and we kind of talked. I stayed the night too." I told him.

"What exactly did she say?" He asked.

"She wants leave." I said. He nodded. When Chelsea yelled at me that day I could tell she was hurting and that she meant what she said. I liked Chelsea more than a friend like she did me. We just weren't dating because I always find a way to mess it up. We've been this way for a year now. Now she wants to leave me.

I shoved the thought away and headed to class. After my classes I started towards the courtyard where I knew she was. But before I could get there I was stopped by Casey. She was the girl who got around quite a lot. She had a huge global crush on me but I didn't return the feelings. "Hey Levi." She said, pushing her chest on me.

"Casey, get off." I said. She only came closer.

"Why?" She asked. I sighed and tried to politely push her out of the way but she stayed put. She leaned in and hugged me. I was stuck because her arms were wrapped tightly around mine. The doors opened and Chelsea walked in with her friends. She saw me and scowled at the sight. She kept walking.

Later on that day after school was out I headed towards the parking lot to Chelsea's truck. I saw her from a distance as she made her way out of the school. She was on the phone with who I'm guessing was her cousin, Raleigh. She was talking and smiling. I walked up to her and placed my arm around her. "Ugh, Raleigh, I got to go. Satan just arrived." She said and hung up.

"Satan?" I asked.

"That's you." She said and removed my arm. She jogged to her truck and got out the keys. I ran to her side and grabbed her keys. "Let me drive today." I said.

"Sure but only because I'm tired." She said. I nodded and hopped in. -Chelsea"Yeah, Raleigh. All over him."

"Now you know that probably wasn't his doing. Casey is a titanic whore. Besides, Levi is in love with you."

"Raleigh! Language! And he isn't in love with me."

"Hey, I'm just saying the truth! And you love him too. I'm just waiting on that sweet day when you two finally get your acts together."

"What do you mean?"

"Levi drives you crazy and you're just plain crazy."

"Yeah, yeah ok Raleigh. Whatever you say, even though that doesn't make sense."

"Hey, just speaking truth here."

I spotted Levi as I almost made it to the parking lot. He came and put an arm around me.

"Ugh, Raleigh, I got to go. Satan just arrived." I told her and hung up my phone.

"Satan?" He asked. I responded then shrugged his arm off. Levi wanted to drive today so I let him. I needed to think anyway. After he came to me last night my thoughts have been jumbled up. I believe I'm ready to break things off with him but something is holding me back. On top of that, Casey was all over him today and that made me angry. Things like that get me thinking about how much I like Levi. So I called Raleigh.

Raleigh was my cousin. She and I were the same age. She was like my sister. She's mixed. Her dad is the mayor of the town and her mom is from California. Her dad is my dad's brother. We looked alike except for our hair and skin tone. Other than that, Raleigh was the sister I never had.

He drove to the school baseball field. He got out and grabbed his stuff and changed. Once he got back I got out. "Are you gonna stay for the first game?" He asked. I shrugged.

"I think I will. Jake is finally getting to play and I want to see my favorite baseball player play." I said. He smiled. "You wanna see me play." He said before making an awe sound. I rolled my eyes. "No I said Jake. Get over yourself." I said and pushed past him to go and find Jake. I saw him walking off from the field. "Jake!" I yelled and started running. He opened his arms for me.

I jumped into his arms. "Jake! I missed you bud!" I said. He laughed. "I missed you too, Chelsea." He said as he hugged me once again. "Ok, that's too much hugging." Levi said as he neared us. Jake laughed. "Don't worry about Satan." I said to Jake.

"Quit calling me that!" Levi said.

"Nope." I said popping the 'P'. I turned to Jake and he was chuckling. "So, Jake, what have you been doing?" I asked.

"The same thing as me." Levi interrupted.

"I'm sorry? The last I checked, Jake wasn't being a pain. Now was he, Satan?" I said. Levi grumbled something under his breath. I ignored it and turned to Jake. "Oh nothing, working out the arm. I'm so excited to play today." He said. I nodded.

"Well I'll make sure to at least watch an inning or two. I have to work tonight." I told him. He nodded with a smile then ran off. It was quiet for a minute. "I can feel you staring, Levi." I said.

"You didn't care for or seem concerned about me when I broke my arm." He said and stood by me. I looked up at him. Man was he tall. "You were being a jerk as usual. You know, Levi, I actually tried to be nice then." I said.

"How about now?" He asked. I shrugged.

"Nah, I'm good." I said.

"Yeah. Since we're a couple we don't have to be friends. We're more than that." He said and wrapped his arms around my waist. I slapped his hands and tried to remove them but he locked his grip. "You're mean." I said. He shrugged. "You say that all the time." He said.

"Levi, let me go." I said.

"No, not until you promise that we can talk tonight. Ooh, and I stay the night again." He said.

"No."

"Then I'm not moving a finger." Levi said and pulled me closer. We were having a stare down. To everyone else we may have seemed like a very cute couple, like they see us already, gazing into each other's eyes but it's the opposite. Someone snapped a picture and it was my friend, Joanna. She wanted us to get together and whenever she could, she'd snap a picture of us. Levi liked her best, of all my friends, just for that one reason.

"Send me that one." Levi said to Joanna. She held up a thumbs up and walked to the bleachers. I looked back to Levi. His face was serious. "So you really want to talk?" I asked.

"I want to talk."

"You serious?" I asked.

"Very." He stated.

"Are you sure you wanna talk?" I asked.

"Chelsea, we have things to discuss." He said. I sighed. "You can come and we'll talk but you sleep on the couch." I told him. His face went from a serious stare to a huge smile. He picked me up and twirled me. "Thanks, Chelsea Jane." He said and kissed my forehead.

"Just go." I said and pointed towards the dugout. He ran off with that smile never leaving his face. I walked up into the bleachers and spotted Joanna. I saw Levi's mom on the way in. "Hey, Chelsea." She said with a smile.

"Hey, Mrs. Brenda." I said.

"Levi is smiling very big. What did you agree to today?" She asked with a knowing smirk. "I agreed to talk with him. Oh and he invited himself to stay again too." I said. She nodded. Brenda knew of Levi's antics. Tonight was the last game and it was also senior night. The seniors from the baseball team were being announced and recognized for their work during the season.

My last softball game was tomorrow and it was also senior night too. "Oh before you go and find Joanna, could you help me carry Levi's other gift to him on the field?" She asked. I nodded. "Sure but if he asks, I did it for you." I said. She laughed. The senior recognition part started. Mrs. Brenda joined her son on the field along with her husband who just arrived. I grabbed the gift and when they called Levi's name I walked on the field.

I reached Levi and tapped his shoulder. He looked down at me and smiled when he saw the gift. He hugged me and kept a hold on me as he got the gift. I heard a huge obnoxious 'awe' come from the crowd. I looked and Joanna had her camera up taking a picture. I smiled for this one. After the senior recognition, I took his gift to the dugout and found his bat bag.

I walked down to the end and found his number. He was number seven. I know that he was coming because I couldn't miss the footsteps. When he reached me, I pulled his glove out and handed it to him. He kissed my cheek and I wiped it off. He kissed it again then I wiped it off once again. This process happened five times.

"Bye." I said. He grabbed my arm. "Where you going?" He asked. I looked at my phone's clock and I had to be at work in fifteen minutes. Well, I guess I wouldn't be able to watch the game. "Work." I said. He nodded. "I'll be there after the game then I'll go home with you." He said. I shrugged. "Ok bye." I said. He leaned in and kissed my cheek again. I just ignored it but gave him a glare. He just chuckled and said bye. I left and found Joanna.

"Hey Joanna if you want a ride to work you better scoot your boot because I'm about to leave." I said. She hopped up and we left.

Chapter 3

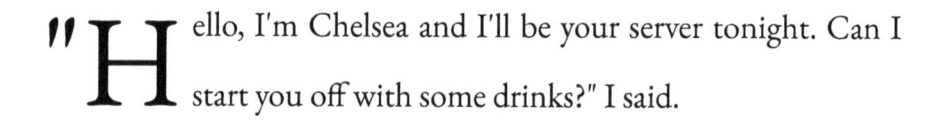

"Hello, I'm Chelsea and I'll be your server tonight. Can I start you off with some drinks?" I said.

"Uh, yeah. I want a Coke." The guy said.

"Water."

"Gatorade."

"Mountain Dew."

"Dr. Pepper."

"Sprite."

"Water."

The baseball team was here and I was stuck being their waitress. Levi wasn't here at the moment so I was grateful. "Just give me my usual, babe." A familiar voice whispered in my ear. I spoke too soon. I turned and Levi was standing behind me all covered in dirt from the game. I glared at him and went to get the drinks.

After balancing the drinks on the tray I walked to the table. "Ok we have two waters, a Sprite, Coke, Mountain Dew, Dr. Pepper, and a Gatorade." I said and set the drinks out. They all thanked me. "Where's mine, babe?" Levi asked.

"Don't call me that. And yours wouldn't fit on the tray." I told him. I left and went to fix Levi's drink. His favorite thing to do was to mix drinks. He liked his Mountain Dew mixed with Glacier Freeze Gatorade. Surprisingly it was really good. I went ahead and placed a straw in it so I wouldn't have to make two trips for the boy. I couldn't resist so I took a sip of the drink.

I walked to the table and set it down in front of Levi. He pulled my arm down so he could whisper in my ear. "I know you took a sip of my drink but anyway, I wanted to say that you look nice tonight." He said. I nodded and patted his head. "Thanks." I said and pulled out my notepad.

"Ok, anyone ready to order?" I asked. -After work, Levi came in my truck to pick me up. I walked out of the restaurant and I could hear the music blasting. That boy was gonna bust my speakers. He was playing a Florida Georgia Line song. It was my favorite too. Anything Goes was blasting. Levi knew this was my favorite.

I turned the radio down and he kept singing. Levi couldn't sing. He only sang around me though. "Levi, I'm hungry." I said.

"I know." He said and put the truck in gear. He pulled up to Wendy's. "You know me well." I said as we got out.

"I know." He said and placed an arm around me. We walked in and made our way to the counter. The cashier greeted us. He was cute. "What can I get you?" He asked while looking directly at me. I opened my mouth to talk but Levi beat me to it.

"I got this babe. She wants a number one with no mustard, onions, or pickles. And a large lemonade." He said. The guy looked at me. I nodded with a impressed smile on my face. After I received my food, we left.

"That was impressive, Levi. How long did it take for you to remember that?" I asked before feeding him a French fry. He shrugged.

"Four years." He said. I nodded. It was true, we knew each other well enough. "I want another fry." He said. I picked a fry and gave it to him. He caught my finger and held on to it between his teeth. "Ew, Levi! Let my finger go, I don't know where your mouth has been." I said.

"Oh babe, like you don't know where my mouth has been." He said.

"Probably all over Casey's." I muttered.

"Did you say something?" He asked. I shook my head. He pulled into the long dirt driveway. Levi parked in my spot. We hopped out and walked into my house. As soon as Levi opened the door Beau came running. He barked and ran straight to Levi. Levi started petting him and playing around with him.

"Levi, how many times do I have to tell you not to get Beau all riled up when you come?" My mom said as she came around the corner. "Sorry, Mrs. P." Levi said. She shook her head.

"Hey momma." I said.

"Hey, Chelsea. Did you get any good tips tonight?" She asked. I shrugged. "Only about fifty dollars worth. Tonight the restaurant wasn't filled like it usually is." I said. She nodded. After talking to her

I went to my room where Levi was already. I went into my bathroom and showered. After putting on some pajamas I went into my room.

I jumped on my bed and laid down. I sat right back up after remembering that I have a game tomorrow. I got up and walked to my closet. Levi watched me as I walked back and forth. "Are you gonna just stare at me all night or are we gonna talk?" I asked. He placed his chin in his hands.

"Don't leave." He said.

"What do you mean?" I asked.

"Chelsea come on. Graduation is next Thursday. College is coming soon and I know that you haven't chosen which scholarship you're gonna take." He said.

"So we're going back to this now?" I asked.

"Yes, we are. Chelsea, let's be honest. Do you really want to go to Florida?" He asked. I thought for a moment.

"You know, I actually thought that Florida was a way that I could get away from all of this." I said.

"You mean from me." He said. I stayed quiet. He sighed.

"Chelsea, I'm gonna be honest. I don't want you to leave. Heck, none of us around here want you to." He said.

"What do I have to stay for, Levi?" I asked. He stayed quiet. "Well?" I asked.

"Me, Chelsea. Stay for me." He said as he got up. He grabbed my hands. "I don't want you to leave. It would hurt so bad if you did. I like you Chelsea and I'd hate to see you leave before our relationship can flourish." He said. I looked up at him. I ran a hand through his hair and brought it down to his face. He naturally leaned into my touch.

"I've never seen this side of you before." I whispered. He touched my hand and a small smile formed. "You know that I honestly like you too." I said. His small smile grew bigger. "And?" He pressed.

"That's all." I said with a cheeky smile and backed away. He grabbed my waist. "Oh no, there's more." He said. I shook my head.

"You want the same thing as me." He said in a sing song voice. I stayed quiet but a small smile formed on my face. "Oh so you do." He said as he brought me closer. I put my head down. He pulled me closer. "Chelsea Jane." He said. I lifted my head and his lips caught mine. Levi was a dang good kisser. We pulled away because both of us couldn't breathe. That was our first kiss together. He rested his hands on my hips and lips hovered above mine. He pecked my lips.

I smiled and backed away. He chuckled and sat down on my bed. Did I mention what Levi looks like? No? Well here we go. Tall, tan, and handsome. Levi Anderson is a stud. He has that country accent and that country boy charm. His jaw is defined just as much as those muscles. Baseball player, he hunts, has the cutest dimples, and most of all, is the devil to me. But he's my devil.

I walked over to my closet to pull out my uniform. My jersey was hanging up so I grabbed it. I had two jerseys so I had to try it on to make sure it was the right one. During high school my body size varied. I pulled my shirt off and pulled the jersey on. I went to the mirror and looked. There was a seven on it.

This was Levi's jersey from tonight and it was clean, my mom must have washed it. His jersey stopped at my thighs since I was tall. But Levi was taller. "Levi why is your jersey in my closet?" I asked with my hands on my hips. I looked at him and he was laying on his back on my bed. I listened closely and that familiar little snore sounded. I chuckled.

I picked up a pillow from the couch and threw it at him. He jumped up. "What the- Oh hey!" He said when he saw me. My arms were crossed. "Whatcha doing?" He asked while scratching the back of his head.

"I'm trying to figure out why your jersey was in my closet." I said. He shrugged. "I don't know, but you look pretty cute in it." He said and held up his phone to take a picture. I frowned as he did. He looked at the picture. "Smile, Chelsea." He said. He held up the phone once again and I stuck my tongue out. He looked at it.

"Chelsea Jane."

"Levi Bradley."

"Stop being difficult." He said.

"Stop being difficult." I mimicked. He hopped up and grabbed me by the waist and spun around. I let out a little shriek as he did. He placed me in front of the mirror. He held the phone up and poked my sides. A huge grin broke out on my face as I laughed. He wrapped an arm around my waist and snapped it. He looked at it and showed me. "Better." He said and sat down. "Now to answer your question, your mom washed it so I brought it up here to put in your closet." He told me.

"Or you were too lazy to go home and put it up." I said.

"Yeah the second one was what really happened. Chelsea, you know me so well." He said with a smile.

"Well when you're around a person constantly for six years, you learn things about them." I said as I pulled the jersey off. "Whoa!" Levi shouted.

"What?!" I asked frantically.

"Them abs baby girl. Where did they come from?" He asked. I looked down. I had faint abs. You see, I'm not a 'skinny as a pole' chick. I'm curvy with a flat stomach that's all. But don't let the figure fool you, my love handles are somewhere in there. "Shut up, you scared me." I said as I found my right jersey. He laughed and winked. I checked to make sure the number five was there.

"You know, it still bothers me that you chose five over seven." He said.

"You had that number so I just had to choose a different one." I said as I put my old t shirt back on. "You didn't have to. We could've been number twins or something. It's the couple thing to do." He said. I rolled my eyes and hopped into my bed. He scooted close to me. "Levi move." I said and pushed him back over. Being his dramatic self, he rolled off the bed. I ignored it and turned my tv on.

Levi got back in the bed. I scrolled through the recordings list and clicked on Pixels. It was my favorite movie at the moment. I watched the movie until I fell asleep. Levi was already fast asleep. I laid on my pillow. All of a sudden Levi flipped over and faced me. His eyes opened.

"It's amazing how we know so much about each other." He said.

"Well, we were together most of the time."

"But you call me Satan." He said.

"Yeah, and that's my name for you most of the time."

"But my name is Levi." He said.

"I know." Sigh.

Chapter 4

I woke up the next morning and there was no one beside me. "Huh, I guess it was a dream." I said.

"What was a dream?" Levi asked when he came out of the bathroom. I jumped. "Good gosh, Levi. You scared me." I said. He chuckled. I got up. "Wait, did you kiss me last night?" I asked.

"Yep and you kissed back." He said with a smirk and I slowly nodded. "That's what I thought." I said.

"Did we even talk?" I asked.

"Yeah, we did." He said a little gruffly. I nodded. I got ready for school and grabbed my uniform. Levi took it from my hands and carried it to the truck for me. My mom was in the kitchen early this morning.

My dad was somewhere in the yard doing something. I smelled the sausage when I stepped into the kitchen. "Deer sausage?" I asked.

"Yeah, your dad just brought this from the smokehouse early this morning. He'll try to make it to the game this evening but he may be late because of some orders. Plus, Tony is coming to start today." She said. "I want you to ask Tony if he wants to come to my game." I said and she nodded.

Tony was a guy who was two years older than me. He works for my dad and someday, he'll be running one of the meat shops. My dad owned a meat shop and was slowly starting a franchise. There were five meat shops in the state right now and one was opening in another state. Levi came back into the house and kissed my mom's cheek. "Levi what did I tell you about kissing my wife?" My dad said as he came back in the house. We laughed. "I can't help it. She cooks great food." Levi said as he helped himself to some sausage.

After eating I gave Levi my keys and he started the drive to school. "Ready for your game?" He asked. I nodded. "It's unbelievable that today is my last game as a high school softball player." I said. He nodded. "It was fun but now we're playing for college teams, babe!" He said excitedly. Levi was gonna stay in the state and go to Mississippi

State to play baseball. He had a scholarship. I also had a scholarship there and one to Florida. (University of Florida)

Next Thursday, I had to reveal and call one of the coaches to let them know who I was going to play for so I could go and start training. It was a hard decision. I like Levi but I'm not sure if I still want to stay. We pulled up to school and Levi ran to my side and lifted me out of the truck. "Levi! You must be excited or happy about something this morning?! It must've been that deer sausage." I said.

He chuckled. "Oh, Chelsea Jane, I'm just excited, baby. School is almost over and my girlfriend is with me." He said and placed his hands on my waist.

"Levi." I said.

"What?" He asked.

"When did you ask me to become your girlfriend?" I asked.

"Um, you know? That didn't come up." He said while scratching his chin. "Mmhm, yeah. I'm going to class." I said.

"Wait, can I kiss you before you go?" He asked. I put my finger on my chin and thought. I leaned in and kissed the corner of his lips then ran. I made it to class then sat at the back.

At lunch I was sitting with Joanna in the courtyard. I told her all that happened last night. "So you still haven't made your decision?" She asked. I nodded and leaned on the tree.

"What?! But you told him about your feelings and everything! The decision should be easy, Chelsea!" She yelled. I put my hand over her mouth. "You want everyone to hear about my situation, don't you?" I asked. She smiled sheepishly. "Sorry, but still Chelsea. Is it not obvious?" She asked. I shrugged and looked as I saw Levi making his way to me. Joanna bumped me. "Ooh, there's your man!" She squealed. I rolled my eyes.

He had my keys in his hands, jingling them around. He handed them to me. "Why are you giving them to me?" I asked.

"So I won't be tempted to leave school. I promise some people are just plain annoying." He said as he sat beside me. He placed his arm around me. "Who?" I asked.

"Casey." He said and I rolled my eyes.

"What did she do this time?" I asked. He sighed and shifted. He laid his head in my lap and started to play a game on my phone. "The usual. She tried to push herself on me. The only girl I like is you and you know that. Then she tried to get defensive and threaten me but you know me, that didn't scare me. So I threatened her." He said. My eyes widened.

"You threatened her, Levi?" I asked. He nodded and waved his hand like it was not a big deal. The guy just threatened a person. Levi wasn't the nicest around school and everyone knew that. "What did you say?" I asked.

"Well, I said that if she didn't leave me alone that I'd snap her neck." He said. I sighed. "Can you at least try to be nicer? That was kind of mean don't you think?" I asked. He shrugged. The bell ringed, signaling us to go to class. Joanna hopped up and said bye to us. I didn't have anymore classes for the day. But Levi had an athletic period.

"Hey don't you have to go to baseball?" I asked. He shook his head. "Not me, my credits are finished. I really don't have to come to school but I come for you." He said.

"Today was my last day. I just had to come and take a few tests this morning." I said and he nodded. We got up and headed towards the truck. "Did you eat today?" He asked. I shook my head. "They ran out of French fries so I gave up." I said and he laughed. "I didn't eat either, wanna grab something?" He asked.

"Yeah let's go." I said and we started towards the truck. After eating, Levi started home. "Hey, Tony is coming to my game!" I said excitedly.

"Oh, yeah, he is." Levi said in a monotone voice. Levi didn't like Tony. It was only because Tony liked to flirt with me and I didn't mind. But Tony knew not to cross boundaries with Levi. Tony was one of the people who helped me realize my feelings with Levi. We pulled up to the house and I hopped out. I ran straight to the shed and cranked the four wheeler. I drove to the smokehouse. Tony's truck was parked outside.

I rushed into the smokehouse and spotted him. "Tony!" I shouted as he looked up. He opened his arms for me as I jumped in them. "Hey, Chelsea!" He said. We hugged for a really long time.

"How have you been?" I asked.

"Oh I've been doing good. I missed you." He said.

"I missed you too. Hey, are you coming to my game?" I asked.

"Why would I miss it?" He said and I smiled. We talked and caught up for the time being. "Where's Levi?" He asked.

"Right here." I heard Levi's voice. I turned and Levi was standing at the door. His arms were crossed and he looked mad. Him and Tony exchanged greetings then Levi turned to me. "Come on, we've gotta get you to the field, babe. Senior recognition starts in an hour and you know how long you take to get ready." He said. I looked at the clock and realized that he was right. I said bye to Tony and left with Levi.

It looked like he walked out here. I hopped onto the four wheeler and he made me move so he could drive. I held on tight to his torso. "So you still don't like Tony?" I asked. He said nothing but his jaw clenched.

"Tony has had a big ass crush on you since last year. No, I don't like him. He needs to learn boundaries." He said and pulled off. I looked at him shocked. "Don't become all protective when you just recently revealed your true feelings to me, Levi. You've been dancing around that subject for however long. And Tony is two years older than me. I have no romantic interest in him at all so I suggest you calm down." I said and hopped off.

I went and grabbed my uniform from the truck and changed. I was so mad at Levi right now. After angrily putting on my uniform and fixing my hair I left. All my anger I had towards Levi right now was channeled into my hair. I did a nice side braid and pulled the rest of my hair into a ponytail. The ponytail fell down my back. I pulled up to the field and hopped out.

After setting my stuff down in the dugout, I took a walk around the parking lot. There was forty minutes to spare before the senior recognition. A black truck pulled up and the guys that I thought that I wouldn't see until graduation hopped out. All five of them. "Chelsea!" They shouted. A huge smile broke out across my face as I ran to them.

I jumped and gave each of them a huge hug. "Hunter, Steven, Luke, Daniel, and Grayson?! What are you guys doing here, I thought you weren't coming until graduation?" I asked.

"We wanted to come see our favorite softball player play her last game." Grayson said. These were Levi's brothers. Hunter was the oldest, then Luke, Daniel, Steven, and Grayson was the baby. He was off at a camp during the last few weeks of school. They were all two years apart. These guys are just like brothers to me. "Y'all are so sweet." I said.

"It was the least we could do." Steven said.

"Yeah, and we get to see Levi too." Daniel said.

"Where is he?" Hunter asked. I rolled my eyes. They chuckled. "What did he do this time?" Grayson asked.

"I rather not talk about it. I'm trying to keep a positive attitude for this game." I said. "That bad, huh?" Luke asked. I nodded. He draped an arm over my shoulder and we all started walking towards the field. "Don't let him get to you." Luke said. I nodded. He walked me to the dugout. They all went and found seats.

I went to the infield and waited with the other seniors for the small program to start. Once my number and name was called, I stepped up and waved. I could hear the loud cheers from Anderson boys and my family. My mom and dad made their way to me with baskets. I hugged them and thanked them for the gifts. After the recognition the game started.

I ran to my spot in left field. The first batter decided to swing on the first pitch. Her ball went flying in between center and left field. "I got it!" I yelled as the ball landed in my glove. The crowd cheered as I threw the ball in and jogged back to my spot. One of the team members scored but that was about to change because our team's turn to bat came up.

I was fourth in the line up and the second batter was at bat now. After advances, I was on deck. I took a few swings. It was my turn to bat and the bases were loaded. I watched closely as the pitcher took her stance. She started and I watched as the ball flew out of her hand. I took the hardest swing ever at that ball. I heard the deafening crack of the impact and took off running. The other runners made their way home.

As I rounded to second I watched the ball fly over the fence. I couldn't help but leap out of joy as I sprinted home. I ran into the tunnel of teammates and hollered as they patted my helmet. The crowd was ecstatic. My last high school softball game was going pretty good if you ask me.

Chapter 5

After our victory, I posed for pictures with the team and individual teammates. I took pictures by myself and some with my family. Also with the Anderson boys. All except one. I headed to my truck and stopped when I saw a big basket and balloon sitting on the hood along with Levi. "Hey." He said.

"Hey." I said. He hopped down and gave me the basket. "Thank you." I said while looking straight at him. "You're welcome. I saw the grand slam." He said and held up the ball that was hit over the field. I smiled at the memory. "I know that you didn't come here only to give me the basket and show me the ball. What's going on Levi?" I asked. He sighed.

"I'm sorry about how I acted earlier." He said. This was the first time Levi apologized openly after doing something to make me upset. "Why are you doing this?" I asked. He looked at me. "Doing what?" He asked. I motioned around us. "This. The basket, the niceness, the apology." I said.

He sighed. "I'm trying, Chelsea. I'm really trying." He said. I just looked at him. "You don't get do you?" He snapped. I jumped back a little but my face stayed neutral. I guess I didn't answer him for a long time. "Get what, Levi?" I asked. He came closer and grabbed my hands. "I'm doing this for you. I want us to be something more." He said.

"Then do something about it." I said and turned to leave. I couldn't deal with this. Every time he told me something like this there was never any action behind it. I drove to the restaurant where the team was meeting. That night was fun. -Today was Wednesday and I hadn't heard from Levi ever since my game. He hasn't been to my house ever since. I see his truck around town so I know that he hasn't left town. Tomorrow I make my decision and decide the contract. It's either Mississippi or Florida. It was one o'clock in the morning. I know that

Levi was up right now so I decided to call him. If he answers and we talk about it, I'll stay but if he doesn't then I know where he stands.

I scrolled through my phone and clicked his name. The phone started to ring. I thought he picked up but instead the stupid voicemail person's voice filled my ears. I tried again and the same thing happened.

Well Levi. I know where you stand now.

I'm tired of waiting. I was waiting for him to make that move. When I said to do something about it, I meant it. For him and I to be together. But he didn't budge. I've always known Levi to be stubborn but not this stubborn. Clearly he didn't want to fight hard enough. But something in the back of my mind was telling me that he wasn't ignoring his phone.

I have no time to wait around for Levi Bradley Anderson. -"It was nice meeting with you." I said to the Florida head coach as I shook his hand.

"You too, Ms. Phillips." He said. I walked out of the office and made my way to my truck. The drive home was quiet except for the tune of the radio. I got home and changed into some comfortable clothes. My phone vibrated and I looked at the screen. Levi's face was there. I ignored it. The last thing I wanted to do was talk to him. He clearly didn't have time for me last night so why now.

It was a reality now. I was going to Florida. The days flew by quickly and before you knew it, I was standing in front of my bed in the dorm room.

My roommate was setting her stuff up since she had just got here. "So, Shaley, you're from where?" I asked.

"New York." She said. I looked her at her amused. "I've never been to New York before. There are plenty of good schools in New York, yet you choose to come here?" I asked.

"I have an academic scholarship here and it was a full ride so this was my choice." She said and I nodded. "I'm here on a sports scholarship." I told her.

"Softball?" She asked.

"How'd you know?" I asked.

"You seem like the softball type plus I saw the pictures." She said. Shaley was actually really pretty. She had long brown hair, green eyes, and was tall like me. She went and pointed to one in particular. "Boyfriend?" She asked.

"Nah. Complicated romance." I said. She was looking at a picture of Levi and I. It was the picture of me and him staring at each other. It was a gorgeous picture, I admit. The sun was setting just right and the light was hitting our faces perfectly. We both stare at each other intently.

She smiled. "Are y'all together?" She asked and I shook my head. We dropped the conversation and started to talk about something else. -Days went by. Then it became weeks, then months, and pretty soon I was leaving to see my family for thanksgiving. After waking up from a three hour nap I got ready to leave. I said bye to Shaley and left the dorm. I wanted to drive back to Mississippi. The scenery was simply beautiful. It was eight o'clock at night right now so I should get home around four o'clock in the morning.

I stopped by a gas station and gassed up my truck. After filling up I hit the road. There wasn't much to look at, considering it was nighttime and I was the only one driving. Night driving helps me think better. -Levi"Then do something about it." She said and left. I turned and walked to my truck. I finally got it out of the woods. I had hide it so I could make an excuse to ride with Chelsea. She was all I cared about now.

The next few days had been quite odd. I didn't stay at Chelsea's house or stop by to hangout. I was always busy and I never got to see her. It was Wednesday and my friend Jake texted me and asked if I was up for a party. I said sure and now I was getting ready. He picked me up and we left.

When we got there, people were everywhere. "Who's party is this?" I asked.

"Will's." He said. Oh great, just great. Will was Casey's brother and I'm pretty sure she was bouncing around here somewhere. I did not have time to deal with her tonight. After going and fixing myself a drink I stood along the wall. For some reason I kept checking my phone.

Three hours later I took a step and things went crazy. I spotted Jake and tried to walk to him but ended up staggering into someone. "Hey! Watch where you're- Levi?" The person asked.

"Yeeeepp. That is me." I mumbled. The person reached out to me and grabbed my hand. I tried to get a good look at the person and when I did, I saw three Casey's floating around. "Oh God, now there's three of you." I said and groaned. "Levi you're drunk." She said.

"Where's that pretty little girlfriend of yours?" She asked but I didn't miss the way she said girlfriend. It made me angry I may be drunk but that didn't matter right now. "Don't say it like that. Chelsea is the best thing that ever happened to me." I slurred. She rolled her eyes from what I can confirm.

"Well let me be the best thing that's ever happened to you." She said and pulled my lips to hers. It was disgusting. I felt my phone vibrate but I couldn't get out of Casey's hold to at least try and decipher who it was. The phone stopped vibrating but soon started again. After finally pushing her out of the way I started to leave. "Levi where are you going?" She asked.

"Leave me the hell alone, Casey! The girl I love is at home where I should be so stop trying!" I yelled. Everyone around us looked at us. I pushed through the crowd and soon two hands guided me to a truck. "I got you bud." The familiar sound of Jake's voice said before I blacked out. -The next morning I woke up with a killer headache. I looked around and saw that I was in someone else's room. Not mine or Chelsea's. "Where the hell am I?" I said.

Jake walked in with some pills and water. He threw them at me. "My house. And you have some explaining to do my friend." He said. I took the pills and laid back down. Soon, I was able to get up and go talk to Jake. "What happened last night?" I asked.

"Well, firstly. You were drunk off your ass. Casey kissed you. You yelled at her for kissing you. And finally, oh this is a good one. You shouted out that the girl you love is at home where you should be." He explained.

"So Casey actually kissed me?" I asked with a disgusted look on my face. "Beside the point, Levi. You love Chelsea don't you?" Jake asked.

I shrugged. "Man I don't know. I've liked her for a long time and every time I think about her my heart beat quickens and when I see her I just feel absolutely better even when I'm having the shittiest days. She makes everything better. Even if we aren't together." I said.

Jake sighed. "You love her don't you?" He asked. I nodded. "Very much and I didn't realize until now." I said.

"Well, before you go running to tell her, what was the last conversation you had with her?" He asked me. I thought back to her last game. I told him about it. "Then she told me to do something about it. After that she left in her truck. Just gone." I said and snapped my fingers.

"That was bait, my friend." He said.

"Bait? We're not talking about fishing Jake, we're talking about Chelsea." I said. He chuckled. "I know this, Levi. That was bait for you. She wanted exactly that so she told you to do something about it. Chelsea wants to be with you too. I'm sure of it. She's probably holding back on her feelings." He said.

I took in what he said. I thought about it for a while now. One week actually. I decided to get up and actually do something about it. I got dressed and drove over to Chelsea's house. I knocked on the door. No one came. I didn't even hear Beau's little pitter patter. I jogged around to Chelsea's balcony. I climbed the side and tried to open the door. It was locked.

I pulled out one of my pocket knives and opened the door. Chelsea's parents never got her an alarm for that door because I was always here. I walked into her room. It looked different. Most of her clothes were gone. Her suitcases were gone. Most of all, she was gone. I looked at her desk and saw something. It was a piece of paper. Like a pink sheet when you fill out stuff and get to keep a copy.

I picked it up and read it. It was the signing papers. I looked at the school logo and my stomach dropped. I sat on her bed. Boy did I mess it up big time. She left. She actually left.

Chapter 6

After hours and hours of driving I finally made it home. Using my house key, I opened the door. When I walked in Beau came bounding towards me. "Hey, Beau!" I whisper shouted. I grabbed my stuff and went to my room. My mom must've knew that I was gonna make around this time. The covers were pulled back. Without thinking twice, I hopped straight into my bed and let sleep overcome me.

When I woke up I looked at my phone and it read one in the afternoon. I eventually got up and got dressed. It was the day before thanksgiving so I know my momma was gonna go shop. I showered and put on some light wash skinny jeans, a shirt from my college, and some converse. My hair was already straightened so I combed it out and placed a cap on my head. It was a gators cap that matched my shirt.

I walked downstairs to find something to eat. When I walked into the kitchen I saw my mom, grandma, Mrs. Brenda, and Levi's grandmother sitting there looking at newspapers. They all looked up and smiled at me. "About time you woke up." My momma said. I went around and hugged everybody.

"Look at you! You look good, Chelsea." Mrs. Brenda said. I smiled and thanked her. After I found an apple to snack on, we left and went to the grocery store. -Levi The drive from Starkville wasn't so bad. Whenever I did wake up, it was around noon. I showered and threw on a pair of jeans and a t shirt with my boots. I walked downstairs only to be greeted by my dad, grandpa, brothers, Mr. Phillips, and Chelsea's grandfather. "Boy, I was just about to come wake you up." My dad said. I shrugged and grabbed some water. We all left and went to get supplies for tomorrow.

I know you're wondering what I did once I went to college. Well, after finding out that Chelsea and her parents drove to Florida that day, I sulked. I let the girl I love get away and I'm pretty sure she was probable pissed off at me. She always was but this time I'm sure it was major so I didn't call.

I picked myself back up and got ready for college. After my parents dropped me off, I had to start over. I met my new roommate, Josh. I made sure my stuff for baseball was done. I did stuff to keep me busy. I worked out many days so I can gladly say I'm more buff. The one thing that was missing was my girl. I started over everywhere else but in the romance department. Call me crazy but I'm stuck on her.

There were girls but they weren't her. I wanted her. I wanted someone who I could argue with then turn around and be completely fine in the next minute. Sure, Chelsea and I argued but after the argument, sooner or later she was by my side. That's why I love her.

After we set up the tables in the field, I had to take the turkey to the Phillips' house. We all had conjoined Christmas' and Thanksgivings every year. I hopped into my truck and drove over there with the turkey. I walked in through the kitchen door and was instantly greeted by everyone. I hugged them all and set the turkey down on the table.

They all went outside to take a walk before they would start cooking. I heard footsteps come down the stairs. I looked and Chelsea came. She was wearing skinny jeans that gave me wondering eyes, converse, and a t shirt. I looked at the t shirt and it was her college t shirt. My body stiffened. She was staring at me just like I was staring at her.

A hint of anger flashed in her eyes when she finally looked me in the eye. "Hello, Levi." She said, her voice hard and strong.

"Hey Chelsea, long time no see." I said. -ChelseaLook at him just sitting there all handsome and stuff. Then he says long time no see? Clearly. Quit the freaking casualties Levi! Where the hell have you been?!

"Sure has." I replied. He sighed and looked at me. "We both know that we need to talk." He says. Ok, that's a given seeing that the last time I saw you was a couple of months ago. "Clearly." I said.

"Ok, let's talk." He said. I motioned for him to follow. We went up to my room. He sat in my beanbag chair and I just crossed my legs on my bed. I have no idea where to start. "I have no idea where to start." He said. Thanks for voicing my thoughts Levi. I shrugged. "How about this? Where'd you go after that night?" I asked.

"Well I really didn't go anywhere. But I did nothing although I was busy for the following week." He said. I nodded. "I called you the night before the signing." I told him.

"About that. That night I was busy." He said.

"Yeah, busy enough not to answer me or call back. What were you doing, if you don't mind me asking." I said. He sighed. "If I tell you, you'll be even more mad than you are right now." He said.

"This is probably true but I'm a big girl Levi. Tell me and we can probably soon fix this." I said. He sighed and before he could say anything I saw the guilty look on his face. "That night I went to a party, got drunk, and kissed Casey. She had a tight hold on me so I couldn't reach my phone when I felt it vibrating." He said.

"Well you're right. I'm just a tad bit angrier than I was a second ago but it's fine. You're with Casey now, right?" I asked. He looked at me like I was crazy. Ok maybe I shouldn't have said that.

"No! Not at all. In fact I told her off." He said. I just nodded. "Well, since you shared some information with me do you wanna know some for yourself?" I asked.

"I um- yeah." He said. I nodded with a sad small smile.

"I called that night and I told myself, talk to him. If we would've talked that night and solved our now even messier mess, I would've stayed and went to MSU with you. Honestly. We could've been together right now. But that was thrown away. Thank you Casey!" I shouted.

I continued. "I was gonna call once but instead I called twice. I don't know, I had some sort of faith in you. But that just went down the drain." I said.

"So you're saying it's my fault." He said.

"No. We both can take the blame but what I'm saying is, maybe it wasn't meant to be. Maybe we were trying to make something that couldn't work happen." I said. I hadn't realized that I was crying until I felt the tear hit my hand. I wiped it and was thankful that I didn't wear makeup.

"You wanted to talk, so we did. But let me say this. I'm sorry for everything I did wrong. Maybe if I wouldn't have been so stubborn we'd be together." I said and grabbed my keys. I reached inside my closet and grabbed my bat. I hopped in my truck and sped off. I pulled up to the batting cages and grabbed my bat. There was a bucket of softballs in the bed of my truck. I grabbed that and a tee from the storage closet. After setting up the ball on the tee I took a few practice swings.

Whenever I was angry I'd come here and hit a few balls. It made my hitting better so I guess I had Levi to thank for that. Today I wasn't angry. I felt at peace with myself. Maybe walking away from Levi was the best thing. I put my headphones in and started hitting.-LeviShe grabbed her bat and left. I knew exactly where she was going. She was going to the batting cages, the question is which one. I knew Chelsea more than anybody. Our conversation wasn't finished and I hoped she knew that. It was just over for the time being. I got up and walked out of the house. After I got home I walked up to my room and laid down.

"Wake up, Levi!" Someone shouted. I slowly opened my eyes and saw all of my brothers with angry expression glaring at me. "What?" I asked.

"Where's Chelsea?" Hunter asked. I shrugged. "That's last time I saw her was when we talked at her house." I said.

"Well she's been gone for too long and we're all worried about her. She's probably somewhere crying over what you two talked about." Steven said. I just sat there.

"I swear, Levi, if she's hurt I'm gonna beat your ass." Luke said angrily. They all looked pretty angry. "I know where she is." I said.

"Where is she then?!" Grayson yelled.

"The batting cages. We will have to find out which one she went to." I said while running a hand through my hair. "Well quit being lazy and get so we can find her, you asshole!" Daniel said. I got up and grabbed my keys. We all split up and started the search. My stomach dropped as I thought about the negative outcomes of the situation. I really hoped Chelsea was ok.-Chelsea "Chelsea! Wake up!" I heard someone shout. I slowly opened my eyes and saw Luke outside my window. I guess I had fell asleep. I opened my door. "Luke?" I asked. He pulled me out and hugged me. "Oh thank God. We were looking all over for you. Have you been here the whole time?" He asked and I nodded.

"Why?" He asked me.

"I came to blow off some steam and think. Where's your idiot of a younger brother, Levi?" I asked. His facial expression turned to an angry one. "Looking for you. Wanna tell me what happened?" He asked. I shrugged.

"Hop in. I'll tell you everything." I said and got back in my truck. He got in and I started my story. After my story I couldn't tell if Luke was angry or sad. "So what are you gonna do now?" He asked. I shrugged.

"There's nothing for me to do. I realize that all we do is hurt each other. That's not good for either of us. I'll just go back to school and start my career like I want." I said. He nodded. "I can't tell you what to do with your life, Chelsea. You're eighteen. You're old enough to make your own decisions but please promise me that you'll make the right decision, ok?" He said. I nodded and leaned over to hug him.

"You know, Luke, I care deeply for Levi." I said. He looked at me. "You love him, don't you?" He asked. I just looked away. "I care for him deeply." I said. He chuckled.

"If that's your way to say that you love him then, ok." He said. I turned to look at him. "Is it safe to say that I'm scared?" I asked. He sighed. "If you're scared, it's ok. People get scared. Just don't let him slip away in the long run." He said. I nodded.

After talking for a bit, we decided to head home. I pulled up into my driveway and hopped out. I walked into the kitchen and was instantly bombarded with hugs and questions on my whereabouts. "Y'all calm down, I was at the batting cages." I said and went up to my room. The next day, I got dressed and was ready to start a new slate.

I pulled on my boot cut jeans, a nice maroon top, and my boots. I curled my hair slightly and put on some earrings. I went downstairs and waited with everyone else for the food to be done. Suddenly I felt the urge to go and visit Lily, my cow. She's gotten big over the years. I walked out to her pen. "Hey, girl." I said and got a moo in response.

I stayed there for about an hour just petting her. I heard a bark and saw Beau running towards me. "Hey, boy!" I said and rubbed behind his ears. Later I went back and we all had dinner. After dinner I went with the Anderson boys to their barn. Levi didn't go. But I wasn't worried. That thanksgiving was nice but I know that deep down it could've been a thousand times better. -"You're back!" Shaley exclaimed. I ran and hugged her.

"Yeah, I'm back." I said more to myself than her.

Chapter 7

"Alright pick up the pace, guys!" I yelled. I fixed my outfit. I had on a pair of sweatpants, a San Fransisco shirt, and a hat along with my tennis shoes. As the team made their way to me I checked the clock. Almost five, I'm doing good. "Ok, we're gonna do a couple of drills then head to the house." I told them as they sipped on some water. "Chelsea, you're doing good today." Mike, one of the other trainers told me. I nodded and thanked him.

I have been working here for three months and the staff already respects me. I work for a training agency who sent me to San Fransisco to be their trainer. I train baseball players, if you're wondering. Well, for any sport. That means I am with them for every practice, home, and away game. It's a lot of work but it's only me so my schedule is flexible. A twenty two year old athletic trainer, wow.

"Alright, let's hit it!" I yelled. The guys came and got ready for the last few drills. I got out the cones and started to measure with the tape measurer for a perfect square. At the starting cone, an individual player would have to sprint to the top cone, shuffle to the right, back peddle, shuffle to the left, then sprint past me in under twelve seconds. It was a simple drill but they'd just have to get through it pretty quickly. I was here to assist with their practices and assess their physical ability.

After they finished that up, I set the cones up for a T run. "Ok, this is the last one and my favorite, the T run!" I shouted. After setting up the cones, they ran through it. "Bring it in, guys!" I yelled and waited while they made a circle around me. I looked down at my clipboard and read over the results for today.

"Ok, you guys did pretty good. Everyone made it through everything just fine so good job on that. We do not meet tomorrow, the rookies do. So go home and get your rest." I said. They all nodded and mumbled agreements.

"Ok, any questions?" I asked.

"Yeah, what are you doing tonight?!" One of the player shouted and the others agreed. I rolled my eyes. "I'm going home after rookie practice." I said.

"Well, what about tomorrow?" They asked. I rolled my eyes again. "If you mind your own biscuits, life will be just like gravy." I told them. They all laughed. "You and that southern accent, Chelsea. We keep forgetting you're from Mississippi." One of the players said. I chuckled and dismissed the players.

It was five on the dot and I was going to head out and get a little something to eat. "See you seven, Mike!" I called out as I grabbed my bag. He waved and I walked out to the parking lot. I hopped into my truck and drove to a Panera Bread restaurant. I took my food and drove back to the field. It was five thirty now so I had plenty of time to eat and stretch to get ready for the rookies.

After eating, I sat around for a good thirty minutes. I got up and took a lap around the field. Once I made my lap, I grabbed my clipboard to look at the list of rookies. I flipped through the pages and one pitcher caught my eye. Levi Anderson. Never thought I'd hear from him again.

I grabbed a bat and went to the onsite cages. I saw a bucket of softballs and a tee. I wasn't mad, I was just stretching out my body. After a few hits, I checked the clock. It was 6:58, I was right on time. Everyone should be here and ready to start. It didn't take me long to make it back to field to meet the players. When I arrived, Mike was talking to them.

Everyone turned to me as I walked in. I had Mike's bat on my shoulder as I walked. After he finished talking to them, he turned and jogged to me. "Stole my bat again, I see." He said. I smirked. "Yeah, thanks for letting me use it." I said and he smiled. Mike was my best friend here. We did our handshake and he let me go start with the rookies.

As I walked towards the group, they all stopped talking and brought their attention to me. "Ok, so I'm guessing everyone is here?" I asked. They all murmured an agreement. I nodded and looked down at my clipboard. "Before we get started, I'm gonna let you know something," I said while looking them each in the eye.

"I do not care if you're here or not. If you don't show up, that's you and it's not my problem. I'm here to help you get ready for the season and am here to assist during the season like your coach asked. Tend to you and your progress and nobody else's. As I always say, mind your biscuits and life will be just like gravy." I told them. I actually heard the southern twang at the end there. They chuckled.

I smiled. "So who's ready?" I asked. They all nodded and spread out so we can stretch. Mike helped me demonstrate the stretches we would do before each session. After stretching it was time for a lap. "Alright, let's take a trip." I said and started to jog. It didn't take long for them to start following me. I led them through the whole stadium. When we started, I separated them into two groups.

"Alright, field positions to my right and pitchers to my left!" I called out. They separated and I started with the field positions. Mike handled the pitchers. "Ok, so let me introduce myself. I'm Chelsea Phillips and I'm your official head trainer." I said with a smile. They smiled back. "Ok so everyone won't talk at once, say 'Hey Chelsea'." I told them.

"Hey Chelsea." They all said. I smiled. "Ok, let's get this thing started." I said. I brought them to some stations I set up for them. They all tested their shuffling skills and their catching skills. I broke them into four groups. "Ok, so when I come to your group, you'll be timed.

But until then, just play around with it to get the feel." I said. They all nodded then went to their stations.

I sat back and watched as they tested out the stations. I took notes on their trial performances. After fifteen minutes I got up and made my way to the first station. I visited each station three times. I then traded groups with Mike. I did the same thing I did with the field position players. It was a little weird because Levi was there but I didn't show any emotion.

After I finished up with the pitchers we all went to the cages. I grabbed Mike's bat and started the introduction of this portion. "Welcome to the cages, gentlemen. In here, you will swing off the tee, hit off a live pitcher, and do specialty swings." I told them. I demonstrated the specialty swing to each of them.

They would do their regular stance swing and the karaoke swing twice. I divided them up into groups and put them each with a trainer. I took my group to the live pitching part. I had a veteran pitcher with me. Each batter got in and I would demonstrate how I felt they should stand. I'd either adjust them or take the bat completely and kick them out of the box to show them. They'd simply chuckle when I did it but understood what I told them.

"Ok, I'm going to the next cage." I told the veteran pitcher. He nodded an continued with the throws. I took my group to the tee section. Here they would hit off the tee then do the karaoke swings too. I grabbed the bat and showed them my regular swing. They practically pushed me to hit. I took a few practice swings and got ready. I stepped in the box and took my swing. The ball flew off the tee and hit the net powerfully.

They clapped as I got ready to show them the karaoke swing. I took my steps and swung. I looked back at them and smiled. "Who's ready to swing?" I asked then started. My group did pretty good. I took all the players back to the field. "Ok, guys, today was pretty good. Tomorrow, we meet in the weight room to build muscle. Please don't be late. On your way out, pick up a schedule." I said.

I motioned to Mike. He had the guys stretch out again and run a lap. He came over to me and sat with me on the bench. "Hey, bestie." He said and draped an arm around me. I hugged him back and went back to my clipboard. "Hey, Mike." I said.

"Hey, how were your groups today?" I asked. He sighed. "Pretty good. Although, you had an admirer. Uh, number seven. Levi Anderson kept looking at you." He said. I rolled my eyes. "Wait, don't tell me. He's that Levi Anderson." He said. I nodded. "Man, this season is gonna be an interesting one." He said.

"Yeah, pretty interesting." I said and he laughed. We got up to meet the team after their jog. "Ok, good job guys and I'll see you tomorrow." I told them. I turned and walked towards the trainers lockers. I walked in and grabbed my backpack. I threw it on my back and walked out while grabbing my keys. I left with some of the players. Even though I was taller than most people, these guys were tall.

As I was walking out the door, I was pulled into an empty hallway. I looked up and saw Levi. "Hello, rookie." I said.

"Hey, trainer." He replied. I folded my arms and looked up at him. "Any reason why you pulled me over here?" I asked. "Long time no see, Chelsea Jane." He said. I nodded.

"That is true," I said, "How's the girlfriend?" I asked.

"I wouldn't know. We broke up a year ago." He said.

"What do you really want, Levi?" I asked.

"To talk. For real this time. None of that running out mess. A real conversation." He said. I shrugged. "I'll think about that after training camp is over. Meanwhile, you should be heading home. Tomorrow won't be as easy as today." I said with a smirk then left.

"Wow." I said to myself once I got in the truck. This boost in confidence hit me unexpectedly. I think I like it.

Chapter 8

Levi Wow she changed. I couldn't help but look at her during the camp. So here I am, a rookie in the MLB. I felt proud of myself. And of all people, Chelsea is my head trainer. I still love her and I'm not gonna let her slip through my fingers. That girl is just so dang stubborn. Over the last years, things have went downhill for us.

After that thanksgiving of freshman year in college, we kept a distance from each other. Sophomore year we became friends. Junior year we fell apart, and I got a girlfriend. She was different but I didn't like it. She wasn't Chelsea. Rachel was very picky and annoying. That relationship made me realize how much I still loved Chelsea. I broke things off with the girl. Senior year was my highlight year.

Chelsea and I drifted apart again but my feelings still remained. I was drafted after graduation and now here I am. I looked as Chelsea walked in. She had a bat on her shoulder and she looked absolutely amazing. I knew she wanted to make it big but an athletic trainer for the MLB was just over the top amazing. I watched as she interacted with the guy who just spoke to us about her.

His name was Mike. Apparently they knew each other well because they did a handshake. I wasn't worried because he had a friendly vibe from him. After they spoke she came and greeted us. Her voice like silk as she talked. When she finished Mike came and showed us the stretches we'd do before and after every practice. We stretched with him and Chelsea. She got up and had us jog or "take a trip" as she says, with her.

She then split us into groups. This whole day I never got to talk to her but I did after practice though. We didn't do much talking like I wanted. She told me that she'd think about it after training camp. Training camp was only one week before they put us with the veterans. I got in my truck and headed to my condo. No need for a house when it's only me there. Hopefully that'll change soon.
-ChelseaI walked into my two bed apartment and headed towards

the shower. After showering I pulled on a pair of comfortable sweats and an old softball t shirt. I looked down at the sweats I had on and noticed some certain lettering. The words MHS Baseball on the leg. "Really." I said out loud. These were Levi's pants. Of all people, these were his pants that I had on.

My buzzer rang and I went to answer it. I looked on the screen and saw him. "Levi what do you want?" I asked.

"Let me in." He said.

"No." I said.

"I have food." He bribed. Buzzzzzzzzzzz

What? The guy had food. How can I turn that down? I heard a knock on the door and opened it. Levi stood there in sweats and a hoodie looking scrumptious. Chelsea! Right, sorry, bad thoughts. I let him in. "So is there a reason why you show up to my apartment with food right now?" I ask.

"Well, I figured that you'd be hungry. Which you always are and that we should catch up." He said. I gave him a 'really' look. He chuckled. "Yeah." He said and handed me a bag from Wendy's. -"This is unprofessional of us." I said as I sipped on my lemonade. Levi looked over at me while he scrolled through channels on my tv. "Definitely." He said.

"So what was that about catching up?" I asked. He sat up. "Oh! Yeah, I wanted to catch up with you seeing that the last time we really talked was almost four years ago. That's way too long in my book." He said. I nodded, remembering that day. It was horrible but let's not dwell on the past. "Ok, so start." I said and sat back. "Ladies first." Levi said with that annoying smirk of his. I rolled my eyes.

"Well, after graduation last year, I went into training with the agency I'm with now. After working for about seven months with them, I was transferred to a MLB team. Your team. I've been their official head trainer for about three months and have been working with them ever since. Tomorrow marks ten months for me becoming an official athletic trainer." I said and he nodded.

"Any romance?" He asked.

"Let's not talk about that." I said and looked the other way. I don't think he'd want to know about that. Not like there was any romance. I never found anyone worth keeping.

"Well I guess it's my turn." He said. I nodded and turned towards him.

"Well after my graduation last year, I went on the job hunt but also signed up for the draft. I had no idea that is get drafted but it was amazing when I found out I did. So after finding out what team I was gonna get signed to, the journey began." He said. His story was short but it made me smile. "Hey, remember when we were twelve and thirteen? You kept saying,'one day in gonna be playing in the major leagues. And you're gonna be with me!'." I said. He smiled.

"Yeah, it was my dream." He said. I smiled. "I guess you can say that your dream has come true, huh?" I asked. He nodded. "Alright, go home Anderson." I said and shooed him off my couch. "What?! But I brought you food!" He argued.

I shook my head. "You have an early day tomorrow and need your rest." I said. He groaned. "Hey, don't be like that. I'm telling you, as your head trainer, go home and get some sleep." I said as I tried to push him towards the door. He stopped and dropped his weight. "Good gosh, Levi! What have you been eating?" I asked, out of breath from pushing him.

He finally sat up and I almost fell over until he caught me in his arms. "Thanks." I said and stood up completely. I'm pretty sure I felt sparks but then again, I'm pretty sure I want to ignore them. He just stared at me. I gave him a small smile and pointed to the door. He smiled and left. After tonight, one question was on my mind. "How in the world did Levi Anderson get my address?"-"Let's take a trip!" I yelled and started the jog. I took the rookies through the usual jog. Today I was gonna set up for fungo for the field positions. I had a trainer situated towards each direction. They'd each hit a ball to them. It could be a long or short distance ball. It could even be a popup or grounder. The goal was for it to be unpredictable.

I was gonna watch the pitchers and create notes on them. This was only the first part and that went by pretty quickly. Now we were all walking towards the weight room. I had my backpack strapped on my back and my clipboard in hand. Right now, I was texting the head coach and letting him know about the process.

Once we got to the weight room, I gave them a small water break. During the break, Mike wanted to see how much I could benchpress. "Come on. Let's see how much this country girl and bench." He joked. I rolled my eyes. "Come on Mike." I said and sat on the bench.

He placed the weights on and it made a hundred. That was my mark freshman year in high school. I moved up one fifty each year and about twenty five a year in college. So that was about six hundred fifty but I never wanted to over do it. I took a deep breath and lifted the bar. I did twenty reps and placed it back on the hooks. Mike placed more weight and I lifted it too. Barely.

By the time we were finished playing around, the guys were ready to start. They were all so quiet, considering that they were watching me benchpress. I laughed to myself at the thought. "Ok, so three rounds of bench pressing, three rounds of hand weights, two rounds of sit ups, the step up workout, and then meet me outside to push the sled. After that, we can get ready to go to the house!" I said excitedly.

We got started. Slowly, each player made their way to me outside for the sled. It was a football sled where I could stand on it. I stood on it and timed how long it would take to make it to the yellow line. After going through each player, we stretched everything back out and jogged a lap.

The next few months went pretty good. The coaches were giving us time to go home before the season. It was that time now. I hopped in my truck and headed home for some rest. Tomorrow I have to catch a flight back to Mississippi. -The next morning I woke up early and showered. I dressed up really cute, considering that I only wear sweats, a t shirt, and hat everyday. I put on a pair of cute dark boot cut jeans, a nice loose feminine button up shirt, and left my hair down. There was a rodeo going on in Jackson and I wanted to stop by it. I locked up my apartment and caught a cab to the airport. I was going to rent a vehicle while I was down there.

I waited for my flight to be called. Once it was called I grabbed my stuff and headed to board the plane. I found my seat and sat down after storing my carry on. Once I sat back I put my headphones in and started up my music. I felt someone's presence beside me. I looked and instantly dreaded looking. Sitting beside me smirking his butt off was Levi.

"Ugh, what are you doing here?" I asked.

"Have you forgotten that we're from the same state, town, and community?" He asked with amusement. I sighed. "I did but I didn't expect you to be on this flight with me, let alone the same seat." I said.

"Let me guess. You wanted to leave earlier than me." He said. I nodded. "Well, I guess you're too late for that." He said with a smirk.

This was gonna be a long flight. I sat back and closed my eyes for the time being.

Chapter 9

"Chels...Chelsea wake up." I heard someone as they shook my shoulder.

"Chelsea Jane." The person said.

"That voice sounds so familiar." I mumbled. They chuckled. "It's Levi, babe. Wake up." He said. I opened an eye and for sure it was Levi. I stretched and stood up to grab my stuff.

After grabbing my things and collecting my luggage I walked over to the car rental place. I noticed Levi following me. I stopped and turned around to meet him. "Any reason you're following me?" I asked.

"Well, when I was booking my flight, there was one thing I forgot to do." He said. I rolled my eyes. "You forgot to rent a car or set up a ride." I said. He nodded and looked away embarrassed. I groaned.

Typical Levi. "I guess you can ride with me." I said. After all, we are going to the same place.

I rented the newest Camaro. It cost a pretty penny for a week. The desk attendant gave me my keys and I hurried towards the car. I opened the trunk and Levi placed our things inside. We got in and I started towards the Coliseum. "Rodeo today?" He asked. I nodded and pulled onto I-55.

I pulled up to the rodeo and hopped out. I gave the keys to Levi so I wouldn't lose them. Levi walked a little ahead of me. I studied what he had on. He was wearing a pair of jeans, his favorite boots, and a black button up shirt rolled to his elbows. In a way we matched. I must say, he was looking good. "Hey, I didn't notice your hat until now." I said as I walked up next to him.

He looked down to me and smiled. "Well I wouldn't come home without my Stetson." He said and I smiled. His cowboy hat fit him well. I had one but it was ruined at a rodeo a couple of years back. I was watching a bull ride when my hat flew off and was stomped on all over by the bull. The rider picked it up and took it with him. After the show, I went down to the pens to get it and when I got there, somebody's cattle had pooped all over it and it was getting chewed by a goat.

We walked up to the box and paid for some tickets. There were so many people here. Levi wrapped an arm around my waist and pulled me closer. "Don't wanting you getting lost, Chelsea Jane." He whispered in my ear making me shiver. I felt a tingly feeling with him this close but I ignored it. But Levi and I were friends, right? I'm not even sure if we were acquaintances at the moment. Was this even real?

The rodeo didn't start until another hour so we walked around a bit. Levi's arm was around me and we just walked through the vendor areas. I saw a hat company. They were making specialty hats. I looked over there and it made me miss my hat. I patted my head absentmindedly. Levi looked down to me and smiled. He pulled me to the table.

"One hat for this little lady right here." He told the man. The guy looked at me and placed a hat on my head. "This would be perfect." He said. He took the hat and started to crease it. I looked up to Levi surprised. He just put his finger to his lips and shushed me. I frowned. Well I'll pay for it, I thought. When the hat was finished, Levi handed the man a credit card.

Once again I looked up to him and he shushed me again. I frowned once again. The man placed the hat on my head. "There you are, sweetheart. I put designs in to match your boyfriend's hat." He said with a bright smile. I smiled at him.

"Thank you sir." I said. He just smiled at me. Levi grabbed my hand and pulled me along to look at some shirts and accessories. I stopped Levi. "Levi." I said. He looked at me. "Chelsea." He said in a mocking manner. I glared.

"How much was that hat? Why did you buy me this hat? I love it but I could've bought it." I said. He sighed. "I know, but I wanted to buy you a hat. Remember what happened to your old one?" He asked with a small laugh. I nodded. "Yeah but how can I repay you for the hat?" I asked. He thought for a minute.

"A date." He said. I looked at him wide eyed. "A what?" I asked.

"A date?" I asked. He nodded and came closer.

"Chelsea, we may go through this over and over but I'm not over you. Give me another chance. That's all I'm asking for." He said while looking me in the eye. I bit my lip and looked at the ground. A chance. "Levi-"

"Just trust me this time." He said. I've always trusted you. I sighed. "So I guess we're gonna go on that date soon huh?" I asked. I guess I wasn't over him myself either. He grinned and hugged me. My feet were dangling off the ground. I laughed as he spun me around. He came closer. "I promise you that you won't regret this." He whispered in my ear. The ladies at the table giggled as they watched us interact. I spotted a necklace. It reminded me of the one Levi threw in the river when we were kids. I laughed at the memory.

I grabbed it and snuck off to the register. "Hello, dear will this be all?" The lady asked. I smiled. "Yes ma'am." I told her. She rung me up and I paid for it.

"Sweetie, this necklace comes with a free engraving. Any name or quote you wanna put on it?" She asked. I looked back to make sure Levi didn't notice me. He was too busy looking at some shirts. I turned back to the lady. "Let's put his name on it. His name is Levi. L-E-V-I." I told her and she smiled. I went with her to the engraving station. She finished up and gave it to me.

"Thank you." I said. She smiled. "Oh you're welcome, sweetie. I'm sure your boyfriend with love it." She said. What's with everyone calling Levi my boyfriend? I nodded and went to Levi. I tapped his shoulder and he turned around. "Ready?" He asked. I nodded. "Yeah, let's go get a seat." I said. He nodded and grabbed my hand. Once we found a seat I tapped his shoulder. He looked at me and I gave him the necklace.

"What's this for?" He asked.

"Remember what happened to your necklace like this when we were younger?" I asked with a smirk. He chuckled. "Yeah. That was a nice necklace but this one is better." He said. I smiled as I watched him put it on. He held my hand throughout the whole show.

"So why'd you want to come to the rodeo?" Levi asked.

"Two reasons. One, it's fun as hell. Two. Have you had any contact with your best friend, Jake?" I asked. He shook his head. "Not lately, why?" He asked. I smiled.

"Come on." I said and pulled him towards the trailers. We walked and walked until I found Jake's trailer. I knocked on it and waited for him to come to the door. I looked up at Levi and smiled. He smiled back. The door opened and Jake came into view. "Hey, there stranger!" I said.

He hopped out and hugged me with a huge grin. "Chelsea! You came! And you brought Levi too!" He exclaimed. He and Levi shared this sort of bro hug. We all went into his trailer. "You did great out there, Jake." I said. He smiled and thanked me. I looked over at Levi. "You remember that one bull rider who wore that mask?" I asked. He nodded. I pointed to Jake.

"That was you man?" Levi asked. Jake nodded. They went into conversation about their lives. I stepped outside to give them a little privacy. They may not know this but I know that over the past few years or so, they hadn't been close like they used to. It's important to have friends who you can count on. Jake was one of those friends. A friend who I felt Levi needed.

I walked around and looked at Jake's trailer. It was a nice one. "Chelsea? Chelsea Phillips?" Someone called. I turned around, my eyebrows instantly raising up. "Who's asking?" I said in a tough like voice. The man came closer and as he did I recognized who he was. His name was Jeremy. We went to college together.

"Oh hey, Jeremy." I said. He smiled as he neared me. You see, Jeremy liked me but I didn't give him the time of day. People said that we'd be a great couple but I didn't see it then and still don't see it now.

"Hey, how have you been?" He asked. I shrugged. "Pretty good, what about you?" I asked.

"Good, good. So what are you doing now?" He asked.

"I'm the official head athletic trainer for the San Francisco Giants." I said. He nodded in approval. "You?" I asked.

"I'm in real estate." He said. I nodded. He cleared his throat.

"Listen, if you're free anytime, you should call me. We could go grab coffee or something." He said. I smirked unintentionally. "Are you asking me out?" I asked. He gulped. "Sort of." He said. The smirk remained although I tried hard to wipe it off. "I don't think that's a good idea." I said. He frowned. "Why not?" He asked. I pointed to the trailer and the door opened. Levi and Jake came out laughing. Levi placed an arm around my waist.

"Who's this?" He asked me. I looked from Levi to Jeremy.

"Jeremy this is Levi, Levi this is Jeremy." I said. I watched as Levi sized up Jeremy.

Jeremy's eyes widened. "You're Levi Anderson. You were drafted to the MLB!" Jeremy exclaimed. Levi nodded. "You know him?" Jeremy asked me. I nodded. "I've know him for over six years." I said. He nodded. "Well it was nice to talk to you." He said. I nodded and smiled as he walked away.

"Weird." Levi said.

"Tell me about it." I said and both guys chuckled. Jake stepped closer to us. "If I'm observing correctly, Levi's arm around Chelsea's waist. This means that Chelsea and Levi are on good terms. And when Chelsea and Levi are on good terms, good things happen. So tell me, are Chelsea and Levi dating?" Jake asked with a hopeful glint in his eyes. Before I could answer, Levi said yes. I slapped his shoulder which caused Jake to laugh.

"No, we're not. We're testing new waters." I said and he nodded. "Well, Jake man. We better get going." Levi said. I nodded in agreement. "Yeah that plane ride kicked my butt." I said.

"Oh hush, you slept through most of it." Levi said. I shrugged. "Same difference." I said. He chuckled. We said bye to Jake and headed to the car. Levi hopped into the driver's seat. I got in and buckled up. "I'm gonna have to invest in one of these when I get back." I said.

"What's wrong with the truck?" Levi asked as he backed out. "Oh nothing, I just want something new." I said. And hey, I could afford it so why not? Levi hit the highway and we headed home. We stopped in town for some food. Levi pulled up to the Mexican place where most people go. He put his arm around me as we walked in. "Table for two." Levi told the hostess. Levi grabbed my hand and followed the waitress.

As we walked in, people looked at Levi with shocked expressions. You could hear them among their tables. "Isn't he the one who was drafted?" Or "I remember when that boy used to cause trouble around town. He's grown up now and he still has that pretty girl on his arm." The last one caught my attention. I wish it were true.

I'm pretty sure Levi heard it too because he smirked. He squeezed my hand. "I heard it and I know that you heard it too." He said. I smiled and nodded. "It's been too long, Chelsea Jane." He said.

After ordering and eating our food, I texted my momma to tell her that we were on our way. When we pulled up to his house, the yard was packed. Once we got out I could here the music form the backyard. Levi grabbed my hand and led me there. His family had a huge house, front yard, and back yard. We walked back there and everyone tackled us with hugs and kisses.

I hugged my mom, dad, and grandparents. Raleigh was even back there. I went over and hugged her. She was over the moon excited to see me. Raleigh pulled me to the side. "So, big shot baseball rookie and his trainer come home together. What's this all about?" She asked with a smirk. "Well, um, you see. Levi and I are giving it another shot like adults this time." I explained. I looked over at Levi who was talking to his brothers. He winked.

Raleigh hugged me out of excitement. "It's gonna work this time. I just know it will." She said. -It around eleven and Levi decided to go to Walmart. "You going?" He asked. I nodded. He grabbed my hand and we walked to the car. When we pulled up at Walmart, Levi grabbed my hand and led me into the store. Even though it was eleven, there were many people in Walmart. Mostly young adults and teens. We went back to the food section. "My parents have no snacks at the house, can you believe it?" He asked. I laughed and nodded.

"They don't want you to get fat and neither do I." I said as he picked up a bag of chips. He smiled at me. "So you're saying that you like my body?" He asked with a smirk. "I guess it's ok." I said with a small smile. He came closer and lifted his shirt. "You sure?" I asked. A group of teenage girls walked by. They giggled and blushed when they saw Levi. I pulled his shirt down quickly. "Levi put that away, we're in public." I said. He chuckled and pulled his shirt down.

We grabbed more snacks and went to pay for it. I helped carry the food to the car. I got the keys and drove home. I ran the car over the speed limit. There were rarely any policemen out tonight. As I pulled onto our road I turned slightly towards Levi. "Going home?" I asked.

"Yeah, we're going home. You know I basically lived with you. Everything hasn't changed." He said with a smiled. I laughed and pulled into my driveway. We walked everything into the house and I went up to shower. When I walked into my old room, Levi was sitting on the bed. I guess he had used the shower in the guest room.

I climbed in the bed and turned the tv on. After watching tv for a while, I laid down to go to sleep. I thought Levi was sound asleep but when I laid down, he turned to me. "You know, I'm glad we're giving this a try." He whispered as he brought me closer. "Me too." I whispered back.

Chapter 10

I woke up to pots and pans clanging downstairs. I groaned. "My momma has no value of sleep." I mumbled. I tried to sit up but was restricted by Levi's heavy arm. I shoved him. "Wake up." I said. He groaned. "I'm sleeping." He said. I rolled my eyes. Typical Levi.

I got up and went to the bathroom to do my business. When I came out, Levi was sitting up. I heard scratching at my door and walked to let Beau in. He came and went straight to Levi. "Hey Beau." Levi said as the dog interacted with him. My mouth formed an 'O'. "Really, Beau? You choose Levi over me?" I asked the dog. He only barked and Levi chuckled. "Whatever." I said and grabbed some clothes to put on.

I got dressed in a pair of jeans, a t shirt, and my boots. I left my hair down. I walked downstairs and sat with my momma for coffee. "What's got you in a twisted mood?" She asked.

"My dog likes Levi better than his owner." I mumbled. She laughed. "Momma." I whined. She tried to contain her laughter but failed miserably. I rolled my eyes and sipped my coffee. Levi came downstairs with Beau not too far behind him. He kissed my momma's cheek and sat beside me. He grabbed my hand and kissed my knuckles. My momma awed. We looked at her. "So I'm gonna guess. Levi and Chelsea want to give it another try." She said.

We nodded. She smiled. "It's gone stick this time. Believe me. Watch." She said with a huge smile as she left out of the kitchen. I looked at Levi who was already looking at me. "Whelp, I guess I gotta get going." I said. He jumped up with me and blocked the door. "Where you going?" He asked.

"To town, it's been a while since I've just been around town." I said truthfully. As soon as I graduated I went straight into work and hadn't been back to Mississippi since then. "I'm coming with you." Levi said and I shrugged. I grabbed the keys and walked to the car. I drove into town and cruised around town with the top down. People shouted out greetings to Levi and I. We waved and kept going. I finally found a park on Main Street. We got out and I went straight to the women's boutique. Levi followed.

I looked around and spotted the prettiest dress. It was the flowing type and stopped right above my knees. I tried it on and quickly purchased it. I grabbed Levi's hand and we left. He got the keys and drove by our old high school. We also drove by the fields. I smiled at the memories of this place. He pulled over and hopped out. Levi opened the trunk and pulled out a glove and ball along with his bat bag. I raised my eyebrow at him.

"I always come prepared." He said with a wink. I laughed and follows him onto the field. He slipped the glove on and tossed the ball in the air. I took a seat in the dugout. I took a picture of him. It was a nice one. He stopped and looked at me. "You know I can't throw by myself, trainer." He said. I sighed and got up. He threw me a glove which I caught easily.

He threw the ball and I caught it. I got in my pitching stance and pitched the ball to him which he barely caught. "Woah, princess, this ain't softball." He said. I shrugged. "That's my game plus I hadn't pitched in a while. Considering that I'm always dealing with Major

League Baseball players." I said with an eye roll. He chuckled and jogged to home plate. He squatted down.

"Well let's see if you still got it, Chelsea Jane." He said. I smirked and reached into his bag. I knew he still carried my old softball around with him. I took a deep breath and got in my stance. I breathed and launched the ball. I heard the familiar snap of the glove. "Whew, that one stung!" Levi yelled. I laughed. After two more pitches, some kids pulled up.

I saw it was my old high school's softball team. They went and sat in the dugout. I loaded again and pitched it to Levi. He threw it to me. I jumped and caught it making my shirt rise up a little. I glared at him and just laughed. "You know I ain't as tall as you. I'm tall but not as tall as you." I said and he only laughed more.

I could hear giggles from the girls. I wonder if they had practice. I loaded again and pitched the ball. A truck pulled up and my old softball coach got out. He walked onto the field and instantly recognized me. I sent another ball flying in Levi's direction. "Chelsea Phillips?!" My old coach yelled out. I smiled and jogged over to him. "In the flesh!" I said and hugged him.

Levi jogged over. "Oh and you brought the troublemaker too." He joked. We laughed. "Nice to see you too, coach." Levi said. We talked for a bit and now we were staying to watch the girls practice. After they finished practicing coach wanted me to talk to them. They all sat down in the dugout with coach. Levi stood at the corner of the entrance and watched me.

"So, hey guys." I said. They all responded with a hey. "So if you didn't know, my name is Chelsea. I used to sit where you're sitting at a while back. I'm not that old if that's what you're thinking. I'm twenty two and in high school, softball was my life. I had to work really hard for the spot I had. So after playing real hard for a while, I received a scholarship to two schools. One to Mississippi State and another to the University of Florida. It was a tough decision but in the end I chose Florida. After graduating I went straight into work as a sports trainer.

Currently, I am the official head athletic trainer of the San Fransisco Giants. That means I work with baseball players all day everyday. From rookies to veterans. Including that goofball over there." I said and pointed to Levi. The girls giggled and smiled. "So I said all that to say this. Don't give up. Play hard and believe that you can do it.

I know coach can be a little aggravating sometimes but trust me, it's gonna help you in the long run. So just remember what I said and I hope that great things come your way. Good luck with your season." I said. They clapped and coach hugged me.

As we all left, Levi placed an arm around me. "So I'm a goofball now?" He asked. I looked up at him. "Yeah, you are." I said with a smile. He got the keys and drove. We pulled up to the baseball field. I guess the boys had practice today also. "So your old coach called my old coach. So now I'm going to speak to the boys." He said and I nodded. We got out and he placed an arm around my shoulder.

We went into the dugout and watched the remainder of practice. The boys jogged in and stopped when they saw us. I smiled at them. They waved back and one even winked. Levi placed a possessive arm around me. I shoved him a little. The boys sat down and I got up to stand at the entrance of the dugout. The guys watched my every move. I snapped my finger in Levi's direction and they turned their heads.

"Ok, so I know you're probably wondering why I'm up here right now. Well, I used to play on this exact field, wear the same uniform, and deal with the same coach as you a while back. My name is Levi.

Some of you may know me. The seniors maybe but that's not the point. In high school, I loved this sport. It's what got me to college. I went and played for MSU and did a pretty good job. I received my degree for my major and was ready to hit the work force.

Just to get a kick out of it, I signed up for the draft. Little did I know I was going to get the call. So I got the call. Now, I play for the San Fransisco Giants. That means that I do this everyday, with just a little more help. There are more coaches and these people called trainers. They help me up my performance. Everyday all day I'm at that field. I know most of you probably have dreams of going pro. Heck, we all do I'm sure.

What I'm saying is this. Keep up your hard work, do good in school, and just keep an humble mind. That'll get you far." He said to them. He came and grabbed my hand. He pulled me in front of the boys. "You see this woman right here? This is Chelsea. She was one of the greatest softball players here in this town. She worked hard, got a scholarship, and she is now the official head athletic trainer for my team. So yes, I get to spend time with this beauty everyday.

Again, not the point. Look at us. Working hard is how we got here. Guys, what I'm trying to say is just work hard. Hard work will pay off." He said. The guys clapped and shook his hand. One even hugged me. Levi ran to the car while I talked to the boys. He ran back and showed up with his equipment. "Ready to finish out those throws?" He asked with a smirk. I groaned and the players laughed. "Levi I have on boots, not cleats." I said.

"So do I now come on." He said and pulled me out to the mound. I warmed back up a bit. I noticed the team was still there. "So y'all aren't going home?" I asked.

"Nah, we wanna watch you throw." One spoke up. I nodded and focused back on Levi. He threw the ball and I jumped to catch it. "I told you I'm not as tall as you." I said. He just laughed. I grabbed some dirt and rolled it in my hands. I wiped it off then took my stance. I launched the ball and heard the familiar snap of the glove. He threw it back. The process went on and on.

Finally it was my last throw. I took a deep breath and threw the ball as fast as I could. The snap was very loud. I smiled as I removed the glove from my hand. The team just smiled and nodded in approval. Levi packed his stuff and everyone headed towards the parking lot. Levi put the stuff in the trunk and hopped in the driver's seat.

"That was fun." I said.

"Yeah." Levi said and placed a hand on my thigh. He gave me butterflies that I couldn't explain. I'm glad that we were giving it another try. "Chelsea, did you hear me baby?" He asked. I looked at him. He smirked.

"You didn't hear me, did you?" He asked. I smirked. "Maybe I did hear you." I said. He looked over at me. "Ok, what did I say?" He asked with that annoying smirk. "Oops, I forgot. Mind telling me again, Levi?" I asked with a sweet smile. He chuckled and nodded.

"I said, how about we go on that date tonight?" He asked. I smiled and nodded. "I would love to go on that date." I said. He smiled and grabbed my hand.

"Good. You wanna grab something to eat before we head home?" He asked. I looked at the clock and it was one o'clock. I nodded. He pulled up to a diner and we got out. Levi led me to a booth. He sat across from me. Our waitress came and took our orders. While we waited, Levi and I had small conversation. The doorbell rang and I turned to see who it was. Casey walked in with a man on her arm. I rolled my eyes.

They sat down in a booth not too far from us. I don't even think Levi saw her. That's good. My thoughts were interrupted when she walked to our table. "My, my, look at here! Rookie sensation, Levi Anderson!" She exclaimed. Levi slowly turned to look at her. "Casey." He said.

"Hey, Levi." She said, trying to flirt. I tried to stifle a laugh but instead a small chuckle came from me. They both turned to look at me. "Oh, hey Chelsea." She said with a fake smile.

"Hey, Casey!" I said. I felt a little uncomfortable around her. I looked back to Casey. "How's your life going?" I asked. She instantly smiled. "Well, I'm engaged to a wealthy millionaire." She said with a smirk. I nodded. "Yeah...." I pressed. She stood there smiling for a bit. "Oh yeah, that's it." She said with a little smile. I suppose she was trying to intimidate me and all. "So are you visiting?" I asked. She nodded. "Yeah, we live at an estate in New York." She said. I nodded.

"Nice." I said. She smiled. "So what about you?" She asked. I sighed.

"Well, after college, I went straight to work for a training agency. I am now the official head athletic trainer for a MLB team with a healthy pay." I said with a honest smile. She looked at Levi and smiled. "What about you?" She asked. He shrugged.

"Living my dream. I play for San Fransisco. Chelsea is our main trainer so I see her everyday and we're back to visit before the season kicks off." He said with a smile. She looked at me and I nodded. She scoffed,"Well, it was nice seeing y'all again."

I nodded. "Yeah, and next time, please don't try to rub your life in our faces." I said. She scoffed once again and walked away. I heard a deep chuckled and noticed Levi looking at me. He reached across and grabbed my hand. "Man I'm glad we're giving this another try." He said and kissed my knuckles. I smiled at him.

Chapter 11

"Ok, so you're going on a date?" Raleigh asked. I nodded. "With Levi." Shana added. I nodded again. We were currently in my room trying to find me something to wear for my date tonight. Shana walked into my closet and dug around. "You have nothing in your closet!" She yelled from inside. I shrugged. "My stuff is in, San Fransisco. You know, where I live. That closet hasn't been filled since high school." I said.

"It's true. I came here one year to rummage through her closet and all I could find worth keeping was a blue tank top." Raleigh said. I rolled my eyes but it was true, I didn't have anything worth keeping. All my stuff was in my new apartment. I laid back and sighed. "Why am I putting so much effort into this anyway? It's just Levi." I complained.

Shana came out of my closet wearing a dress from years ago. "Because. This is most likely the last first date with Levi you'll have. I believe that this time you and him will be together." Shana said as she twirled around. I sat up.

"But still. Levi has seen me for most of his life. How is dressing up for a date different?" I asked. Raleigh sighed,"You have a reason to. You and Levi are no longer the bickering teens you once were. Time to step up your game and do things grown-up style." She said. I nodded but soon gasped. "I bought a dress today." I said. They shooed me out the room to go and get it. I came back and tried it on.

"Cute. Perfect for your date." Shana said. Raleigh nodded. "Yeah, you don't look too conservative and you don't look to slutty. Wear that dress with your boots." She said. I nodded and went to shower. After showering I pulled the dress on. The girls started on my hair and makeup. When they soon finished, I looked in the mirror. I looked good.

"Awe, you look cute." Shana said. I thanked her and Raleigh for their hard work. They went downstairs to see if Levi was there yet. I heard footsteps running back up the steps. They burst into the room. "Girl, he is down there and looking good." Raleigh said.

"Relationship goals. Y'all matching too." Shana said and I asked what he had on.

"Just wait and see." They said. I nodded and walked to the mirror. I took a deep breath. "Chelsea! Did you hear me?" Shana asked. I turned to look at her. She and Raleigh came to my side. "She asked if you were ok. You looked like you were gonna have a panic attack." Raleigh said. Just then the door flew open and the girl I hadn't seen in forever ran in. "Joanna!" I yelled.

"Hey, Chelsea!" She said before she jumped on me. I laughed at the impact. I hadn't seen Joanna ever since sophomore winter break in college. We were both busy girls. Joanna was in the same program as me until we had to both leave and work for a major league team. Now she's back. "What are you doing here?" I asked.

"Well, you know I've been team Levi and Chelsea since forever. Raleigh and Shana called me to tell me that y'all were going on a date. I just had to drive out here and see it for myself." She said and I laughed. "Yes, it's true. I'm pretty sure you saw Levi downstairs." I said. She nodded. "That man looks fine!" She yelled. We all burst into laughter. I looked at the clock and it almost seven.

"Ok, I would love to stay and laugh with y'all but if I don't go downstairs right now I'm pretty sure there won't be a date." I said. They all nodded. "Ok, girl go do your thang." Joanna said. I turned around as they all hopped on my bed. "And I expect y'all to be gone when I get back." I said. They laughed and shooed me off.

I walked downstairs into the kitchen. I was a little thirsty so I grabbed some water. While I was drinking it, I heard voices in the living room. It was my mom, dad, and Levi. I finished up my water and walked in there. They stopped talking and looked at me. "Hey." I said with a smile to them. "Hey, Chelsea. You look very pretty." My momma said. I smiled. My daddy complimented me too. Levi just stared. "Well, you coming or not?" I asked with a smirk. He hopped up making all of us laugh.

"We'll be back later." Levi said to my parents. They shooed us off and went to do something. Levi grabbed my hand and we walked to the car. I noticed that Levi and I actually did match. He had on jeans and a white button up rolled to the elbows. I noticed he had on the necklace I got for him. I smiled at the memory.

I looked to Levi only to see he was looking right at me. I smiled and gave a small wave. He chuckled. "You look great." He said.

"Thanks, so do you. I notice that we're matching." I said and he smiled. He kept driving and soon we pulled up to a steak house. After dinner we went to a movie. During the movie Levi did simple things like hold my hand, rub my thigh, and kiss my cheek. When that movie finished, we took a walk in the park.

He grabbed my hand and laced his fingers with mine. Levi stopped and came to a bench. "Chelsea, I had a great time tonight but I can't do this." He said. My smile fell. "What do you mean?" I asked. Did he want to break it off when we barely started? "I don't want just petty dates and small outings with you. I want them with my girlfriend. Chelsea, when we go back, I don't want to fight off guys from my girl. You're mine and I don't want to share. Will you be my girlfriend?" He asked.

I smiled. "Of course I'll be your girlfriend." I said and he smiled. "Dang it, now I owe the whole coaching and training staff two dollars." I said. Levi looked at me confused. "Oh, so we made a bet before we left for the break. The coaching staff and training staff noticed us before we even noticed us, if you know what I mean. They pulled me aside after one practice and all had this big discussion. Coach took a notice that we've become chummy, his words not mine.

He said to all of us that by the time we came back for break, you and I would be a couple. I bet that it'd take more than a week. They bet on it and so did I. Now I owe them each two dollars." I said. Levi looked amused. "My girlfriend made a bet on me. That's something every boyfriend wants to hear." He said as he scooted closer. "Well, if it makes you feel any better, I'm glad it only took a week. I will gladly give up those two dollars." I said. He smiled and placed an arm around me.

"Finally I can put my arm around you without you scowling at me." He said and I laughed. "I know I'm a handful so let's just take this at a good pace." I said. He smiled and nodded. I remembered those days in high school. "Hey, tomorrow, me and your brothers were gonna go do some target practice. Wanna come?" I asked him. "So you and my brothers were gonna go for some target practice without me?" He asked. "Wanna come or not?" I asked.

"You know I wanna come." He said and I laughed. We got up and found the car. Levi drove to his house. We walked in holding hands. His parents looked up and smiled at us. "About damn time." His dad said. Levi's mom smiled. "Brenda how long have we been waiting on this?" Joe asked his wife. "Since they were eleven and twelve. They had Hoppy at the time and they were so adorable." She said. I laughed.

Levi grabbed my hand and pulled me to the backyard. "Hey, it's quiet around here. Where are the guys?" I asked. Levi shrugged. "They wanted to go out to eat. Hunter decided to suddenly go out. I guess it's his way of coping." He said and I nodded. Hunter, Levi's oldest brother, had been through a breakup recently. The girl cheated and Hunter was left heartbroken.

Levi came and stood behind me. He wrapped his hands around my waist and pulled me close. I felt great. I felt happy. Levi and I were finally together. "About time you guys got comfy." Someone said, making me jump. We turned around and all of Levi's brothers were standing there. I jumped to hug them all. "Hey y'all! When did you get in?" I asked them.

"Oh I got here a couple of days ago." Hunter said.

"Daniel and I flew together." Steven said.

"I drove." Luke said.

"I live here." Grayson said. We all went and sat around a small bond fire that Luke started. "So when are y'all going back?" Daniel asked.

"I'm not sure. Levi when are we going back?" I asked him. He looked down at me. "Saturday. So I can sleep in on Sunday." He said. They all nodded. We talked for a while and soon I started yawning. Levi stood up and pulled me along with him. We went in the house and up to his room which he barely slept in. "This is the first time I've been in here." I said.

"There was no need for you to. I was always at your house." Levi said with a smile. I smiled. As kids, Levi never let me in his room. At all. He'd always sneak into my room at night. One night, my parents caught him sleeping in my room and made him go home. Levi went home at first but an hour later he snuck back in. He was always the mischievous one out of the Anderson brothers. What am I saying? Their all mischievous.

I jumped on his bed and picked up the tv remote. I could not figure out how to turn on the tv. Soon it turned on but I didn't do anything. "I must be magic." I whispered to myself while examining my hands. "Nah it's just me." Levi said. I looked at him blankly. He chuckled and came closer and trapped me between his arms. He leaned in. "Just you." I said.

"Yep." He said, his lips brushing over mine.

"Just me." He said before bringing his lips to mine. His lips were soft. How long has it been since I kissed this guy? Wow. We pulled away for air and I hopped up. "Where are you going?" He asked. "To change." I said and reached into his closet. I peeped my head in and looked to the far left. My little hello kitty bag was sitting there under his clothes. I grabbed the bag and walked out into the room.

"Where did that hello kitty bag come from?" He asked.

"My house. When I was sixteen, I snuck into your room and placed a bag in your closet. I swore to myself that I would come into Levi Anderson's room and stay the night. I packed a little bag and hid it in your closet." I said as I pulled out the stuff. "How could you do that when we were together constantly?" He asked.

"I lied one time and told you I had practice the same day as you." I said. He looked shocked and amused at the same time. "You little sneak. What's in the bag anyways?" He asked. I shrugged. "Oh some things I'd usually take if I went to stay at someone's house." I said. I had deodorant, a toothbrush, toothpaste, perfume, underwear, clothes, and pajamas. You know, the usual stuff.

I pulled out the sweatpants and a t shirt. I went into his bathroom and changed. I noticed the sweatpants fit but they were loose. After checking them out I noticed they were Levi's. I walked into the room and swooped up my bag. I placed it back into the closet. "So that's where my favorite grey sweatpants went to." Levi said. I shrugged and smiled. He patted the spot beside him and I sat beside him. He kissed my forehead, cheeks, my nose, and finally my lips. I could tell that Levi and I would be just fine.

Chapter 12

"Yes momma, we landed safely." I said into the phone.

"Well where is Levi?" She asked.

"Right here momma. He's getting our stuff." I said. I looked and Levi had already grabbed up out stuff. He was making his way over to me. I kissed his cheek then we left. I quickly ended the conversation with my momma. She was so worrisome sometimes. Levi dropped me off at my apartment and headed off to take a nap. Later we were gonna go bowling, which I suck at.

I started to unpack and wash my dirty clothes. After putting up my things, I plopped down on my couch. Turning on the tv, I grabbed a bag of trail mix to snack on. Soon, I got up to shower. After showering I put on some comfortable clothes and laid back on the couch. An hour later, my buzzer buzzed. "Who is it?" I asked into the buzzer. I didn't bother to look at the screen. "It's me, babe." Levi's voice came through. I let him in and hopped back on the couch.

I unlocked the door so I wouldn't have to get up. The door opened and a nicely dressed Levi stepped in. "Really?" He asked. I shrugged. "What?" I asked. He motioned to me laying on the couch. "You gotta get dressed." He said.

"Oh yeah." I said and got up. I walked into my room and straight into my closet. I spotted a pair of dark skinny jeans. I pulled them on and found a capped-sleeved coral crop top. I paired the outfit with some flats. After putting on a little make up and placing a gold necklace around my neck, I was ready. I had pulled my hair into a messy bun. Levi walked into my room. "I was just about to come get you." He said. I nodded and grabbed a clutch.

We left my apartment after locking it and headed to his truck. Levi drove off to the bowling alley. After getting the shoes, we found an empty lane. I was an insanely competitive person and seeing Levi win every time made me slightly upset. We were now sitting in Hooter's. I was completely against coming here but I lost against Levi. The winner got to choose where to eat and this was where he chose.

I wanted to go to Dave and Buster's. But since I lost, I had to sit here in Hooter's. I sat across from him with my arms folded across my chest. Levi looked up and smirked. "Don't be a sore loser Chelsea." He said. I rolled my eyes. "I'm not a sore loser, Levi." I said. He just nodded and said ok but it was sarcastic. The waitress girl came and took our order. She pushed her chest in front of Levi's face. I was enraged but kept my cool and casually sipped my lemonade.

"Chelsea."

"Hmm?" I answered.

"Look at me." He said I looked at him. This guy had straws up his nose. "No one told me I was dating a twenty-three year old kid." I said with a small laugh. He grabbed my hand. "You like this kid though." He said. I smiled.

"Very true." I told him. He grinned. "I can't believe you're my girl-friend." He said. I smiled at him. The waitress came back with our food. More pushing of the chest in Levi's line of view. I took a deep breath and folded my hands to keep from slapping the mess out of her right now. "Excuse me." I said in a polite but not so polite way.

She slowly turned to me. I jumped a little in my seat. This girl had more make up on than a clown. To tell the truth, she scared me.

"Here's a tip for you. Stay out of his face and maybe you'll have a chance. Lay off the makeup before you scare the customers away. And this guy right here likes it all natural. So keep the implants at a distance. Ok, hon?" I said with a fake smile. She looked angry but at the moment I didn't care. The girl stomped and walked away. I shrugged and started on my food.

I noticed Levi looking at me. "Is there a reason you're looking at me, Levi?" I asked.

"That was amazing. Come here so I can kiss you." He said. I made a small laugh. "Ew, no. I'm eating." I said. He fake pouted. I smiled. "Cute." I told him. After dinner we went to my house. I popped in a movie and we cuddled on the couch. -Today is the first game and I was very excited. Levi was unbelievably nervous. He had a press conference this morning so he and I hadn't talked for a good bit. Our families flew in for the big game. Right now, I was getting ready to drive to the stadium. "Ok, make sure that you guys lock my door and put the code in." I told my parents, Raleigh, Shana, and Joanna. "Ok, Miss Bossy. Go!" Shana yelled and basically pushed me out the door.

I jogged to my truck and drove to the stadium. Once I got there I went to the locker room. I put my stuff down and got out the necessary items for warmup. "Ok, warm ups are in fifteen minutes! Everyone should be dressed in their practice uniform!" I shouted. After setting the things up, I walked to the press conference room. Just as I walked in, I caught Levi's last questions.

"Levi! Anyone special here today?" The reporter asked.

"My girlfriend, Chelsea. She's here along with my family." He answered.

"How long have you been seeing this girlfriend of yours?" She asked.

"We've been together for over three years. We made official two months ago. No more questions, thank you." He said and got up. I met him and some of the other players outside the door. "Ok, guys go get ready for warm ups." I told them. They jogged to the locker rooms. Levi grabbed my hand and gave me a kiss. "Three years, huh?" I asked. He smirked.

"We both know how long we've been together. More years than we can count. All that matters is that I'm with you, right?" He asked. I smiled at him and nodded. "Of course, Levi." I said and leaned up to kiss his cheek. We walked into the locker room. The whole team said awe all together. I scrunched my face up at them. It was a habit. Ever since we revealed that we were dating, the team and coaching staff has been giving us flack about it.

After the guys got dressed I took them to the field to get ready. During their stretches, I spotted our families finding their seats. "Let's take a trip!" I shouted and started the jog. They followed in behind me. I took them through the stadium. Some of the fans saw them and went crazy. I led them to the locker rooms to get dressed. The guys came out dressed so the coaching and training staff led them to the field.

Man the stadium was filled to the max. They lined up for the opening ceremony and I situated myself in the dugout. After the national anthem and prayer, the game started. Right away, we weren't doing good and I getting frustrated. "What the heck are you doing, defense?!" I yelled.

"Get your asses down!" I yelled. The next ball was hit. It flew towards right field. "Get the ball!" I yelled. The right fielder caught it and threw it in. I clapped my hands. "About damn time." I said and plopped down on the seat. The coaching staff was looking at me.

"You ok there, Chelsea?" The head coach asked me. I nodded. "I'm fine. It's just that I get frustrated when I don't see defense techniques on the field. I mean, what do they come to practice for if their not going to use at least one of the techniques that are taught to them. Plus I'm sort of a baseball fanatic. " I vented. He chuckled nodded.

"True, but their knuckle headed men who don't listen. The last trainer had problems but you seem to hold your own and we're all baseball fanatics here." He said with a smile. I just nodded. It was time for the other half of the inning. When the team came in, the coach sat them down for a talk. "Get your head in the game. We have no room for careless mistakes. Play like you got some sense." He said and dismissed them. They got in their batting order then got ready for the rest of the inning. I walked to the fence and watched as someone from our team batted. -Well, our team pulled through. I watched as they took a picture. After the pictures were taken and interviews were given, they headed into the locker room where the coach gave a speech. Now, I was packing my things and headed out for some drinks. As I put my things in my backpack someone's arm wrapped around my waist. "Unless your name is Levi Bradley Anderson I suggest you unwrap your arms." I said. He chuckled.

"Hey babe." He said and kissed my neck. I turned and hugged him. I grabbed my backpack and headed to the door. Levi caught up and grabbed my hand. We walked out to our trucks. "Come stay with me tonight." He said while I leaned on my truck. I shrugged. "Another day. We have family here, remember?" I asked. He shrugged as he stepped closer to me.

"They'll understand." He murmured on my lips. I moved my head and frowned. "Levi. Your parents and brothers are staying at your place." I said. He pulled me back. "I didn't say we had to stay at my place." He said. I smiled at him. "I'll think about it." I said. He smiled. "You're gonna say yes." He said. I rose an eyebrow. "What makes you so sure?" I asked.

"Cause you like me." He said before putting his lips to mine.

"Awwweeeee!" Someone yelled. We turned and saw our families standing there with huge smiles on their faces. I rolled my eyes and turned back to Levi. He just shook his head while laughing. "Hey, y'all." I said with a smile. They all said hey. I shook my head and got into my truck. Levi hopped in with me. "What are you doing?" I asked.

"Riding with you." He said.

"Who's driving your truck?" I asked.

"Steven. Hunter. Daniel. One of them." He said. I shrugged and started my truck. Everyone followed us to a bar restaurant. Everyone here was able to drink so we did. After dinner we all went to Levi's place. When we walked in, I went to his bedroom and laid down. "Tired?" He asked when he walked in. I nodded. He laid beside me. "Me too." He said.

"You stink." I said.

"So do you." He said. I covered my nose. "You need to shower." I said.

"Come with me." He said.

"In your dreams, country boy." I said and got up. He laughed. "Don't worry, it'll be a reality one day." He said. I shook my head and found some of my clothes. After I showered, I found most of our families sleeping around the living room looking quite comfortable. The only ones I didn't see were Levi's parents and my parents. I smiled and continued to Levi's room. He was laying up watching tv. A smile came to his face when he saw me. I crawled into the bed with him and snuggled his chest.

"I never knew twenty-three year olds still watched cartoons." I said, a small smile playing on my lips. I felt him shrug. "Only the ones we watch together." He said. I looked at the screen and spongebob was on. A smile crept a way to my face. "Cute." I said.

"You say that every time. Find a new adjective." He said. I shook my head. "Cute is fine." I said while stifling a yawn.

"Go to sleep, baby." He whispered. I shook my head. "I want to watch spongebob." I murmured. "I know." He said before I drifted to sleep.

Chapter 13

I loved the random moments we had. They brought me happiness. A feeling that I felt whenever I was around or thinking about Levi. I looked at our joined hands on the console and smiled. Levi and I were "taking an adventure". He decided that we should explore our city. He ended driving on the countryside somewhere, not that I was complaining. Three months into our relationship and things are doing good.

"Baby lock the door and turn the lights down lowPut some music on that's soft and slowBaby we ain't got no place to goI hope you understand." I sang.

"I've been thinking 'bout this all day longNever felt a feeling quite this strongI can't believe how much it turns me onJust to be your man."

He sang back. I laughed because Levi couldn't sing. I'm not trying to be mean but the guy couldn't sing. He knew this but would bust his butt trying to. It was funny.

"I love it when you sing to me." I said to him with a huge smile. He laughed.

"You and I both know that I can't sing, babe." He said. I nodded. "True, but it's the thought that counts. I think it's sweet." I said. He smiled and kissed my knuckles. "You make me happy." He told me.

"I'm glad I do." I said. We were all smiles that whole day. Levi even bought me ice cream. When we got back to his place I hopped on his couch and turned the tv on. His buzzer sounded. "Babe, can you get that?!" He yelled from the kitchen. I got up and looked at the buzzer. I let them up. There was a blonde standing there. She looked like a model with striking grey eyes. "Hello." I said. She eyed me.

"Yes, where's Levi?" She asked.

"Who are you?" I asked.

"His fiancé. Where is he?" She asked. I eyed her. I took a deep breath. This girl said fiancé. Did I hear her right? "Wait right here." I said and closed the door. I quickly shuffled to the kitchen. My whole mood changed just that quick. "Levi." I said. He turned and looked at me.

"Tell me why there is a pretty girl at the door saying that she's your fiancé?" I asked. He furrowed his eyebrows.

"You said pretty?" He asked with a smirk. I rolled my eyes.

"Levi don't play." I said. My arms were crossed by now and my weight was shifted to my left leg, making my hip jut out. "Let me go see." He said and put down the towel he had in his hands. I looked and saw that he was making a fruit bowl. I stole a grape and walked to the foyer. "Gwendolyn what the hell are you doing here?" I heard him say. I walked around the corner.

"That's all I get? I traveled across the country for you and you ask me why I'm here?" She asked. Levi crossed his arms. "What do you want?" He asked.

"I decided it was time for me to come be with my fiancé." She said. I scoffed and they both looked at me. Levi gave me a knowing look and Gwyneth, whatever her name was, gave me a hateful look. "You should really keep your help under control." She said. I rolled my eyes and fixed my mouth to say something but Levi stepped and placed an arm around my waist.

"She's not the help. She's my girlfriend." He said.

"I had no idea you had a mistress, Levi. Just pay her off and we can start over." She said a smile. I raised an eyebrow, What the hell? "Look, you have five seconds to tell me what you want, Gwendolyn." He said in a threatening tone.

"I figured that Beatrice would like to meet her father. It has been two years after all." She said with a sly smile. Beatrice would like to meet her what?! I took a deep breath and slowly stepped out of Levi's hold. I pulled him down so I could whisper in his ear. "I'll let you handle this." I whispered then shuffled to his bedroom.

A kid?

Really Levi? I paced the bedroom praying really hard. I prayed that Levi would take responsibility if the girl really was his child. I prayed that if the girl wasn't his child, that her mother would find the father. Through all of this I paced the room and calmed myself down. Lastly, the issue came to mind. This girl said that she was Levi's fiancé. That has to be sorted out.

I sat down on the bed and closed my eyes. The door opened and soon there was someone beside me. I turned over. "It's time to talk." Levi said. I nodded and sat up to listen.

"Gwendolyn is an ex from college. I dated her for a week after Rachael-"

"The girl you brought home." I muttered.

Side Note: Hey guys, it's Chelsea! Let me tell you about Rachael. She's the girlfriend that Levi had during his junior year in college. He even brought her home. Imagine the awkwardness! Everyone looked at her weird and everything. She constantly touched on Levi and got snippy with anyone who tried to talk to him. Including his own grandmother! Long story short, old girl was crazy! Didn't like her that much anyway. End of Side Note:"Did you really have to bring her up?" I asked.

"Well, I had to so the story could build, Chelsea." Levi said.

"I don't like her." I told him.

"I know, but babe please listen." He said. I nodded and waited for him to finish.

He took a deep breath. "After Rachael, I dated Gwendolyn. For like two weeks. She's crazy and controlling. She was convinced that I love her but that's not true. And she also tried to get me to marry her. About the child, she's not mine. I know this. But if she is mine I'll step up and take the responsibility." He explained.

I just nodded. "I'm gonna go." I said and got up. He grabbed my hand.

"Where are you going?" He asked.

"To my place. Clearly we both need some time to think over this." I said as I grabbed my stuff. "Don't leave me on my own through this, Chelsea." He said. His words seemed sincere. I don't know. "I won't. You just have to sort out your situations. I'll be around though." I said.

I walked out the door without looking back at Levi. When I got to my truck, the same girl who was at the door earlier stopped me. "Hey, I'm sure we got off on the wrong foot earlier. I'm Gwendolyn." She said with an outstretched hand.

"Nice to meet you." I said and shook her hand. I quickly got in my truck and left. That night, I sat in a bubble bath and thought long and hard. I got up early for practice the next day and hurried to the stadium. I put up my stuff and took a seat in the stands to run over some drills. I felt the presence of someone beside me. "Hey, Mike." I said.

"Hey, bestie. What's got you down?" He asked. I shrugged.

"Come on, it's something. I know you too well to let that pass." He said. I sighed and told him everything.

"Damn. Just when I think everything was gonna be fine with you two." He said. I shrugged once again.

"A child, Chelsea?" He asked. I nodded.

"He told me about their relationship. Said she was crazy and tried to get him to marry her. I sort of believe it. At first, the girl was rude then in the parking lot she apologize and tried to make amends. Like what the hell?" I said, very frustrated. He rubbed my back in a soothing manner.

"We go off on the road for the next month. How can I stay focused on my job when something as big as this comes up?" I asked.

"You'll make it through. Where's the strong Chelsea I know?" Mike asked.

"She shriveled up and died. This doesn't even concern me and I'm stressed." I said.

"Looks like you're not the only one." He said and nodded his head towards the field. I spotted Levi looking sad and depressed. I could tell that he didn't sleep last night and that he was in deep thought. "Boy aren't you guys quite the couple. When one is down, the other is too." Mike said. I let out a small chuckle. "We're emotionally attached. Remember that I've known Levi ever since I was twelve." I said.

"Come on, let's start practice. The coaches just arrived." He said. I nodded and stood up. I dragged tail all the way down to the bottom row. "Mind stretching them for me?" I asked. He nodded and proceeded to the guys. As they stretched and did warm ups, I doodled on my clipboard. I even came up with a few more drills. A little progress, I thought to myself.

I guess the guys were finished because they were standing in front of me. I scooted back and pushed my back to the next row. "Ok, guys, we go off for the next month. This means harder practice. Let's do our best for these games, ok?" I said and got up. They were split into groups and put with different trainers and coaches. The head coach was with me.

"Coach, how does the progress look to you?" I asked him.

"Well, Chelsea, our numbers are better than last week's. Better hustle this week. I'd say that progress is definitely working." He said. I nodded. "I got this new drill that I planned out today. Mind if I teach it?" I asked and handed him the clipboard. He took and while he looked, I watched the players go through this defense drill.

"Is this for defense or offense." He asked.

"Defense, of course. We both know that our defense can always become better." I said. He nodded. "I agree. Let's teach it to them now." He said.

"Bring it in!" I yelled. They jogged to me and coach.

"Today we're gonna learn a new drill." I said. After explaining and demonstrating the drill, we went to work with it. After practice, I headed straight to collect my things. I was pulled into a hallway. Levi grabbed my hands. "I hate it when you ignore me." He said.

"I'm not ignoring you." I said while looking at the wall behind him. He turned my head with his hand. "Yes you are. What's the matter?" He asked. "Nothing." I said and tried to shake from his hold. He wouldn't budge.

"I also hate it when you lie to me." He said. I just looked at him. It seemed that we stared at each other for a good moment. I took in a deep breath. His phone ringed. He pulled it out and looked at the screen. I looked down at it and it said Gwendolyn. "You should answer that." I said.

"I don't want to." He said. I got the phone and spoke into it. "Hold on for one moment please." I said in a nice voice and muted it.

"Talk to her, ok? Do what you have to do. Go home and get some rest. We have a plane to catch in the morning." I said, kissed his cheek, and walked off. Wow, they move fast. It was just yesterday when she showed up on his doorstep. I got in my truck and went home to pack. Two big suitcases and some hours of sleep later, I stood outside the airport getting the suitcases out of the taxi. After paying the man, I grabbed up my stuff and walked in.

I spotted the coaches and trainers in a waiting area. I saw Mike and sat beside him. "I saw him pull you into that hallway yesterday." He said. I nodded. "You see a lot of things." I said with a yawn.

"You left. What happened?" He asked.

"She called and he didn't want to talk. I answered the phone and made him talk. Before that we were just staring at each other. He said that he hated when I ignored him. I told him that I wasn't but he said that he didn't like me lying either." I explained. He just nodded.

"I don't know what to say." Mike told me.

"Why don't you talk it out with him, though?" He asked and pointed towards the entrance. Levi walked in with his stuff. I thought he was alone as usual until blondie ran in behind him. I got up and walked past them to Starbucks. I could feel his eyes on me. After getting my coffee I headed back towards the waiting area. More of the team started to show up. I was stopped by Levi.

"What did I tell you about ignoring me?" He asked.

"You hate it." I said as I casually sipped my coffee. He grabbed it and drank some.

"She was with you this morning." I said. He sighed and nodded. "She insisted that I see Beatrice last night. I went and met her but didn't tell her that I was her dad or anything like that. After seeing her, I went home. Gwendolyn showed up to my apartment this morning as I getting ready to leave. She tried talking about marriage." He said. My turn to sigh. I frowned.

"Hey don't do that. She has no value to me, you do. Only you." Levi said and pecked my lips. I nodded. I just hoped he was right.

Chapter 14

Stepping foot off that airplane, I took a deep breath. We boarded buses and were taken to our hotels. After I was given my key, I hurried to my room. Mike's room was across from mine. Levi's was on another floor. There was a knock at my door. I groaned and answered it. Levi was standing there. "I can't sleep." He said.

"At three o'clock in the afternoon, Levi?" I asked tiredly. "Is it a bad thing to miss my girlfriend?" He asked as he walked in and laid on my bed. I shrugged and laid beside him. He placed an arm around me and I drifted to sleep. -Last month's games went great. We only lost two. I actually forgot about the whole Levi possibly having a child thing. That was until his ex kept calling everyday, all day. Like seriously. She wouldn't even call about the child. She'd call about some irrelevant stuff like what color she should wear often, the type of soup he likes, and marriage. Freaking marriage! Me of all people should know what they talk about. Levi and I are together all time and when she calls he puts it on speaker.

I was currently in the grocery store picking up some things for dinner. Levi and I were going to cook pasta tonight at my place. He wanted to stay over so I figured why not? After collecting the necessary things, I left. A black car sped out of the parking lot really fast as I walked out. During the drive home, I felt uneasy about something. I took a deep breath and switched the radio on.

CRASH!!

Glass went flying everywhere. Warm liquid cascaded down my head. My vision became blurrier by the second. I heard people's voices but they were slowly fading away. My eyes slowly closed. Soon darkness overtook me. -Levi "Where the heck is Chelsea?" I muttered to myself. I finished packing my overnight bag and left. After locking my door, I headed towards my truck. I was stopped by Gwendolyn. "Levi!" She called out. I groaned.

"What do you want?" I asked.

"It's been months since you've seen Beatrice." She said. I sighed. "Why does it matter?" I asked.

"Because you're her father." She said.

"As far as I'm concerned, I have no real proof that she's mine. Until that test comes back, I'll be nowhere near her." I said harshly.

"Then you'd want to look at these then?" She asked and held up an envelope. She handed it to me. I saw the clinic's name at the top and opened it. I read the information. Long story short, I was Beatrice's father. I crumpled the paper and shoved it in my pocket. Gwendolyn had a satisfied smirk on her face. I got in my truck and drove off.

I was angry. I wasn't angry that I was Beatrice's father. I was angry that I had to deal with her mother now. This isn't fair but the deed was done and now I have to take care of my responsibility. Two hours later, I found myself slumped in a booth at a bar. Thinking. Just thinking with a full glass of beer I front of me. It was probably piss warm but who cares. I wasn't gonna drink it anyway.

Chelsea ran across my mind the most. What would she think? How would she react? Would she stay? I picked up my phone and texted her.

Hey, babe. Sorry I'm not there yet. Something came up. We need to talk

I sent the message and waited for her response. Knowing her, she'd take the time to analyze the message then figure out if she wanted to reply back or not. I love her and I know she loves me. We just hadn't voiced our thoughts yet. My phone buzzed and it was an unknown number.

Hey, Levi it's Chelsea. Tonight wouldn't have been good, last minute meetings came up for me. Text me from this number. Got a new one today;)

I sighed and saved the number. After about another hour I went home. When I got there, Gwendolyn was at my door about to knock. She has Beatrice with her. "I have a meeting. Can you watch her?" She asked. I sighed and nodded. The little girl looked up at me and I gave a small smile. Gwendolyn quickly left. I opened the door and we walked in.

She sat on the couch and started to play with the teddy bear in her hand. I sat beside her. "Hi Beatrice." I said.

"Hi." She said in a small voice.

"Call me Levi." I said. She nodded and continued with the bear. This was gonna take some getting used to. -Once Gwendolyn came back I received a text from Chelsea. She has to leave town immediately for a training tour across America and Europe. It would take a year. Sadly we weren't able to see each other.

I love you, I texted.

I love you too.

After she left I got ready for my next practice. Wasn't much I could do. My best friend was gone. At least she knows I love her. -Three months laterChelsea was still gone and the only thing we did was text. I miss her like crazy and it was driving me insane not to see her. Practice was weird, not having her there. The players just looked at me sympathetically. Her friend Mike wasn't his usual playful self anymore. With Chelsea leaving, the atmosphere within the place had changed.

I just hoped she came soon.

I locked my door and walked into the building for practice. Things weren't the same for me anymore and Gwendolyn made it no better. She constantly bad mouthed Chelsea and it took a lot of control to not strangle her. I nodded at Mike and continued to the locker rooms.

After getting prepared for practice I placed a kiss on the picture of Chelsea in my locker. I placed my hat on my head and left. Hopefully things can go back to the way they were and my baby can come back.

-ChelseaI remember it like yesterday. I was supposed to go home. I was supposed to see Levi, the love of my life. I was supposed to do a bunch of things. They said that wreck damaged my head pretty bad. Luckily, no memory loss just that I might receive severe headaches sometimes. Thank God, it could've been worse. I was out for two months. My last monitoring days are winding down. I wouldn't be nervous or anxious to get out if it weren't for that little visit earlier this week.

Flashback"Ms. Phillips, you have a visitor." My nurse said. I nodded and met them come in. I hope it was Levi this time. Gwendolyn walked in. The nurse left and Gwendolyn took a seat.

"Hey, how you feeling?" She asked. I shrugged.

"Why are you here?" I asked cautiously.

"I guess I should cut the act huh?" She said. Gwendolyn got up and while she this, she smirked. A chill went down my spine. She came closer. "I'm here to warn you." Gwendolyn said.

"About what?" I asked.

"Levi. Stay away from him. He wants nothing to do with you. Levi would've came to tell you himself but he was busy playing with our daughter." She said with a sadistic smile.

"That doesn't make sense." I said.

"Don't believe me? Here's some texts to help you out." She said and tossed me a phone. I looked and saw texts. I soon picked up on them and saw that they were between Levi and her. Apparently they loved each other. She chuckled.

"Now that you're awake and alert, you'll understand this." She said.

"Listen here. If you come near Levi ever again, I won't hesitate to have you killed next time." She said and quickly left.

End of Flashback

A tear rolled down my cheek as I thought about that day. I was already mad at Levi. He should've been by my side. Now I find out that he was playing with Gwendolyn. So Beatrice was their daughter. Good for them, I hope.

Today was the day that I get discharged. My first order of business was to head to the stadium. My insurance paid for a new vehicle. After being discharged, I left and headed straight to that stadium. When I walked in, people looked as if they'd seen a ghost. My face had a look of determination on it. I hated that in order to get to the head coach's office, I had to walk by the locker rooms.

I had rather not but toughed up some. I walked through like a boss. When I passed Mike, I smiled at him. He looked as shocked as the others. I knocked on the door and was welcomed in. When the coach looked up, he gasped. "Chelsea Phillips?!" He said. I nodded. "In the flesh, sir." I said.

I took a seat. "We have much to discuss. First tell me. Where the hell where you for the last three months?" He asked.

"The hospital." I answered. He looked shocked. I showed him the discharge papers.

"I was in a wreck. The police looked into it. It was a hit and run. Someone was after me." I explained. He nodded and sat back. "Ok, now explain to me why there was a letter of resignation on my desk?" He asked. I shrugged. "Sir, I have no interest in quitting this job." I said. He nodded.

"The accident sounds pretty serious." He said. I nodded. "I probably shouldn't tell you this but it's been eating away at me and I need to get it off my chest. I was threatened." I told him. I proceeded to tell him about the Gwendolyn situation. After talking with him, my butt was officially saved. My job still stood. He even gave me a card for a private investigator to sort this thing out. I called him right then and there. When I walked out of the office, the players were being dismissed.

I quickly walked to my vehicle. One thing was for sure. I was avoiding Levi Anderson. -Levi

Unless I was hallucinating I'm pretty sure I saw Chelsea. Three months and she finally appeared. I missed her a lot. She walked into the head coach's office. After being in there a while, she left. She practically rushed out of there. I at least expected her to look for me but she rushed quickly.

Maybe she wanted to do something special. When I walked outside, Gwendolyn was by my truck. I groaned. "Hey, babe." She said and tried to hug me. I dodged her and took a step back. "What do you want, and don't call me babe." I said. She's been doing that a lot lately. Her car door opened and Beatrice hopped out. "Levi!" She said.

"Hey, Bea!" I said. The little girl hugged my knees. She was starting to grow on me. "Why did you get out?!" Gwendolyn yelled. Bea flinched back and hid behind my legs. "Why are you yelling at her like that? She's only two." I said.

"She needs to learn how to follow orders." Gwendolyn spat. I sighed. "Listen, what do you want because I need to go see someone." I said impatiently.

"I hope it's not Chelsea. From the looks of it, she doesn't want to see you." She said snd pointed towards a parking space. Chelsea's truck sped out of the parking lot. Whenever she passed me she didn't even wave like usual. Something was up. I got in my truck and left. When I pulled up to Chelsea's place, I checked to see if she was home. Her truck was here and her car was here too.

I walked up and buzzed the buzzer. "Who is it?" I heard her ask.

"It's me babe." I said like I usually did.

"Go away!"

"It's been three months, I want to see you." I said.

"Just leave. I have a bunch of meetings in the morning I want to get some sleep," she said and clicks off. I turned and left. Chelsea was acting weird today. I'm sure it's nothing. -ChelseaWhy did I just lie to him? That does not make things easier. I didn't have meetings in the morning. In fact, I was free for the whole day except for an afternoon practice that was scheduled. I called Mike. "Hello?"

"Mike?"

"Chelsea Jane Phillips. You have an enormous amount of explaining to do."

"I know, I know. I called to schedule a hangout for us tomorrow night."

"I'm free but I won't hangout until you tell me what has been going on."

"Trust me. This isn't something to tell over the phone. Let's hangout tomorrow and I'll stay at your place. I'll tell you then, ok?"

"Deal. Also, I want you to meet my new girlfriend too."

"Girlfriend? We definitely have to catch up. I'll see you tomorrow, ok?"

"Ok, bestie."

I hung up and let out a huge sigh. What has my life become? Things used to be easier than this. I got up and showered. I had a small headache so I took the medicine that was prescribed to me. After settling down, I put on a movie and got in my bed.

I pray that things get better.

Chapter 15

"Ok that's it!" I yelled. The head coach talked to the team while I headed to the lockers with the other trainers. I caught up with Mike. "Hey, bestie." I said. He slung an arm around me.

"Hey." He said. We walked in and grabbed up our things. On the way out, we were stopped by Levi. "Hey, babe." He said and tried to hug me. I dodged his hug and walked off. The nerve he has try and hug me. Mike looked at me weird. I just sighed and kept walking. I drove my car today. After arriving at Mike's house, I took a shower. When I finished, I combed out my wet hair and put a little oil on it.

I walked out and heard two voices. When I stepped foot into the living room my eyes got wide. "Shaley?!" I gasped. She turned. "Chelsea!" She exclaimed.

I ran and hugged her as tight as I could. "Oh my gosh it's so good to see you!" I said.

"You too! You look great!" She said. I thanked her and we started a conversation which was soon interrupted by Mike.

"So you two know each other?" He asked.

"We were roommates in college. Freshman year dorm buddies and soon to be living mates in an apartment." Shaley explained with a smile. I nodded. Mike looked surprised. "Sweet, I don't have to bother with the introductions now." He said. We both slapped his arm. He chuckled.

"I'm just happy to see my best friend again." Shaley said. We hugged again. "Um, stop right there babe." Mike said and pulled me away.

"Chelsea is my bestie." He said.

"I've known her longer." Shaley said.

"We work together." He argued.

"We lived together." She fired back.

"I see her everyday." Mike said.

"I know her better." Shaley responded.

Oh here we go, I thought with an eye roll.

"What's her favorite food?" He questioned.

"Pizza. With extra meat and cheese."

"Where is she from?"

"Mississippi." She answered with ease.

"Middle name?"

"Jane."

"Ok. Last one and it's gonna be hard. Which arm did she break and what age did she break it?" He asked with a raised eyebrow and smirk.

"She never broke her arm." Shaley said with a smirk. Mike's smirk fell but then he smiled. "I guess we can share her." He said and pulled her into a hug. I laughed.

"That's what I thought you guys would do." I said and pushed myself into their hug. They laughed but hugged me back anyway. Mike looked at me. "So, are you gonna stall all night or do what you said you would do?" He asked. I nodded. "Ok, I will. As long as Shaley stays." I said. He nodded and motioned to the couch.

I sat down, took a deep breath, and told the story. "He what?!" Shaley practically yelled in my ear. I nodded.

"No, Shaley. He didn't come see me in the hospital. I could've died and to find out that Gwendolyn was the one who did it made me angry. It made me even angrier when I found out they were canoodling behind my back. Then he tries to hug me like everything is normal?! What the hell?!" I yelled.

"So that's why you were gone for a long time. I thought my best friend quit. Chelsea I'm just glad you're ok. But don't ever say canoodling again." Mike said and hugged me. "Me too, Chelsea." Shaley said. I let out a small laugh.

"Yeah I'm fine but I'm just confused. I thought Levi would, you know, be loyal. It hurts to know that he wasn't there for my dark times." I said. I know what you're thinking. Am I giving up on Levi?

To tell the truth, no. I'm not gonna leave him in the dark like this. It's too hard, I love him too much. It's gonna take a long amount of thinking. -Levi I texted, called, and did everything to try and reach Chelsea. She generally didn't want to see me. The next day, I showed up early to practice. When she walked in I stopped her. "Excuse me." She said and tried to move around me. I blocked her. "Excuse me." She said a little bit more forceful. I didn't move.

"Levi move." She said.

"I called you and texted you yesterday." I said. She sighed and looked at her phone.

"There are no missed calls or texts. If you stopped me to tell me those lies then you seriously need to move." She said. That hurt. I looked at her phone.

"You sure you didn't get a call?" I asked.

"Yes, I am sure. Now move, I have many things to do." She said and brushed past me. I need to figure out what her problem is. I went to the locker room and got ready for practice. We did all the usual stuff and started drills. After practice I made it my mission to talk to her. I stopped her when she was about to leave and pulled her into a conference room.

"What did I do?" I asked.

"You want to know what you did?" She asked quietly after a few minutes. I nodded. "Very much, yes because it drives me crazy when we're not together." I said truthfully.

She sighed and sat down in a chair. "Three months ago, I was in a wreck. My head was damaged pretty bad. I was in a coma for two months and had to be under constant monitoring for a month. My question is, where were you? Where were you during all of this? I never got a text, call, or even a freaking visit. Although, on my last day someone came. And that someone was Gwendolyn. Information was given. The girl is crazy. She told me how you two were together now and how much you love each other. Even showed me texts." She said. My emotions skyrocketed.

I love this girl so much and to find that she almost died kills me.

"The girl had someone hit my car, Levi. She threatened to have me killed the next time I was around you. But you don't have to worry about that because the only time you'll see me is at work. Just take care of your daughter and have a nice life." She said and started to leave. I stopped her. I wasn't gonna let her go that easy.

"I am so sorry. If you were in a wreck then I should have been notified. What Gwendolyn said about me and her isn't true. I don't love her. Yes, Beatrice is my daughter but that doesn't change what we have." I said while looking her in the eye. I'm pretty sure I was crying by now but I didn't care. I could've lost her. I got angry and punched the wall. A hole was made and my hand throbbed like crazy but I didn't care. "I could've lost you!" I cried out.

I hugged her tight. It took her a moment before she hugged me back. We just sat at there, hugging then eventually slid to the floor. She reached up and wiped my tears. I pulled her closer. One thing crossed my mind. If Chelsea was in the hospital for three months, who was I texting? "Chelsea?" I called.

"Yeah, Levi?" She answered.

"Did you by chance get a new number?" I asked her. She sat up and shook her head.

"No, still the same number." She said. She pulled out her phone and showed me the automatic contact of her number. I pulled out my phone and looked at the number that was supposedly her new number. "What's wrong Levi?" She asked.

"That's funny. I got a text the day of your wreck from someone posing as you. Look." I said and showed her. She scrolled through the messages and her eyes widened. "Levi." Chelsea said. I looked at her. "I should slap your head right now." She said in a serious tone.

"These are the freaking texts that Gwendolyn showed me that apparently proved that you loved her. She showed me these in the hospital." She said. My eyes widened. So this whole time, I was texting Gwendolyn? Ew. "Chelsea I'm so sorry." I said.

"Yeah, yeah. Give me the phone." She said and took it. She texted something and handed me the phone. "Go home. I'll be there in an hour." She said.

Before she opened the door I called her name. "Yeah?" She answered.

"I love you." I said.

"I love you, too, you idiot." She said and left. I smiled and left.-Chelsea I've come to an understanding with Levi. There's no defined forgiveness yet. I'm still deciding. I love Levi very much and it hurts not to be with him. I walked into my apartment and got a shower.

After showering I dressed up really nice. I put on a dress and sandals. I checked my make up and left. On the way to Levi's, I called the private investigator.

"Hello?" I answered. He asked me a question.

"Yes, everything will be set up. I have it right now." I told him.

After arriving at Levi's place and setting up my plan, I waited. Levi walked out of his room and stopped when he saw me. I smiled. He came over to me. "Hello." I said with a smile. He smiled and leaned in to kiss me. I welcomed it. I hadn't seen Levi in so long. "I missed you." I said.

"You have no idea how much I missed you." He said in a husky voice. He was about to kiss me again when the buzzer sounded. I looked at the clock and smiled. "Right on time." I said. Levi looked confused.

After quickly explaining everything to Levi I opened the door. Gwendolyn looked up and I smiled. "What are you doing here?" She asked. I motioned for her to come in. Levi frowned at her while she smiled at him. I rolled my eyes. Levi followed my act and led her to the couch. "Gwendolyn, you'd tell me the truth right?" Levi asked. She nodded and batted her fake lashes. "Ok. Did you know that Chelsea was in the hospital?" He asked.

"Yes." She said.

"Why didn't you tell me?" He asked her.

"I want you to myself. You love me. It's here in the phone. You said it. I love you too, Levi." She said. He shook his head.

"No, I don't. I don't love you. I love Chelsea." He said. Her face contorted to anger. She then looked at me. "I knew I should've killed you when I had the chance. But no, you survived. Listen to this, listen real good. You better watch your back. I'm gonna get you. Beatrice will have her father, and I will have my husband." She said angrily.

"Yeah about that, there was a misunderstanding with your little Doctor here." Levi said.

"What do you mean? It's said it in here, you're her father." Gwendolyn said. Levi chuckled and pulled out a piece of paper. "This is Dr. Scott. He is the doctor from the clinic. I called his office the other day when you gave this to me. I've been meaning to tell you this. He says that you never came to his clinic. This signature is forged." Levi said, "I'm not her father but she is a wonderful little girl. If she was mine, she'd have brown eyes like me. Not grey like you. Other reasons too but that's not important right now. You're going to jail for this." He continued.

Someone knocked at the door so I opened it. The detective stood there. "Hello, detective Morris." I said. He nodded to me and made his way to Gwendolyn. "Gwendolyn Waters, you are under arrest for forging someone else's signature, and for the kidnapping of Grace Turner." He said.

"Kidnapping? Grace Turner?" Levi asked, confused. The detective nodded. "We've been hunting down this woman for five months. She kidnapped her sister's child. We will gladly take her off your hands." He said then headed towards the door.

"Thank you, detective." Levi called out. Gwendolyn was taken away. I turned to Levi only to find he was looking at me. "I'm sorry." He said.

"For what?" I asked.

"For everything. Gwendolyn, the wreck, this drama, everything." He said. I walked towards him.

"I love you, Chelsea. One day, I promise we will get married. I'm gonna marry you. I know this, I knew it from the first day." He said. I smiled as he came closer.

"I love you too, Levi. And I'm looking forward to that day." I said. He smiled before he kissed me.

Chapter 16

"Good news!" Levi shouted as he walked into our apartment. We live together now! "Ok, what is it?" I asked.

"I get to stay home for the rest of the day!" He said and kissed me. I laughed. "Oh great. A whole day of just looking at your face." I said sarcastically. He backed away and looked hurt.

"You're mean."

"I'm just playing, baby." I said.

"Yeah but when you play, you make it sound real." He said. I laughed and wrapped my arms around him. He did the same. "So, what do we wanna do today?" I asked.

"Plan our wedding." He said while he played with the ends of my hair. "How are we gonna plan a wedding when you haven't proposed yet?" I asked. He shrugged. "That's a minor detail." He said. I chuckled.

"So wedding planning huh? Ok. Let's plan my wedding with my dream fiancé, Ryan Gosling." I said with a dreamy look.

I closed my eyes and but my lip. "Mm, mm, mm. That man is gorgeous." I said. I opened my eyes and Levi was staring at me. I laughed nervously. "Love you." I said with kissing lips. He waved me off and walked away. I followed him into our bedroom. "I'm not mad because I know you love me and that you'll never meet Ryan Gosling ever in your lifetime." He said with a smile as he took his suit jacket off. I laughed.

"What if I get lucky one day?" I asked.

"Then, Ryan Gosling would be very lucky to meet my woman. Too bad he can't have her." He said before he spun me around.

"I love you." He said.

"I love you, too." I said. He finally kissed me. After he changed clothes we settled down in the living room. "Levi?" I called.

"Yeah?" He answered.

"How'd you know?"

"Know what?" He asked.

"That we would be what we are right now?"

"Some things you just know. It was no secret for me. I've loved you forever." He said. I smiled at him. He smiled down at me. "Let's go get some ice cream or something." He said. I nodded and slipped on some shoes. He grabbed my hand and we left. Once we pulled put to the ice cream place I basically rushed out of the truck. Levi quickly caught up with me and ordered our ice cream.

Quickly, we made it back home and were laying on the couch once again. "This ice cream is so good." I said. He nodded as he got up to turn the tv on. Levi and I laid around all day. "I was supposed to propose today." Levi said suddenly. I looked at him.

"Way to ruin the surprise, Levi." I said with a small laugh. He smiled.

"You were gonna say yes." He said. I smirked.

"What makes you so sure?" I asked. Levi turned around to face me. He placed his head in his hands and looked at me. "I can see it in your eyes. All of it. The love you have for me, when you're angry, when you're irritated or annoyed. I know you." He said slowly. I leaned in absentmindedly he chuckled and pulled me close. "You were gonna say yes." He said.

"True. I'll say yes a million times." I said.

"Will you marry me?" He asked.

"No."

"You just said that you'd say yes a million times." He whined. I laughed.

"I still want a nice proposal." I said. He nodded and kissed my cheeks. I guess we fell asleep because later I was woken up by the buzzer. Levi was asleep. He was always a heavy sleeper. Me too but today that wasn't the case. I opened the door and there was Shaley and Mike. They jumped on me and hugged me. I laughed as they did.

"Hey guys." I said while wiping my eyes.

"You two were asleep? Such a married couple." Shaley said.

"Wake up man!" Mike yelled then sat on Levi. His eyes popped open and he groaned. "Mike what have you been eating man?" He asked as he pushed him off. Mike fell to the floor with a thud. We laughed. "Michael, Shaley. Why are you here?" Levi asked.

"We came to find some trouble." Shaley said.

"Let's go get into some trouble!" Mike shouted.

"No. Last time we went out with you two I came back drunk and Chelsea got lost." Levi said.

"Not our fault that your girlfriend has no sense of direction." Shaley said.

"Watch it." Levi warned. I chuckled. "Ok, I know! Let's go to this new bar that opened up downtown." I said. They all thought for a minute. "I'm down." Shaley said.

"Me too."Mike voiced.

"Where Chelsea goes, I go." Levi said. I nodded and clapped my hands.

"Let's go." I said and headed towards the door.

"Chelsea." Levi said. I turned and looked at him.

"Are you forgetting that you have on your ducky pajama pants?" He said with a small laugh. I looked down and gave a sheepish smile. "I'll be right back." I said and left the room. After changing, we left. When we got there, the placed was packed but not too packed.

We all found a table that accommodated us all plus one more person so everything worked out pretty good. The waitress took our orders and went to put them in. An hour into hanging out, I wanted to dance. "Come on Shaley." I said and grabbed her hand. Mike and Levi were too engrossed in a conversation to notice us leave. An upbeat song started and our hips went to moving. I looked at Levi and he winked.

"This reminds me of our college days." Shaley said. I nodded in agreement. My gaze shifted to the door as it opened. I stopped abruptly. "Oh my gosh! Oh my gosh! Oh my gosh! There's my future fiancé!" I shouted at Shaley. "Levi? Yeah there's your man. I see mine too." She said. I rolled my eyes.

"No. Either I'm hallucinating or I see Ryan Gosling at that dang door right now." I said. She turned and her eyes widened.

"Girl. That's Ryan alright." Shaley said. I watched as his eyes scanned the room. His eyes caught contact with mine. My stomach did a flip. He left and entered the VIP room though. Oh I'm definitely being a fan girl right now. "I need a drink." I said and headed back to the table with Shaley. I was bouncing in my seat. "Babe, either you have to go to the bathroom or you're excited about something. Which one is it?" Levi asked.

"She's just giddy because she saw Ryan Gosling." Shaley said.

"Oh really?" Levi asked. I nodded my head rapidly. He chuckled. We ordered drinks and sat around to talk.

"Hey, Shaley, remember when we were in college and went out drinking?" I asked. Her eyes widened and she nodded.

"Girl yes! And we'd always end up at someone else's house." She said and laughed. I laughed along with her. "Yeah, at least the dude was nice enough to let us stay." I said and she laughed.

"Hold up." Mike said.

"What guy?" Levi asked.

"Oh you know, a guy from one of wild adventures in college." Shaley said. Both guys looked at us skeptically. "But nothing to worry about." I said with a sweet smile. Wink. -"Chelsea, wake up." I heard someone say. I was being shaken. I slowly opened my eyes. I was in the truck. Levi was standing outside my door. "Wake up. You kept murmuring something about Ryan Gosling and your man." Levi said in an annoyed tone.

"I was asleep?" I asked. He nodded.

"Yeah." He said.

"We didn't meet Ryan Gosling?" I asked. He shook his head. "No." He said.

Dang it.

Really? So it was just a dream. -"Wake up!" I yelled as I put the last piece of bacon on Levi's plate. I heard him groan. "Give me five more minutes babe!" He yelled. I shook my head and walked into our room. Levi was curled up into a ball. I pushed him and he groaned. "That's ok, I'll eat your bacon. I'm pretty sure this was the last of the bacon we had anyway." I said and started to walk away.

"Don't. Touch. My. Bacon." Levi said as he sat up slowly. I smiled and placed the plate on the nearby table. I grabbed my clothes and headed into the bathroom. After showering, I got dressed in a pair of ripped skinny jeans and an old college t shirt. I slipped my converses on and walked out. "You leaving?" Levi asked. I nodded as I put on some lip balm.

"I'm coming." He said. I nodded. "Yeah you should come. Who else is gonna pay for the groceries?" I asked with a cheeky smile. Levi squinted his eyes at me. "Cute." He said then disappeared to get ready. He soon came out and was ready. As I walked along the aisles, Levi pushed the cart not too far behind me. He called my name and I turned around to see what he wanted. I his hands he held a box of cupcakes. "Can I get them?" He asked.

"Why are you asking me? You have the money." I said. He nodded. "But you're the boss lady." He said with a wink. I laughed. "Ugh, you sound like my dad." I said. He laughed.

"As your trainer, I say no. But as your girlfriend, I say we can share them." I said with a smile soon followed by a laugh. Levi did a small victory dance. We continued out trek through the grocery store. A bunch of groceries later, we were back on the couch. "Let's do it again next weekend." Levi said. I just laughed.

"Sure. Who knows whenever I can spend an off day with my man again?" I said with a smile. He just pulled me closer. "Can I kiss you now?" He asked and ran a thumb across my bottom lip. I laughed and nodded.

Chapter 17

Levi leaned in to kiss me before I headed to the trainer's room. When I walked in a bunch of congratulations were given to me. "Thank you?" I said, confused. I walked over to Mike. "Um, what's going on?" I asked. He shrugged.

"They think that Levi proposed." He said. I laughed. "How'd they know he was gonna propose?" I asked.

"Levi told them he was going to. I guess they thought he did already." Mike said. I chuckled. "Levi told me he was gonna propose yesterday. He did but I declined." I said.

"Why?" Mike asked.

"I want to marry him. I just want a nice proposal and I'd kind of like it to be a surprise." I said. He nodded as we walked on to the field. There was a game tomorrow so the practice wouldn't last long. After stretching the players and testing their physical ability for the game, we left them for the coaches. The other trainers and I headed to our break room to meet about a new practice schedule. We didn't do much so after we met we just chilled.

Soon practice was over and we all went home. -"Let's elope." Levi said when I walked out of the bathroom. I laughed. "Our parents would kill us." I said. He shrugged.

"I'd die a happy man." He said with a smile. I chuckled. "You really have your heart set on marrying me, huh?" I asked. He nodded. "And I won't stop until I do." He told me. I smiled and crawled into the bed.

"I'm hungry." Levi said.

"No you're not." I said. As if on cue, his stomach growled. I laughed. "Really?" I asked and looked at him. He just shrugged and smiled.

"I'll cook. What do you want?" I asked. He thought for a moment.

"A cake. Bake me a cake, Chelsea Jane." Levi said.

"A cake, Levi?" I asked. He nodded. "Yeah, like one of those cakes your mom makes." He said. I laughed and got up as I shook my head. I made my way to the kitchen and got down the ingredients. Luckily, there was some chocolate cake mix in the cabinet. And some frosting too! I mixed the cake and popped it in the oven. Shortly I reappeared into our room. Levi was watching tv. I sat beside him. He kissed my cheek.

"Mm, you smell like chocolate. I love chocolate." He said and licked his lips. I laughed and played a game on my phone. Once the time went off, we both made our way to the kitchen. Levi sat at the bar and watched as I iced the cake. "Levi, I can't focus when you're just staring at me like that." I said. He chuckled. "You're so irresistible." He said. I laughed.

"Nah, you just like the fact that I made you a cake at ten o'clock at night." I said. He looked at his watch. "Anytime is cake time, babe." He said. I rolled eyes as I sat the cake in a cake plate. I'm so glad my mom got me a cake plate as a housewarming gift. Levi tried to sneakily put his finger in the cake. I slapped his hand. He looked at me. "Stop." I said. He pouted. "It's hot." I told him.

"You're hot,"He said,"but I can still touch you." He complained. I rolled my eyes and walked away. He soon caught up with me and lifted me up from the ground. "Would you stop rolling your eyes? It's a eleven year trait I've gotten used to. I see it everyday and it's kind of getting old." He said. I looked at him and rolled my eyes once again. "Has it really been eleven years?" I asked. He gasped.

"Have you forgotten our best friend anniversary." He asked, shocked. "You weren't my best friend. Even now, you're not my best friend." I said. He feigned hurt. "You're more than that. For now, you're my boyfriend." I said.

"I love you." He said with a smile before he crashed his lips onto mine.

"Dang, I can't say I love you back?" I asked after he kissed me. He sighed and huffed. "Fine. Go ahead if you must." He said. I nodded and smiled.

"I love you too." I said. Levi wasted no time and kissed me again. - The reporters swarmed around the stadium waiting for the gates to open. Levi and I had just arrived. He had his game face on. I looked at him and he looked down at me and smiled. That grin of his always made me smile. I squeezed his hand tighter. We made it to the conference room where he would do yet another interview. I stood at the back by the door as always.

Levi winked at me before the interview started. Question after question was asked and Levi answered one after another. Soon he was finished and we were walking back to the locker rooms. I walked in and gave some instructions. "Make sure you are dressed and ready for warm ups in fifteen minutes." I said.

The game went pretty good. It was after the game and I was looking everywhere for Levi. "Have you seen Levi?" I asked a player.

"He's still on the field I think." He said. I nodded and thanked him. I wonder what Levi could be doing on the field. I saw him on the mound. I went and tapped his shoulder he turned around and smiled. "It's beautiful isn't it?" He asked. I looked around and saw that the sun setting indeed was a gorgeous sight. He grabbed my hands.

"I love you so much. We've been through everything together for the past eleven years. Twelve now. I remember that day clearly. Twelve years ago I moved to another small town. I met this little girl there the first day. All I could remember was my little heart thumping so fast when I saw her. As time goes by me and this little girl hang out. We went through high school together, attempted to stay in touch for college, then reconnected later in life." He said. He was talking about us.

"Who'd a thought that she'd be one of my bosses. But, hey, I see her smiling face everyday. And for that, I'm grateful. Now we come to the part of our story where we move things along. Today, on this twelfth anniversary of us, I'm proposing to her. Chelsea Jane Phillips, will you marry me?" He asked. A single tear fell down my cheek as I said,"Heck yeah!"

I jumped on him and hugged him. He laughed as I did. When he finally put the ring on my finger I kissed him. His hands found my waist and he pulled me closer. We heard cheering. I looked and saw the whole team and coaching staff. "About time Levi put a ring on it!" Someone shouted causing us to laugh. I'm pretty sure that was Mike.

After the commotion settled down, everyone went out to eat together. There was so many of us that the team rented out a restaurant. I stuck on Levi's side all night, which I'm pretty sure he didn't mind.

Every now and then I kept glancing at the ring. It was gorgeous and it was finally a reality. I'm engaged to Levi Anderson.

Twelve years now that we've known each other. It feels longer. We've been together for almost a year now but it feels longer. I looked at Levi only to find him looking at me.

"Ugh, are you guys gonna be that couple who always stares at each other lovingly?" Mike interrupted. We turned our heads to Mike. "Michael, why you gotta ruin my moment?" I asked him.

"Because he a butthole." Shaley piped up. I nodded in agreement, so did Levi. "Shaley is just mad because I didn't propose." Mike said. I shook my head and looked at Shaley for confirmation. She just rolled her eyes. That was a yes. I rolled mine too to tell her that everything would be just fine.

On the way home, Levi sang every song on the radio. We called and talked to our families. They were over the moon excited when they found out about the engagement, which I'm sure they already knew about. Tonight was the last game. We have a whole summer to ourselves. Training starts back up towards the end. Levi and I had planned to leave for Mississippi the day after tomorrow so we could make it back for his birthday.

I danced my way into our apartment with Levi not to far behind me. "I'm getting married, I'm getting married." I sang quietly to myself.

"I can hear you." Levi said. I turned and he was standing by the door. I shrugged and kept singing and dancing. "You surprise me everyday." He said as he wrapped me in his arms.

"No that's you who surprises me. It's something new everyday, huh?" I asked.

"It's a different day everyday, sweetheart." He said. I smiled as he turned me around to face him. "I love you." I told him.

"I love you more." He said.

Chapter 18

"Hey family!" I shouted as Levi and I made it into the house. My mom and dad turned their heads. "And there's that loud child of mine." My dad said. I laughed as he hugged me.

"Hello, sweetheart." My mom said while I hugged her. They both hugged Levi. For a minute, they just stared at us. "Ugh, you two are getting married!" My mom said excitedly. I shrugged my shoulders up and down while I did a happy dance. "That's right!" I said.

"How was your flight?" My dad asked us. Levi shrugged. "It was ok, although your daughter slept the whole way." Levi said.

"Plane rides make me sleepy." I said and proceeded towards the kitchen. Levi chuckled. "Well at least you two made it safely. Congrats on the last game of the season, Levi." My mom said.

"Thank you." He said. We all sat down for a light lunch then headed to see Levi's parents. "Levi! I knew you weren't gonna be a wimp all your life, congratulations on the engagement son!" Joe shouted as he came out the house. I laughed as Levi's dad gave him a huge bear hug. After hugging Levi he came and gave me the same hug. I laughed as he did. I've always enjoyed his hugs.

His mom came out and hugged us. "So what now? Another party?" My mom asked Levi's parents. "You know it!" How said.

"Another party?" I asked.

"We all hosted a party to watch the game last night." Brenda said. I nodded. As our parents talked, Levi pulled me into the house and up to his room. "Let's take a nap. I'm sleepy." He said.

"I'm not sleepy." I said. He pulled me down anyway. I yelped as he did. "You know I can't sleep without you." He murmured in my ear. "I guess." I said. He sighed contently and drifted to sleep. I planned on sneaking out of his hold but he wrapped his legs around mine as he spooned me. I sighed and snuggled up to him.

Later

Levi "Awe, look at them, their asleep." I heard someone whisper.

"We'll leave them alone, they need to sleep."

"Well ok."

I heard my room door close.

"Our parents can't whisper." Chelsea murmured. I sighed. "True." I said. She sat up and wiped her eyes like a kid. I stretched my muscles out. I wrapped my arms around her. She kissed my cheek. Chelsea was so beautiful. I've always known that we'd be together. Now we're getting married and I couldn't be happier. I love her so much.

"Why you staring at me like that?" She asked as she wiped away some drool. Yep, beautiful.

"I'm the luckiest man in the world. I'm so lucky to have you." I said to her. She smiled and leaned in.

"You sure are. I'd be glad to have me too." She said with a smile. I playfully glared at her. "That sarcasm of yours is unbelievable." I said. She just shrugged. -ChelseaI looked out the window and it was almost dark. I heard the music downstairs. "Our parents are throwing a party." I said as I looked out the window. Levi came and looked out the window with me. "Whelp, would you look at that. Your brothers just pulled up." I said. He peered out the window and watched as

Hunter, Steven, Luke, Grayson, and Daniel proceeded towards the house.

"Here come your cousins and friends." Levi said. Raleigh and Shana came too. Even Joanna. I hopped on the bed. "I'm not in the mood for a party right now, babe. Let's watch tv." I said. Levi wasted no time and sat close to me. I turned the tv on and placed the channel on. Duck Dynasty was on so we decided to watch that.

"You're coming with me this duck season." Levi said. I shook my head. "No can do. I can sit in a deer stand all day long but waiting for some ducks? That's a no no. Sorry babe." I said.

"What if I told you Kaitlin was coming?" He asked. Kaitlin was his dad's friend's daughter. She threw herself on him every time she saw him.

"Then I'm coming." I told him.

"Why change your mind all of a sudden?" He asked.

"Because Kaitlin is a major whore. Worse than Casey and she's not coming nowhere near my man." I said as I latched on to his arm and he chuckled. As I did this, the door opened and there was a huge group standing there. "Get out." Levi said. They all came in anyway.

"Hey guys!" I said. They all greeted me and Levi. Levi just told them to get out again. I slapped his shoulder. "Quit being mean." I said. He only shrugged and I rolled my eyes. "Oh I see the engagement changes nothing for you two." Grayson said.

"Yeah, Levi is still an asshole and Chelsea still rolls those eyes." Steven said. We all laughed. "What do y'all want? As you can see, before you guys interrupted, I was trying to enjoy some alone time with my fiancé." Levi said gruffly.

"Oh please, you guys should get enough alone time in San Fransisco. Our time now." Raleigh said. Levi pulled me closer. "Can y'all please get out?" He whined.

They all voiced their no's. Levi shrugged and started to kiss me. "Ew, stop!" I heard Grayson stop. Levi deepened the kiss.

"Y'all nasty." Shana said. Levi kissed me harder and flipped us over. He was hovering me now. "You know, I think it's time for us to leave. Let's go kids before they start creating juniors." I heard Hunter say. Once the door shut, I pushed Levi off of me. "You barbarian." I said as he laughed his head off. "Your facial expression is funny, babe." He said in between laughter.

I laughed sarcastically. "Yeah, so funny. The next time you decide to suck my face off, tell me." I said and got up to straighten out my clothes. "I'm sorry." Levi said with a pouted lip. "Well your birthday is tomorrow so I won't go crazy." I said. He smiled and hopped up. Levi wrapped his arms around my waist and kissed my forehead.

"I kind of liked the kiss though." I said to him while looking at him through the mirror. He smirked. "Oh really?" He asked. I nodded. He leaned in to kiss me but I dodged it. "I'll kiss you on your birthday. But until then, I have a party to go to." I said and walked towards the door. "Wait, I'm coming. I don't want any guys looking at my fiancé." He said. I chuckled and waited for him.

As we walked downstairs, I looked at my engagement ring. It was gorgeous. I still remembered what Levi said to me the morning before we left for Mississippi. "You will wear this ring, be proud of this ring, and love this ring. It's all for you, baby. I hope you love it because I paid a lot of money for it."

I laughed out loud at the memory. "Wanna share what's so funny?" Levi asked.

"Oh nothing. I just thought about what you said about my ring." I said to him. He smiled and wrapped an arm around me. Once we hit the bottom step, everyone smothered us in hugs and kisses along with congratulations on our engagement. It was around six thirty and the place was packed. Levi's dad and my dad were grilling and our moms were cooking up a storm in the kitchen. But I was hungry at the moment.

"Levi." I said at the same time as he called my name.

"Hungry?" He asked.

"Hungry." I replied. He grabbed my hand and slipped one of his brother's keys off the key hook. We hopped into the truck and left. "Who's truck is it this time?" I asked.

"Luke's." He said. I shook my head at him.

"You are very mischievous." I said.

"You make me this way." He said.

"I hope our kids aren't as mischievous as you." I said with a small laugh. He was quiet. I looked at him and he was smiling. "You wanna have kids with me?" He asked.

"Well duh. Who else would I have them with? I love you and only you." I said. His smile grew bigger with each word. He reached over and rubbed my stomach. "Our kids are gonna be good looking." He said. I slapped his hand away and he laughed.

Levi pulled up to the old diner we always visited as teens. We walked in and grabbed a booth. "Levi! Chelsea!" The waitress said excitedly as she neared us. "Hey Bertha." We greeted. "What's new?" She asked us. Bertha has always asked us this question.

"Well, I'm engaged now." Levi said.

"Who is the lucky lady? I hope it's Chelsea. She's the only one I approve." Bertha said. Levi had a mischievous glint in his eyes so I played along.

"I'm actually engaged too, Bertha." I said.

"Goodness me, you two have been busy." Bertha said.

"Yeah, my fiancé is great. She's smart, beautiful, and just down to earth." Levi said.

"My fiancé is better though. He is sweet, funny, and loves me very much." I told her. Bertha nodded. "They sound wonderful." She said.

After taking our orders and quickly bringing them out we devoured our food. We both walked to the cash register to pay for the food. "It's on the house." Bertha said. We looked confused.

"Seriously, go on now. Think of it as an early wedding gift." She said. We looked at her surprised.

"That rock ain't hard to miss, honey." She said and pointed to my finger.

"Plus, who else would put up with this knucklehead? And who can handle such a feisty fireball like yourself, little miss missy?" She asked.

"You're right, he is a knucklehead." I said. Levi scoffed. "I'm a knucklehead just as sure as she's a feisty fireball." He said. She laughed. "Y'all go on now. Go enjoy that party your parents are throwing." She said.

"You know about the party?" Levi asked.

"They put it on Facebook and they throw the best parties in the county." Bertha said. We laughed then left.

"Who would've thought that our parents would throw the best parties?" Levi asked. I shrugged. "Looks like their capable of it." I said and pointed to the yard as we pulled in. We walked in and was instantly swarmed with people. "You two disappeared." My momma said.

"Um.." I started.

"And you've been to the diner." She said.

"Well you see..." Levi started.

"Just go have fun. I know that you guys will raid the kitchen later. But y'all better do that a little earlier, Levi's brothers are staying the night for his birthday." She said. We nodded and made our way out back where more people were dancing and having a good time. More people congratulated us. The DJ stopped the music and someone grabbed the microphone. It was Daniel.

"I just want to say congratulations to my little brother, Levi, for his engagement-"

"Noooooo!!!!" Someone shouted. We all turned out heads to the direction of where the voice came from. It was Kaitlin and she was crying.

"Someone get her out of here, why is he even here?!" I yelled and the crowd chuckled. Levi pulled me close to him. Everyone knew how I felt about that girl. It was no secret.

"Anyway, congrats Levi and Chelsea." Daniel finished and the music started back up. A slow song came on and Levi led me to the dance floor to dance. I laughed as he mimicked me on what I said earlier. "Ugh, I'm marrying a kid." I said.

"I'm not a kid." He argued. I laughed.

"Yeah, right. How old are you turning, again?" I asked.

"Twenty four." He said with a broad smile.

"Four, got it." I said with a smile. He shook his head at me then kissed my forehead. As the night stretched on, we danced and danced. "Hey, look, it's midnight. Happy birthday, Levi. I love you, baby." I said to him as I hugged him tight. He tilted my chin towards him and planted a long sloppy kiss on my lips. "Nasty." I said and he chuckled then pecked me on the lips.

After everyone that was at the party left, I showered. I walked downstairs humming a song. "You're the one I want, you're the one I need." I sang to myself. I even shook my hips. The microwave dinged so I took my food out. There was extra on my plate because I knew Levi would want to eat off of my plate. The Anderson boys piled into the kitchen and ate the rest of the food.

"You guys eat a lot." I said.

"This is nothing new." Luke said as he bit a piece of steak. They all nodded. Levi entered the kitchen and grabbed another fork to eat with me. "There's the birthday boy." Hunter said.

"Get ready, 'cause in the morning we are going for an adventure." Steven said.

"Can I rain check?" Levi asked.

"Nope." Steven said.

"You sure? I'm pretty sure Chelsea needs me." He said and looked at me for help. I shrugged and said nothing. He sighed. "I guess." He said and continued to eat. Levi and I finished the food and went to the living room. There was a huge sectional big enough to fit the whole family comfortably. We settled into a corner of it and started to watch tv. One by one, the Anderson boys came in.

"Don't you two look cozy." Grayson said. They chuckled. I smiled and laid my head on Levi's chest. He kissed my forehead. Man I can't believe I'm marrying this man. The guys were anything but quiet the whole night. They kept making noises and remarks on everything Levi and I did.

"Ok! The next Anderson brother who makes a joke about Levi and I will square up and box me!" I said and looked then all in the eyes.

"I find it cute how Chelsea and Levi always hold hands. They're so sweet." Grayson said in an annoying baby voice.

"Alright, baby Anderson. Let's box." I said. He hopped up. The guys moved out of the way. Grayson had me in a headlock at first but then I tickled him and he let go. After that, I tripped him and sat on him. "Three! Two! One!" Luke counted.

"And baby Anderson loses to the future Mrs. Anderson for the sixth time in a row!" Steven announced. We all laughed. Levi wrapped his arms around me. Later on, I found myself singing Levi songs in his room. "Ugh, why am I doing this?" I asked.

"Cause it's my birthday." Levi said and buried his head into my neck. He planted small kisses along my neck as I sang. I drifted to sleep as he did.

Chapter 19

One year later We wish you guys the best on your wedding -The Giants

"Awe, Levi come look! The team sent a really nice card!" I shouted. I heard Levi's footsteps come down the stairs. "What'd you say?" He asked. I pointed to the card I sat on the table. He smiled after he read it. "Sweet, ain't it?" I said. He nodded and wrapped his arms around me. "Any mail for me, babe?" He asked.

"No, not much." I said.

"Well, come on. We gotta be at your parents' house in two hours." He said. I sighed and trudged up the stairs. Levi and I lived together in a house. We had a house in Mississippi and a condo in San Fransisco.

"Levi! Hurry quick it's an emergency!" I yelled. I heard his heavy footsteps bound up the stairs.

Once he made his way into our room he looked around for me. "What's wrong?" He asked with deep concern on his face.

"I need to tell you something." I said with a serious face.

"Ok what is it?" He asked.

"I just wanted to say that I love you." I said with a smile. He playfully rolled his eyes and walked out. "Say it back!" I yelled after him.

"Love you too, baby!" He shouted. I laughed and got ready. -"Oh my babies are getting married in a month!" Levi's mom gushed. Levi pulled me closer into him. "And I can't wait until Chelsea becomes Mrs. Anderson." Levi said. I smiled brightly. I looked down at my engagement ring. Randomly, a thought came to my mind. "Levi, has it ever occurred to you that you have never bought me a promise ring? It's the couple thing to do, you know." I said. He looked at me weird.

"I didn't need to buy one." He said.

"How come?" I asked.

"Because I already knew that I was going to marry you. Did I need to make a promise when it was already set in my heart? I love you, and no promise ring can tell you that more than me. Plus I promised that to you already." He said and kissed me. My momma awed loudly. I smiled at him. "Nice save." I said.

"I know right?" He said and took a breath. I laughed cuddled closer to Levi. It seemed as if we were already married. We had a routine that went on from day to day. While we were down here, that routine got perfected. He would get up and go to the gym every morning, I'd get up around nine and he'd be back an hour after that. Then, we'd go do wedding stuff. Planning a wedding is no joke. I'm just glad it's in a month. The wait is killing me also.

"Hey y'all, what if I bust out of my dress today?" I asked with a snort. My mom and Levi's mom looked at me then laughed. "We got you sweetie, there's a back up." My mom said.

"Well what if my tie comes untied?" Levi asked.

"Let's not play the what if game." His mom said.

"She's right. Besides, I can come tie it for you. I tie it for you all the time anyway." I said. Levi nodded with a smile. "No, no little missy.

You are going no where near Levi and he isn't coming no where near you." Brenda said.

"Why not?" Levi asked his mom.

"We all know that Levi has little self control around you. He can't help but to put his hands on you, kiss you, or something. Plus, it's bad luck for him to even see you in the dress." My mom said.

"In my defense, your daughter is irresistible." Levi tells her. She just playfully rolled her eyes and jumped into conversation with his mom. Since we didn't have to be at our fittings until later, we left. I watched as Levi unlocked our home. "Has anyone ever told you that you have a big butt?" I asked him and pinched his butt. He jumped a little.

"Not really, why?" He asked. I poked it over and over again.

"It's big, babe. It must be because of baseball." I said. He chuckled and grabbed my hands.

"It just might be. I may have a big butt but so do you." He said and pinched mine. I laughed. "You're weird." I said with a smile.

"Aren't you the one who started the conversation about butts, Chelsea?" He asked.

"Well, I guess we're both weird, Levi." I said with a smile. "I love you." He said with a smile as he gazed into my eyes.

"You say that all the time." I told him. He laughed and followed me to the kitchen. "Why are you so sassy?" He asked. I shrugged. "Some people need someone sassy in their life. Here I am!" I said with a smile. He laughed. "Well I don't think they said anything about too much sassiness." He said. I rolled my eyes. "See, there you go again with the eye rolls. You can't go a day without them." He told me.

"I know, but you make me do it." I said.

"How?" He questioned. I thought for a moment. "You just do, but I wouldn't trade it for nothing in the world. I love you too much for that." I said. He smiled. Levi wasted no time and placed a big one on my lips. I broke away and plopped down on the couch. "Hey guess what?" He said. I asked what. "We get married in a month. That's like four weeks." Levi told me. I smiled and kissed his cheeks.

"And you can't wait." I said. He nodded and kissed my lips. Levi was very touchy. Not that it was new but I've noticed this lately. The man was touchy. He's either have a hand on me or his lips. Which I didn't mind. "You're touchy you know that?" I asked and changed the channel. He nodded as he pulled me closer. "You don't mind it." He said. I sighed.

"You know me so well." I said. He laughed and kissed my cheeks.

-Later after the dress and the fittings-

I slammed the door and rushed to our room. "Ugh!" I screamed out of frustration. The door downstairs closed so I sat on the bed and waited for Levi to come up. "I swear the next time someone tells me about my freaking job, I'm gonna whoop some butt." I said as he walked in. He looked at me confused as he sat beside me. "What's wrong babe?" He asked.

"Today after the fitting, we went out to eat. We saw one of my mom's acquaintances." I said and took in a deep breath. He rubbed my shoulders. "Ok, what happened?" He asked.

"The little witch tried to tell me that I couldn't work with the team anymore since I was getting married." I said and cracked my knuckles. "It's my job, I should know!" I yelled.

"Calm down. What else did she say?" He asked.

"She was like, 'Oh honey, poor Levi. He's gonna have to support you for the rest of your life.'" I told him. He breathed out. "I said to her exactly, 'Oh no he's not. Because I actually have a degree and am able to work at any place that requires an athletic trainer or physical therapist. I can support myself just fine.'" I explained.

"Then she caught an attitude and said that I was being rude and that I should learn some manners to make you look good. To say I was pissed was an understatement. So I took a breath and tried to calm myself down. She wouldn't let it go. She started to tell me about how my job wouldn't pay enough to support us, how it wouldn't give me a chance to be a good mother, how it'd put a ridge in our marriage, and a bunch of other bull. So I politely got up and left." I said. I shaking with anger by now.

"That offended me Levi. Very much." I said with a shaky voice. "I got in my car and cried because I was so mad." I told him. He had me in an embrace by now.

"You should've called me." He said. I just sniffed. "I could've handled it. No one, and I mean no one, can predict our future. I'm sure that you'll still be able to work with the team, your financial support is none of her business, neither our future children or our marriage.

She doesn't matter, everyone else doesn't matter. It's just us." He said and kissed my forehead.

"It got me thinking though. I'm lucky to have you. As I sat in my car, I thought about you. I actually calmed down until I saw her come out to leave. She spotted me and waved." I said. He rubbed circles along my back. "You are an amazing woman." He said and wiped my tears. I looked up at him. "It kills me when you cry. I love you so much. Don't ever let anyone get in your head about us, ok?" He said. I nodded and he hugged me tighter.

"Cheer up, chickadee, our wedding is almost here." He said, making me chuckle. For the rest of the evening Levi and I just watched movies until we fell asleep. -One week until our wedding and I'm already nervous. Levi is more excited and I'm more of a nervous wreck than an anxious bride. "Good gosh, Chelsea, you cut yourself." My mom exclaimed. I looked down and my finger was bleeding. I was helping my momma cut veggies. "You're so clumsy that you didn't even realize it." She said.

"Oh, yeah." I said, dazed. I looked out the kitchen window as she helped clean my hand. I saw Levi sitting under the tree with his brothers, dad, grandpa, my dad, and my grandpa. Some of my cousins were there too. "Chelsea, are you ok?" My mom asked. I slowly nodded. She squinted her eyes at me then sighed. "Go upstairs and lie down in your old room. Clearly you need some alone time." She said and shooed me off.

"I'm twenty three, mother. Not sixteen." I said as I went. "Oh hush up and go upstairs before I call Levi." She said. I laughed and trudged up the stairs. I found a beanbag and plopped down in it. A few minutes later, Levi walked in. "There you are, I was looking for you." He said. I looked up from the book I was reading and smiled a little. "What's wrong?" He asked and sat beside me.

"How can something be wrong?" I asked.

"You just gave me a smile. That's not your, 'I love Levi so freaking much' smile." He said I laughed. "Well I do love you very much but I don't think there's a certain smile for it." I said. He nodded and came closer. He positioned himself between my legs and looked into my eyes. "Yes there is. Your eyes twinkle, you show more teeth, a small simple forms in the left cheek, and you shower me with kisses afterwards." He said. I laughed and peppered kissed all over his face.

"Hey, guess what?" I said.

"What?" He asked.

"Chicken butt." I said and he gave me a really look and laughed. I calmed down.

"Anyway, I was saying that there are only a few more days until I become Mrs. Anderson." I said.

"Oh so that's what you've been thinking about." He said.

"What?" I asked.

"Your momma sent me up here while I was looking for you. She said something about you being in a daze. She also said that you cut your finger because you were dazed." He explained. I played with the tail end of the braid my hair was in. "Chelsea, tell me. Were you thinking about the wedding?" He asked. I nodded.

"Will things change once we become husband and wife?" I asked.

"No, not at all. At least for me. You'll still be the hot tempered beauty I fell in love with and I'll still be your devilishly handsome man." He said. I laughed and nodded. "I'm glad things are gonna be still partially the same." I told him.

"What do you mean by partially?" He asked. I sighed.

"Things won't exactly be the same, Levi. I'm no longer working with the Giants next season." I said and looked towards the ceiling, trying not to cry.

"What do you mean?" He asked.

"I got a call from the agency two days after I requested for a name change. My director says that I cannot work there anymore but because I'm a good trainer, I'll still have a job. Just elsewhere. But the bad part is that I probably won't be in the same state again." I explained. Levi's jaw clenched.

"How long have you known this?" He asked.

"For about a week now. I just didn't know how to tell you, Levi." I said.

He looked away and got up. Levi walked to the balcony doors and walked out. I heard him sigh and sit in one of the chairs. I sat there in the bean bag and folded my arms. I bit my lip and laid my head in my lap as the tears poured. I really hope things would be okay.

Chapter 20

This was supposed to be a happy week. My wedding was in two days and I hadn't talked to Levi since Sunday. We'd walk by each other and say small greetings. I feel as if I lost him. The back door closed and I heard Levi's footsteps echo through our home. He walked in the living room towards the stairs. He looked at me and gave me a small smile then trudged up the stairs. I sighed. This would be the only greeting is probably get for a while.

-Levi I stopped when I saw her sitting in the couch. She looked so sad when she looked at me. I gave her a small smile and kept going. We really haven't talked this week. The wedding was in two days and I hadn't touched her at all except for when we sleep. I'm not mad, I'm just confused as to why she wouldn't tell me something like that.

She doesn't know it, but I hear her when she lets out every sigh, sob, or word. There's a possibility that she would have to move to another state. I'm not sure what to feel right now. I stripped and jumped in the shower. After showering I put on a pair of boxers and sweatpants.

I walked downstairs to find Chelsea. Hopefully she wasn't gone. When I reached the bottom of the stairs, I smelled food cooking. I walked into the kitchen and found Chelsea sitting at the bar with her head down. There was a pot on the stove with something simmering in it. She looked up then put her head back down. "Chelsea." I called.

She turned her head and opened her eyes to look at me. Her head was still down. "Yes, Levi?" She answered quietly.

"Come with me." I said and stretched out my hand. She slowly sat up and grabbed my hand. I tried not to look at her butt as she did because she had on some tiny shorts and one of my t shirts. I pulled her to my chest and hugged her. She looked up at me. "Levi, why-"

"Come on, put some shoes on and let's go." I said and let her go. She walked upstairs. When she came back, she had on shoes and a shirt in her hand. I slipped my shoes on and led her to my truck. "Levi, where-"

"Just come on, babe." I said and helped her in. I started to drive. Soon, we were at the ball fields. I turned to her. "We need to talk." I said. She nodded. "I know. I miss you." She said.

"I miss you too. But we need to discuss some things. What's going on Chelsea?" I asked her.

"The agency emailed me this week and sent me some teams to choose from this time. I still haven't made my decision yet." She said. I nodded.

"Were you mad?" She asked.

"What?" I asked.

"Were you mad when I told about this on Sunday?" She asked.

"I wasn't happy but I wasn't mad either. I want you to tell me things like this, Chelsea. That's what I'm here for." I told her.

"And I know that. I was scared that you might not want to get married after that. I don't deserve you, Levi. When I got that call the first thing that came to mind was you. I don't know why, but I felt like I was gonna lose you." She said. I sighed and got out of the truck. I opened her door and grabbed her face. I kissed her hard with passion. She finally kissed back after five seconds.

I pulled away and placed my forehead on hers. "Do not doubt my love for you, Chelsea. It's me who doesn't deserve you. You're not gonna lose me because I love you so much. You're stuck with me for a long time, baby girl." I said and she giggled. I hugged her.

"Don't doubt my love, Chelsea." I said. She wrapped her arms around me.

"I won't, Levi." She said. -Chelsea After Levi and I talked, he told me was hungry. "There was some food cooking at home." I said.

"Not anymore. I turned it off." He said. I rolled my eyes. He drove to a restaurant and was about to hop out of the truck when I stopped him. "Even though I love the view, I don't want other women gawking at your abs." I said and threw him the shirt I grabbed. He chuckled and slipped the shirt on. "Well here, take these because as much as I love the view, I don't want other men gawking at your butt." He said and handed me a pair of sweatpants. They were his.

After locking the truck, he and I both went into the restaurant. "Table for two please." I told the waitress. She sat us down and our waiter came to the table. He was nicely dressed and had the most vibrant blue eyes. "What can I get for you two, tonight?" He asked with a smile.

"Two cheeseburgers and an order of French fries." Levi told him. He jotted that down. "What to drink?" He asked. I gave him our drink orders with a smile. He smiled back and went to put in the order. I was looking around when I caught Levi staring. "Why are you staring?" I asked.

"That smile. That smile you gave him." He said.

"What about it?" I asked.

"It's a little too friendly. That's your flirting smile." He stated.

"My flirting smile?" I asked.

"Yes. That is your flirting smile. The corner of your mouth turns up and you have that look in your eye." He says.

"Is it safe to say that I don't notice it?" I asked.

"You're just a little flirt." He said with a smirk. I laughed. "And you're not?" I asked. He shook his head.

"I'm a saint. You, my darling, are a temptress." He said. I nodded and smirked. "Ok, I tell you what. Smile and wink at one of those women at that table over there. They've been eyeing you ever since we walked in. You'll have them passing in numbers in five minutes, I swear." I said.

"No thanks, I'm good." He said. I shook my head. "Oh? I thought Levi never backed down from a challenge?" I teased. He shifted in his seat. "I don't." He said. The waiter brought our food. We dug in. "You sure about that?" I asked, "What happened to my fearless man. Levi Bradley Anderson, have you gone soft?" I asked.

He leaned over and kissed my cheek. "I love you very much." He whispered in my ear and turned towards the women. I smiled. He caught their attention easily. Levi flashed that golden smile of his and wink. The ladies winked back and started to scribble on napkins. Soon, the napkins "magically" found their way into Levi's lap.

"You're lucky I love you." He muttered. I laughed. "See, that wasn't so bad now was it?" I teased. "Yeah, yeah. Come on, we have to leave." He said and paid for our meal. I just stared as he got up. He reaches his hand on. "Come on, babe. We gotta go." He said. I grabbed his hand and we left.

"Where are we going?" I asked.

"I gotta stop by the house and pick up our luggage. We're leaving to go to our wedding location tonight." He said. I nodded. "That's why you wanted me to pack early last week?" I asked. "Yep." He said. I remembered that we both decided that Levi should choose the location of the wedding and honeymoon. I chose the colors and theme for the wedding.

After grabbing our things and hitting the road Levi and I talked all night. "I love you." He said and kissed my hand. I sat up and looked out the window. "I love you too." I told him.

"What if I told you I was a vampire?" He asked.

"You're so random." I said with a small laugh.

"No seriously." He said.

"Then I would tell you not to watch me in my sleep." I told him. He let out a small laugh. "Levi, are you sure you don't want me to drive?" I asked.

"Yes, because I do not want you knowing the location until we get there." He told me. I nodded and sat back in the seat. -"Wake up babe." I heard a voice. I was being shaken. I opened my eyes and saw Levi. "Welcome to Paris." Levi said. My eyes widened.

"Paris, France?!" I asked with a huge smile.

"No, Paris as in Paris, Texas." He said with a even bigger smile. My smile sort of faded.

"I'm just playing babe. Can't you see the sign?" He asked and pointed outside the window. I looked and saw a sign that said,"Welcome to Georgia!" I smiled. This is great. Plus, the sunrise looked beautiful.

"You brought me to Georgia?" I asked with a smile. He nodded. "It's the only place we haven't been to with each other. Everywhere else we've been. In each state and Capitol except Georgia. Why not make our last state our last step in this relationship?" He asked. That was so sweet. I leaned over and kissed his cheek. "Hey, I deserve a little more than that now. Give me some sugar babe." He said. I laughed and leaned over to kiss him this time.

After about an hour of driving, Levi and I stopped for food. I had on his jacket and was huddled up in the corner of our booth at Waffle House. "Come sit with me. I know you're cold." He said and opened up his arms. He didn't have to tell me twice. I scrambled out of the corner and went to his side. Levi wrapped his arms around me and kissed my cheek.

Our food came and we stuffed ourselves. "Now, can you let me drive?" I asked. He sighed. "I guess so." He said. I thanked him and grabbed the keys.

I walked to the truck with Levi not too far behind me. I climbed into his huge truck and started it. Once Levi was in, he put the gps on so I could get to where ever we were going. I looked over at Levi and he had his head in his hands just about on the brink of closing his eyes fully. I placed a hand on his thigh and he slowly looked up. "Levi, go to sleep baby." I said. He gave me a small smile and kissed my hand.

I've seen Levi tired many times before and I hated it every time. I had to make him go to sleep like a child. Most times I ended up sitting out side our door with the tv remotes, his phone, and no way for him to get out. After about five minutes he'd be out. This man works very hard at the things he does. Whether it's something for me or work. And I know that his work causes him to give forth everything he's got. I looked over to a sleeping Levi.

Wow, I really love this man.

Chapter 21

"What the heck?" I exclaimed as I pulled into the gas station. I slapped Levi's arm to wake up him up. After excessively stretching his muscles he looked over at me. "You brought me to a dang gas station." I said. He nodded. "You didn't think that I'd let you drive all the way there did you?" He asked with a smirk. I rolled my eyes and got out of the truck. I hopped into the back seat. Levi got in and turned to look at me. "What are you doing?" He asked.

"That was mean, Levi. I think I'm gonna sit in the backseat." I told him.

"No get up here." He said. I shook my head and stretched out. He started to tickle me but I didn't budge. "Are you trying to persuade me to move by tickling me?" I asked with a small smirk.

"Is it working?" He asked.

"Maybe." I said.

"Chelsea stop playing and get up here now." He said in a stern voice. I rolled my eyes. "Okay, okay. No need to be all pushy." I said.

"I have to be when it come to you." He said. I huffed and crawled into the front seat. He started to drive. Soon I fell asleep but was soon woken up by Levi tapping my shoulder.

"Yes, Levi?" I asked, sleepily.

"Can you wake up? I need someone to talk to." He said.

"Call Jake." I said and turned back over. I heard him let out a breath. "I want to talk to my fiancé, not my best friend." He said. I turned over and looked at him through sleepy eyes. "Ok, Mr. Anderson, what do you want to talk about?" I asked.

"I don't know. Um, how about kids?" He asked. I nodded and motioned for him to continue. "Ok, first. How many kids do you want?" He asked.

"I'm not really sure but I know that I want more than just one child." I said.

"Are you willing to have more than three?" He asked.

"Are you trying to start a football team here?" I asked with a small laugh. He chuckled and shook his head. "Nah, I just think that we will have a lot of kids." He said.

"Why?" I asked.

"I have a lot of love to give." He said with a wink. I smiled and stared out at the scenery.

"Sweetheart, I believe that you will be a great mother." He said and placed a hand on my thigh. I looked over to him. "You think?" I asked.

"I know." He said with a smile. I couldn't help but smile back. His smile was contagious. After hours of driving, we finally made it to somewhere. There was a huge gate and after Levi entered the code to the big gate, my mouth opened. "Oh wow, this is beautiful." I said in awe of the scenery before me.

"Welcome to our wedding location." Levi said as he parked. The place was huge. It was an old southern mansion and it was gorgeous. Once we parked the doors opened and our family came running out. I got out with my mouth open. "Oh wow." I said. Levi wrapped his arms around my waist. "All for you." He said. I smiled and leaned up to give him a big kiss.

After we were all settled in, I was whisked away by my bridesmaids. "Where are we going?" I asked.

"To the girls' side of the mansion. You are forbidden to see Mr. Levi unless you are with the whole family. This starts now and ends until after you two say I do." Raleigh said. I rolled my eyes. I can just sneak away. "And no you can't sneak away." Joanna said. I sighed and decided to be pulled along. -I can't take it. The last time I had seen Levi was when we got here. Well at least it was dinner time now. I skipped to the dining room and looked around for Levi. I spotted him talking to my dad. He noticed me and winked. I smiled brightly and made my way to him. As we were about to kiss, someone yelled. "Nope! No kissing." Raleigh said.

"But you can hug though." Shana chimed in. I shrugged my shoulders and hopped on Levi as he wrapped his arms around me. "I missed you, baby." I said into his chest. I could feel his chest rumble with laughter. "Yeah, I could tell." He said and kissed my forehead. We sat down with the rest of the family as they passed the food around to everyone. During the dinner Levi rubbed his hand up and down my thigh.

After dinner, we all sat around a bonfire in the backyard. Soon I was whisked away again. The next day, everyone split up to do wedding things. I was stuck in my room. It was the day before our wedding. That night, after coming home from my bachelorette party, I changed and quickly got into bed.

There was a knock at the door so I got up reluctantly. "Whoever this is better have a good reason to ruin my sleep. My wedding is tomorrow." I grumbled angrily. I opened the door and Levi was standing there. "Oh it's just you." I said and turned around to get back in the bed. I crawled under the covers and watched as Levi stepped in and closed the door.

"Hey, baby." He said.

"Hi." I said with a smile. He came and sat beside me. "Wait, how did you get over here without getting caught by the groomsmen or bridesmaids?" I asked. He chuckled.

"They were too drunk to function." He said. I laughed out loud but quickly covered my mouth. I laid down and so did he. "You know, it's bad luck to see each other before the wedding." I whispered. He smiled. "We don't need luck. I have faith and my love for you, baby." He said. I smiled. The door opened and I quickly covered Levi with the covers to hide him.

A drunk Joanna sauntered in. "Chelsea? Are you in here?" She asked with a slight giggle. "Yes, Joanna. What do you need?" I asked.

"Oh nothing. Just checking on you." She said.

"Oh, well I'm here." I said with a nervous laugh.

"Hey, what's that lump in your bed?" She asked. She was talking about Levi.

"Oh, those are my pillows. I miss Levi so much so I had to make a replica of him from pillows. I miss cuddling with him." I lied quickly.

"Oh, hehe, I can cuddle with you if you like." She giggled. "No I'm just fine. You go ahead and go to sleep." I reassured her. She mumbled an ok and left the room. Well tried. Joanna bumped into the door twice before she could finally leave. Once she did, I lifted the covers and Levi sat up. He let out a laugh. "I swear my friends are so weird." I said.

Chapter 22

"Wake up chickadee, you're getting married!" My grandmother yelled as she walked into my room. I sat up and looked around for Levi. He was gone. "He left early this morning sweetheart." She said.

"Who?" I asked trying to confuse her.

"I'm not dumb. I know Levi was in here with you. I ran into him in the hallway." She said. I let out a nervous chuckle.

"It makes so much sense, sweetie. You already know that Levi wasn't going to follow those stupid rules. Now get up so you can go eat breakfast." She said. I got out of the bed and grabbed my robe. We walked downstairs and everyone was there except the men. "Morning, Chelsea." Everyone greeted. I greeted them then dug into my breakfast. After eating, we all showered and got dressed into matching sweat pants and shirts.

The wedding was at five so we had a couple of hours on our hands. I went back to the room I was staying in to look over my vows. Levi and I decided that we should write our vows. The wedding was going to be a romantic one. The colors were red with accents of black and gold. But mostly red. It was going to be beautiful.

Our wedding was going to be held here at the mansion in one of the courtyards. I pulled out my notebook and sat at my desk to look over the vows. They looked pretty good to me so I decided to watch tv for a bit.

The door opened and my dad walked in. "You ready, baby girl?" He asked. I sighed and nodded with a smile. He came and sat on my bed like he used to do when I was younger. "Levi is a good man, you know." He started off.

I nodded. "Yes he is." I agreed. "He loves you too." He added. I nodded once again but with a smile. "Listen, I know that I probably haven't said much of this lately but I wish the best for you and Levi. I know he can be a knucklehead sometimes but you also have to keep yourself in check too. Marriage or any type of relationship has three parts. That should be you, Levi, and God. Keep God first in all you do and you'll be just fine. I love you sweetheart." He said and kissed my forehead. I smiled and hugged him.

"Thanks daddy." I said.

"Don't mention it." He said. The door opened and Raleigh stepped in. "Oh, there you are. Come on, it's time to get ready." She said and disappeared to go get ready. My dad left with her. I took a deep breath and got up to leave. I was gonna get married to the love of my life today.-Levi"You ready man?" Jake asked me as we hit off the tee. I nodded. "As ready as I'll ever be." I said before swinging. "But come on, I get that it's Chelsea. Y'all have been together for longer than I can count. Doesn't it feel a bit different now that she's gonna be your wife?" Hunter asked. I shrugged. "There's no difference for me. Other than the fact that she'll have my last name. I love her and she loves me." I explained and took another swing.

After hitting for a while mother came and called for us to get ready. As I was getting ready, I was thinking about Chelsea. I pressed the button on my phone and a picture of us popped up. It was a picture of us at one of my games. She was fixing my jersey and I was looking down at her with a smile. I cannot wait until this wedding.

After getting ready, it was time for the photographers. We all took pictures while doing a little goofing around. It seemed that at last hour, things went wrong. Shana ran into the photoshoot looking around frantically. She went and got Jake along with Mike. After whispering something in their ears, they rushed out. I walked over to Grayson. "Did you hear anything they just said?" I asked.

He shrugged. "All I heard was something about finding someone and not to tell you." He said. I sighed. "I hope it's not Chelsea." I said and left to follow them. As I got closer I could hear their conversation as they rushed through the big mansion. "The last time I saw her was when she went to her room to look over her vows. We came to get her so she could ready. After she got ready, she went to the bathroom but hasn't been back. We've looked everywhere." Shana explained.

"Ok, well we will help you find her. I'm sure she hasn't gone too far." Jake said and Mike nodded his head.

"All I know is that you three better find my fiancé or you won't make it to the next day." I growled at them, making them stop and turn around. "Hehe, hey Levi." Shana said.

"Shana, just please find your cousin." I said. -ShanaOk, Levi scared me. I almost jumped out of my freaking skin. Whenever and wherever we find Chelsea, I'm gonna give her the worst whooping ever. After a complete thirty minutes of looking for her, I stopped by the kitchen to get some water. The fridge was open so I went to close it. I tried to close it but someone was in the way. "Ow!" A female voice said as I tried to close the door. I opened the door wider and saw Chelsea with a doughnut stuffed in her face.

"Chelsea!" I yelled angrily. The guys ran in quickly.

"Where have you been?" I asked.

"Here." She replied blankly while chewing her doughnut. "Why? Everyone has been looking for you." I said to her.

"I was hungry, and I left a note for y'all to find easily." She said.

"Where did you leave it? And who leaves notes anymore, Chelsea?" I asked. She rotated me and got something off of my back. Chelsea held up a sticky note with the words Went to the kitchen for some food;) on it. My jaw dropped. "How in the world were we supposed to see that?" I asked. She shrugged and kept eating. I grabbed her arm and escorted her to the room where we were once getting ready.

"Oh my god, Chelsea. Please don't move for the rest of the day." I mumbled before flopping down on the couch. Everyone watched as she got ready. Her dress beautiful, her skin was flawless, and she was ready to marry her fiancé. She was truly beautiful.-LeviOnce Jake and Mike appeared I cornered them to ask if they had found Chelsea. "Relax, man. She was in the kitchen stuffing her face." Mike said with a laugh. I sighed and thanked them for helping to look. As time went on, it was time for us to head to the waiting area while the bridal party took their pictures. We were ushered to the room while they made their way to the photoshoot. The started to arrive so I'm guessing that we'd be ready to start pretty soon.

Forty five minutes later, the guests were seated and it was time to start. I entered along with preacher into the beautifully decorated courtyard. The music started played and the first bridesmaid and groomsmen walked in. It was a reality now, I was marrying the love of my life. There was no doubt in my heart that she was the one. I have always believed it.

Chapter 23

I smiled and poses as the photographer asked me to. The only thing that kept me smiling was the thought of Levi. It had been too dang long since I saw him and I was ready to marry that man. I was really close to just sneaking away again but instead I complied and stayed. "Ok, that's it ladies. You look beautiful, Chelsea." The photographer told me. He was the photographer for Levi's team. "Vance, could I look at that last picture?" I asked. He nodded and handed me the camera.

I pushed the button to find my photos and stopped on the last one I took. It was gorgeous. "Put this one in black and white." I said. He nodded with a smile and headed to the courtyard to take pictures as the wedding started. Slowly, bit by bit, I was the only one left in the waiting room. My father walked in and kissed my forehead. "Ready?" He asked.

"Yes, daddy." I said with a big smile. The users opened the door and once that door opened, everything else went away. My focus and only focus was on Levi. Standing at the alter at this very moment was my future husband. He had a huge smile on his face and looked like he was about to cry. I smiled back at him.

Soon, we were standing in front of Levi and the priest. "Who gives this woman away to be married to this man today?" The priest asked. My dad cleared his threat. "Her mother and I." He said proudly.

I stepped up and Levi took my hands. Then, we started. "Dearly beloved, we are gathered here today to witness the marriage of this man and woman in holy matrimony. Let us pray." The preacher started. We bowed our heads for the prayer. The preacher finished up his few words and then it was time for the vows. Levi went first.

"Chelsea Jane, I choose you to be my wife, my partner in life. I promise you my unconditional love, my fullest devotion, my most tender care. Through the pressures of the present and the uncertainties of the future, I promise to love you, honor, respect and cherish you all the days of our lives. We've been through ups and downs but we are still here. There is no one I know that can handle me like you. After staying together for so long, I'm glad I will finally be able to call you my wife. I love you so much." He said. A slight, small, little tear came from his eye. I reached up and wiped it before starting mine.

"Thirteen and a half years ago a house was built right across the street from my parents' home. There was a family of eight that lived there. A married couple and their six sons. After I met their family, one of the sons just kind of stuck with me. Yes, Levi, I'm talking about you. Our love came naturally and that's what I love about our relationship. Even if sometimes we get mad at each other and argue, we always come right back to each other. I love you very much and nothing will change that. I take you as my husband and promise to love you, care for you, and to be there for you when ever you need me. No one can or ever will love you as much as I do." I said with tears freely flowing.

He reached down and wiped my tears. I love you. He mouthed to me. I just smiled.

"Do you, Levi, take Chelsea to be your lawfully wedded wife?" The preacher asked.

"I do." Levi said confidently.

"Do you, Chelsea, take Levi to be your lawfully wedded husband?" He asked me.

"I do!" I basically screamed. Everyone laughed.

"By the power invested in me, I now pronounce you man and wife! You may kiss your bride!" He told us. Levi leaned in and kissed me with so much passion that it made my knees buckle.

"Ladies and gentlemen, I present to you Mr. and Mrs. Levi Bradley Anderson!" He announced. We kissed once again and walked back down the aisle hand in hand. "We did it. We finally got married." Levi said once we were alone.

"Took us long enough." I said before he crashed his lips onto mine again.

Chapter 24

"I actually have a surprise." I said to Levi as we walked to the reception area. There was a path to it through one of the gardens here.

"You're pregnant?!" He exclaimed and placed his hands on my stomach. "No, get off." I said and slapped his hands away.

"It's about my job." I said.

"Chelsea, we just got married. Let's not put a damper on our day with that issue." He said. I sighed. "You're right, but sooner or later you're gonna find out about it." I said. He stopped us abruptly. Levi grabbed my face in both his hands. "Listen, I know there was a lot of emotions dealing with that subject but babe, can we please focus on the fact that we just got married? I love you, Mrs. Anderson and that's all that matters right now. That and the fact that I'm hungry but still. I love you, now come on. We're missing our reception." He said and kissed me. Levi resumed to pull me along with him.

As we got nearer to the reception, the music could be heard. We walked straight in but no one noticed us. Levi and I were soon on the other side of the courtyard. "And I now present Mr. and Mrs. Anderson!" The DJ announced. Everyone looked towards the entrance. "We're over here!" Levi shouted. There was a spotlight shining at the entrance waiting for us to appear. The funny thing was is that we already walked in together.

"Yo! We're here already!" Levi shouted and waved his hand. Everyone turned and clapped when they saw us. After a few opening statements, the reception started. The servers started to bring out trays of food. "Oh yeah, this is what I've been waiting for all day." Levi said before he started eating.

"Sometimes I think you love food more than you love me." I said.

"And sometimes I think you love my athletic skills more than me. Who would've thought that you, Chelsea Jane, would marry a Major League Baseball player?" He joked.

"Me." I answered seriously but then soon broke into a smile. After we ate, some of the guests and members of the wedding party were asked to give speeches. They were all amazing speeches. Some made me laugh, some made me cry, and some I can't remember because Levi was messing with me the whole time.

Someone started to tap the microphone. "Is thing on?" My mother said quite loudly into the mic. "Yes, its on, Mrs. P!" Levi yelled. She helped a thumbs up to him. "Thank you Levi. Always so helpful." She said to him.

"Always." He said with a wink.

"Watch it." My dad said and everyone laughed. I leaned into Levi as he pulled my chair closer to his. I may as well sat in his lap. The man wouldn't let me go. "Ok, I'm not gonna be long. I just wanted to say a few words to and about my daughter along with my son in law." My mom started. I smiled brightly at her.

"For thirteen and a half years now, I've watched this couple grow. From coparenting a stray bunny, getting into messy adventures, and eventually falling in love, I was there. I believe that there will never be another couple like Chelsea and Levi. Their too unique. I say that to say this. Levi, don't give up when Chelsea is in one of her moods, ok? We both know it'll pass over within an hour. Chelsea, when Levi is being stubborn, don't blow up. We both know he'll eventually give in.

So, congratulations Mr. and Mrs. Anderson. Now bring some grand babies home." She finished. Everyone clapped. Levi and I both hugged her as she went to her seat. During our first dance as husband and wife, Levi started bouncing. "Levi, either you have to go to the bathroom or you're feeling some type of way about this song." I said.

"Both. Come with me." He said and grabbed my hand. We left and entered into a hallway. He still kept bouncing so while he went into the restroom I checked myself out in the mirror. Dang, I make a good looking bride. "You sure do." Levi said as he came out of the restroom. He threw his paper towel away and pulled me close. "You heard that?" I asked.

"Yeah, you kind of said it out loud." He said with a chuckle. "Oops. It doesn't hurt to tell the truth." I said.

"And you say I'm conceited." He joked. I grabbed his face and pulled him closer. "So what's next?" I asked. "First, I'm gonna kiss you like there's tomorrow, then we're gonna say bye bye to our guests, and after that we're leaving." He explained. I nodded. "I'm fine with that as long as I can change clothes after this." I told him.

He nodded, not really listening to what I said and kissed me. He really did kiss me like no tomorrow. Levi led us back to the reception to say goodbye to our guests. "Ok folks, I think it's time my wife and I head out. We will see you soon. Thank you all for coming and making our day special." Levi said into the microphone. I was currently changing in one of the rooms but I could hear Levi's loud voice clearly.

I changed into a pair of khaki shorts and a dressy coral top with gold sandals. When I met Levi downstairs, he was sort of matching with me. Before the doors opened to let us leave, we hugged our parents. The door opened and as we ran out rice was thrown. Levi opened the door for me and I hopped in. Once he started to drive I sat back in my seat.

"Oh no you don't. Do not go to sleep." He said. I sighed. "I'm sleepy." I whined.

"No. I want you awake for this." He said as he drove. I huffed. He reached over and grabbed my hand. "Come on now, don't be upset.

It's our wedding day. I just wanted to see your face when you found out where we were going." He said with a smile. I frowned.

"Smile." He ordered. A smile slowly formed across my as he handed me an envelope. I opened it and gasped. "Naw, this can't be happening!" I squealed in excitement. He laughed.

"It's clearly printed on the ticket, sweetheart." He pointed. I slapped his hand away and stared at the tickets in amazement. "Paris, France. Oh wow, Levi. This is a new adventure just calling our names." I said.

"I know. That's why I got the tickets, the room, the services, the-"

"I get it, Levi. Baby, this is wonderful. Thank you so much." I said and reached over to give him a hug. He hugged me back as much as he could, considering that he was driving. I sat back and watched as we made our way to the airport. -After getting our passports stamped and stepping foot on that plane, sleep took over. The next thing I knew, Levi was shaking me away. When we arrived to our hotel there wasn't too much of a wait to get into our room. I walked to the balcony with a champagne glass in hand. Levi came and wrapped his hands around my waist.

"Ready to tear this city up?" I asked.

"As long as I got my wife with me while I am." Levi said and kissed me.

Chapter 25

Six Months Later

"Remind me to never cook chicken Alfredo again." I groaned as I vomited into the toilet bowl.

"No can do. That's one of my favorite meals." Levi said. I rolled my eyes and was about to say something when more vomit decided to make its presence known. "Ugh, Levi I'm sick." I told him.

"Nah, you're not sick." He said with so much simplicity that it scared me a bit. I sat up to brush my teeth and flushed the contents. "Ok then what?" I asked as I put paste onto my brush.

Levi just smirked and I raised an eyebrow. "Is there some type of telepathy I'm supposed to pick up here?" I asked. He just smirked. "I told you I had a lot of love to give." He continued.

"Chelsea do I have to spell it out for you?" He asked with that stupid smirk. I rolled my eyes. I gasped. "Levi." I said slowly as I wiped my mouth.

"Yes?" He answered slowly.

"You don't mean-"

"Yep." He said.

"You sure?" I asked.

"Positive." He stated.

"But you used-"

"Nope." He said popping the 'P' with a huge smile. He looked at his watch and smiled brightly.

"Happy birthday, Chelsea! You're-"_____

"-pregnant." The doctor said to me.

"That son of a gun was right." I muttered.

"Excuse me?" My doctor asked.

"Um, not you. My husband." I said as I pulled out my phone.

"Helloooo?" Levi answered.

"Congrats, daddy Levi, you were right." I said as I filled out some papers for my doctor. He pulled the phone from ear as he whooped and hollered. "I'll be at the field in about thirty minutes." I said and hung up.

We came straight back to San Fransisco. I knew that when we got back from Paris I felt different. That went away for a while though but then lately things changed once again. That explains why Levi was giddy when I first threw up.

That little sneak knew what he was doing. After filling out my forms and picking up my medicine I headed to the field. I walked in and greeted everyone as they came off the field. It was gonna be different when I come back to work. I was no longer working here but I was working for the San Fransisco 49ers. I waited for Levi in the stands but it wasn't much of a wait because he came running to me. He had the biggest smile on his face ever.

Levi picked me up and twirled me around. He kissed me and I playfully shoved him. "So I was right?" He asked. I nodded with an eye roll. "Yeah, you were. The doctor says I'm only a month. I guess I was too busy to notice the changes." I told him. He nodded, the smile still evident on his face. I continued to talk and to tell him what the doctor said but stopped when I saw him just staring at me.

"Levi. You're not listening to me." I said. -Levi"You're not listening to me." She said. I couldn't because all I could do was stare at my beautiful wife and mother of my child. I grinned. "It's hard to listen when my happiness is in overdrive right now." I explained.

"Well maybe we could talk about this later. I'm going home to take a nap." She said and grabbed her keys. I grabbed them before she could. "No, I want you to come with me real quick." I said and grabbed her hand. I led her to the coach's office and knocked. After being called in I walked in with her. "Well look at here! Hey, Chelsea!" Coach said.

"Hey, Coach." She said with a smile.

"Hey, I just wanted to stop by and tell you that my wife and I are expecting our first child in a couple of months." I said with a smile. The coach's face was priceless. "Congratulations! And happy birthday." He said. Coach was like a father figure to us. After talking to him, I walked Chelsea to her car. I was going to follow her home.

"I'm going home to take a nap." She said and yawned.

"No, not on your birthday." I said. She rolled her eyes. I chuckled and shook my head. "Stop rolling your eyes." I said and brushed some hair out of her face. She sighed. "Then what?" She asked.

"Just-just go home and shower. Put on something nice and wait for me. I'm coming right behind you. Do not go to sleep." I told her. After rolling her eyes and kissing me, she left to go home. I stopped by the flower shop and grabbed up some red roses. When I got home I rushed upstairs to take a shower. After showering, I got dressed in casual jeans, a polo, and my boots.

As I was getting dressed, Chelsea walked out of her closet dressed and ready to go. She had on jeans, a polo, and her boots also. "Trying to match me, wifey?" I asked.

"Naw, you're trying to match me." She said with a smirk as she picked up her hairbrush. She looked absolutely beautiful.

"So how does it feel to be twenty-four?" I asked. She shrugged. "I don't know, how does it feel to be twenty-five?" She asked smartly.

"Uh, so I've been twenty-five for about three months. But in short, I don't know." I said as I pulled my boots on. She turned and looked at me. "Ok then, I feel the same way." She said and placed the brush back on her vanity.

"You look gorgeous, Mrs. Anderson." I said and picked her up to kiss her. -Chelsea "Why thank you, Mr. Anderson." I said as he placed me back on my feet. We locked up our home and got into Levi's truck. My birthday was going pretty good if you ask me. It's been six months since we got married and I'm truly happy. It has only been a few hours since I found out that I was pregnant. That was the best birthday gift but coming from Levi, it was weird how he just sat there and smirked the whole time. That little weirdo. He's mine though.

We pulled up to a steak house and went in for dinner. After eating, we went to the movies. "Only G-rated movies for my babies." Levi said and rubbed my stomach. I laughed and slapped his hands away. I believe that as this pregnancy goes on, Levi will become even more touchy. Lord, help me.

The movie was great but Levi would not leave me alone. "I love you." I said to him as he unlocked the door.

"I love you too, baby." He said.

"You've made this the best birthday ever. And I'm not just saying that." I told him and sat down on the couch. He sat beside me and pulled me close. "I wouldn't have it any other way. I love making you smile." He said.

"You're so cheesy." I said and made a face. He laughed. "I know, but you love it." He said.

"I know." I said before he kissed me.

Chapter 26

"I can't stand you, Levi!" I yelled as I looked through the fridge. Levi's hearty laughter could be heard from inside the kitchen. He was in our room watching a game and I was on a mission to find my pineapple I'd hidden the night before. He ate it all. My bump was visible now and my monthly checkup was tomorrow. I try my best not to get into a fist fight with Levi but it's tempting when he steals my fruit. I always try to remind myself that he's my husband and I love him.

I walked into our room and Levi was still snickering. "You're mean." I complained. He shrugged and rolled over onto his back. Levi stared at me upside down. "And you have a temper." He stated with a smile. I rolled my eyes and made my way to the bed. I tried my best to hop into the big bed but failed. "Levi, a little help here?" I asked. He looked at me then turned his attention back to the tv.

"You can't stand me, remember?" He asked. Usually, he'd wrapped his big hands around my waist and lift me into the bed but today he was being stubborn. "Really?" I asked. He just looked at me once again. I huffed and reached for the stool I had stowed away. "You're so difficult." I muttered as I climbed the stool.

"And you're a big meany." He said. I just laughed like he did earlier. Levi sat up and looked at me incredulously. I blew him a kiss and he pretended to dodge it. I blew another and he did the same thing. I pulled out my phone and blew a kiss to his picture which was my lock screen. The picture showcased a smiling Levi. "At least this Levi loves me." I said and stuck my tongue out him.

He crawled towards me and flopped beside me. "You know I love you." He said with his head on my shoulder. He kissed my shoulder and leaned down to kiss my belly. "And I love you too, peanut." He said to my stomach. "Awe, look who's being a sweet daddy." I gushed with a huge smile. I pinched his cheeks. Levi just looked up at me. "You were just being mean to me not too long ago. Choose one, momma bear, so I can choose my next steps wisely." He said.

"Well, right now, I just wanna love on my husband but you seem to not want that." I said and folded my arms. He unfolded my arms and placed a gentle kiss on my lips. "You can love on me all you want. After all, I do have a lot of love to give. Ain't that right peanut?" He motioned towards my belly. I just laughed.

-

"Wake up, momma bear. We got an appointment to get to."

I groaned and pushed Levi's face away. "Aw, come on. Don't be like that now. Get up so we can leave." He said. I opened one eye. "And we have one eye open. That's progress. Come on and open the other one." He teased. I groaned once again.

"Do I have to?" I mumbled.

"Yes, baby. We have to go and see what peanut's gender is." He told me. I sat up slowly and got out the bed with Levi's assistance. I walked to my closet and picked out a nice sundress that showed off my bump. After showering and putting on the dress, I paired it with sandals and left my hair down in a natural wavy look. "Beautiful." Levi said and we left.

"Anderson." The nurse called. Levi and I got up to follow the nurse to a room. While she was taking my vitals I saw the way she was looking at Levi. He winked at me while she was taking my blood pressure. "Excuse me, nurse?" Levi called.

"Call me Amy." She said flirtatiously. Levi smiled politely. "Amy. Could please hurry when you leave and get the doctor? My wife hates the cold offices here." He asked. She cringed at the word wife. She looked at me and smiled politely. "Sure thing." She said and left after finishing. I looked over at Levi. He smiled. "You ain't slick. Didn't think I'd notice huh?" He asked. I turned my head and started to poke around with things in the office.

"Babe, I know she was checking me out. You were too but I didn't miss the way you looked at her." He said and came closer to me. Levi leaned down and kissed my lips. "I love you and you only." He said. I smiled.

"Ok now, let's see what we have here. Mr. and Mrs. Anderson?" The doctor said as she walked in. We looked up from our love fest and smiled at the doctor. "Yes ma'am, that's us." Levi said. She nodded and looked over her clipboard. "Ok, so we're finding out the gender today, right?" She asked. We nodded.

"Ok, well Mrs. Anderson, I'm gonna need you to lean back and lift up your shirt. This is gonna be cold when I put it on you, ok?" She said. I nodded and did as she said. She was right. That gel was cold. Dr. Morris took her little tool and rubbed it along my belly. "If you look here on the screen, you'll see your healthy baby boy." She said and pointed to where he was located. I awed. "Look, momma bear, there's peanut." Levi said to me, making the doctor and I laugh.

-

"That was fun." I said while looking at the little pictures.

"Sure was. Now we're gonna have a little family. You, me, and our son." He said. I smiled. "Yeah, another Levi around here would be great wouldn't it?" I asked with sarcasm. "Hey now, having another Levi would be just plain awesome." He said with a grin. I laughed. Levi and I headed out for lunch. We stopped by an Italian restaurant. After eating a hearty meal we headed to the grocery store. Our refrigerator was running out of food.

Levi helped me out of his truck and grabbed my hand. He grabbed a buggy and gave me the list. "Where to, Chelsea Jane?" He asked with a smile. I pointed to an aisle and that's where we started. I saw a box of cupcakes and tried to reach them. I started to jump when hands were placed on my waist. "You better not jump." Levi said. I rolled my eyes and readied myself to jump.

As I attempted to jump, Levi's hold on me tightened. "Chelsea Jane Anderson. Stop." He whispered in my ear. I slowly nodded. He reached up and grabbed the box and handed it to me. As I put the box into the buggy I saw someone tap Levi's shoulder. "Excuse me." The lady said. She was fairly pretty and had brown hair with hazel eyes to match. "Yeah?" Levi asked.

"Can you please reach that from the top shelf for me?" She asked and batted her eyelashes. Not again, I thought. Levi got whatever she asked for and gave it to her. "That's it?" Levi asked her with a smile. I hate that he could be nice sometimes. "Yeah, and your number." She said suggestively. Levi shifted from foot to foot. He backed away and grabbed my left hand. "I don't think my wife would like that." He said and showcased our ring fingers.

The lady then looked embarrassed and scurried away. I laughed as she did. Levi looked down at me and shook his head. "Levi." I said.

"Yeah, baby?" He answered.

"What's with everyone flirting with today? That's the third time it happened." I said. He shrugged. "They weren't my type anyway." He said.

"What's your type?" I asked.

"Beautiful, black, and pregnant with my child." He said and kissed me then my stomach. I laughed. He could be sweet sometimes. We continued to shop until my feet hurt. Once we came home, the cabinets and the refrigerator were stocked. I made my way upstairs to my room and used my stool to get into the bed. Levi came in not too long after that and laid beside me. "What's next, momma bear?" He asked me.

"I need you to call Shaley and tell her to come over." I said. He nodded and pulled out his phone. "She said she'll be over in a few." He said. I thanked him and attempted to sit up. After miserably failing, he stopped his laughing and helped me. This was gonna a long four months.

-

"Hey, hey, hey!" Shaley said as she burst into the room.

"Hey, Shaley." I said. She came and hugged me.

"What's up, girl?" She asked.

"I thought you might want to know your godchild's gender." I said with a smile. She gasped and nodded. I pulled out the pictures and showed her. "Awe, he's gonna look like Levi." She gushed. I rolled my eyes.

"So what have you been up to?" She asked.

"Um, well ever since Levi left for practice I've been here just watching tv. I go to work tomorrow." I told her. She nodded and started to tell me about her day. "So has Mike popped the question yet?" I asked. She shook her head and made a face.

"No. We're supposed to go and visit my parents back in New York this weekend. It's like every time I bring up marriage, he gets uncomfortable." She complained. I sighed. "I'll be completely honest. He is either waiting for the right time to propose or he doesn't want to get married. Mike loves you, choose the latter." I said and smiled. She smiled and we decided to drop the topic.

As we were making our way downstairs, the door opened and Levi walked in along with Mike. "Hey, momma bear and Shaley." Levi said as he made his way towards us. He hugged Shaley then stepped aside to kiss me. Mike came in and hugged me. He kissed Shaley and we all sat down on the couches.

"So what is the married couple up to, tonight?" Mike asked. We shrugged. "There isn't much to do. My feet hurt." I said. Levi rubbed my shoulder. "I'm with my lady, plus she has to go to work in the morning." He said. They nodded. After hanging out with Mike and Shaley for awhile, they went home. Levi and I got ready for work tomorrow.

-

I woke up extra early for work and got out my clothes. I showered and went to put my outfit on. It consisted of a pair of sweatpants, a 49ers shirt, and converses. I brushed my hair and left it down. After putting on a little lip balm and spraying some body spray, I was ready. I grabbed my keys from the dresser and made my way to the door. "Wait." I heard Levi said. He got out of the bed and kissed me. "Now you can leave. Didn't think I'd let you leave without my kiss did you?" He asked. I laughed and turned to leave.

I still remember when I told Levi about my job. He was shocked that I was still gonna be able to work in San Fransisco. I was just happy that I wouldn't have to leave. My husband was here and I was gonna stick with him.

I started my car and drove to a nearby cafe to grab breakfast. After grabbing breakfast and eating it on the go, I headed to the practice field. Working with football players would be a bit of a challenge. All I had to do was run ability tests during the season and help get the injured players ready for action.

My new boss didn't want me doing much since I was pregnant. I arrived at the stadium and got out to sign in. Once I found my way to my boss's office I knocked before entering. "Good morning." I said to him with a smile. He smiled and greeted me. We went over the plan for today and he let me go so I could get started.

Chapter 27

I walked in and the players looked up. Some stared at my face and others noticed my stomach. My stomach showed fairly through my shirt plus the way I walk had changed. There was a slight waddle. I clasped my hands and started my introduction. "Hello, my name is Chelsea Anderson and I'm your new athletic trainer. Before we get started, is there anything you'd like to know about me?" I asked.

"What was your previous job?" One of the guys asked.

"I was the head athletic trainer for the San Fransisco Giants." I said. After their questions, we got started. We soon finished up with the session. I was getting ready to start the suicide runs. I blew the whistle and the first row started. Tweet!

Someone called my name as I blew for the second row. I turned and saw one of the coaches standing with Levi. I motioned him over and blew the whistle for the third row. "Hey, hold on." I said and turned back to the guys. Tweet! They took off.

After the fourth row went it started. As each row ran, I wrote down little notes on each player if what could be improved and what looked absolutely fine. Once they finished I dismissed them and grabbed up my stuff. Tomorrow, I'd just have to start working with the injured players to get them I had a back pack. I smiled at Levi and gave him a long hug. It was as tight because of the limited space my belly provided. He kissed me and grabbed my hand. We walked to the head Coach's office.

"Hello?" I asked as I walked into his office. He looked up and smiled. "Hey, Chelsea. Who is this you have with you?" He asked.

"This is, Levi, my husband." I said with a big smile. "Nice to meet you, Mr. Anderson." Coach said. They shook hands.

"Call me Levi." Levi told him. They indulged into the conversation they were meant to have. Long story short, Levi had to stick around for while. As long as I am working here and am pregnant, Levi is my certified go to person for help. He doesn't have to come everyday but has to make sure that I get rest and that I'm not on my feet all day.

After Levi finished up his conversation with the Coach we headed home. When we got home, I started dinner. I was gonna fry chicken just like Levi liked it. I made homemade mashed potatoes and macaroni. During dinner Levi kept complimenting me on the food. "Send my compliments to the chef." Levi said again while leaning back in his chair.

"You said that five times already." I said.

"And I ain't gonna stop. Baby, you know just what I like and how I like it." He said with a grin. I laughed and picked up the plates to do the dishes. There wasn't much to do since I started the clean up after I finished dinner. "What's for dessert?" He asked as we dried dishes together.

"Um, there's some ice cream in the refrigerator." I said with a smile. "What about chocolate cake?" Levi asked with a smile. I shook my head.

"You ate it all, remember?" I said.

"I don't recall." He teased with a smirk. I rolled my eyes. "You're gonna end up fat one day if you keep eating all those sweets." I said.

"Pfft, please Chelsea. Look at me. Do you really think I'll end up fat?" He asked and held up his shirt. Those toned abs that I've seen many times before were showcased. "Put your shirt down, Levi." I said and tickled him.

"I'm not ticklish babe." He said with a serious face. "Your face says one thing but your eyes say another." I said and sauntered away. He quietly followed. I walked upstairs and got into bed with the help of Levi. "Momma bear." Levi called from the bathroom.

"Yes?" I answered.

"I don't have to go in tomorrow. I'm taking you to work and I'm gonna stay with you." He said. I nodded as he walked out the restroom. He got into bed and I scooted closer to him. I laid my head on his chest and snuggled up even more to him. "That sounds good. You can use the track for your running if you want." I told him.

"Sounds good." He said. He started to rub my stomach. "Our son is gonna have the greatest parents ever." He said to me. I smiled. "You sound really confident." I noted. He looked at me with a frown. "You sound unsure. What's wrong?" He asked.

"We're new parents, Levi. I'm a little scared about this whole being a mother thing." I explained. An eyebrow rose and his face turned serious. "Chelsea Jane Anderson, do not doubt yourself or us as parents. I got you, you got me, and we have us." He said with a serious face. I love this man so much. I grinned. "I'm guessing that made you happy?" Levi asked. I nodded and captured his lips in a kiss.

He kissed my forehead. "Get some sleep, momma bear." He whispered and turned the light out. -"Come on, momma bear. Wake up."

I tried to turn to my other side but was stopped by Levi. "Wake up, Chelsea." He said.

"I don't wanna." I whined.

"You gotta, babe. You have to work with your players today." Levi reasoned. I groaned. "As long as you come with me." I mumbled.

"That's what I planned." Levi said as I made my way to the bathroom. I showered and got dressed into my work attire. I was gonna be working with five players who needed tests for their injuries. I would be working with these players for the next five weeks. Their progress determines if they are gonna be able to play or not during the season.

Levi locked the door and I waited by his truck. Because his truck was lifted, I had to have help to get into it. This was a struggles but as long as Levi helped me, I was good. "I hate your truck." I said as he helped me in.

"You used to love this truck." He said a he got in. I sighed. "That was before I was pregnant. I able to climb in it." I said and he chuckled.

"What am I supposed to do?" He asked.

"Let's get a minivan." I said with a smile. Levi looked at me blankly.

"Come on! It would be so cute!" I gushed. Levi shook his head. "Baby, we are not getting a minivan. You have a truck and car, and I have my truck. If we get anything else it would be another truck. Not a minivan." He said. I laughed. "Why? Don't think the minivan would look good?" I asked. Thinking of Levi driving a minivan made me laugh even more.

He as massively tall and to picture him driving a minivan would be hilarious. "Chelsea." Levi said.

"Hm?" I answered.

"We are not getting a minivan. End of discussion." He said. I smiled and zipped the imaginary zipper of my lips then threw away the key.

-"Ok guys, you are doing good. To end our day, let's see if you can take two laps around the track. Jog or walk it if you can. The worst thing you could do is not get some motion going." I said and let the players go. The players I am working with all have injuries either dealing with the knee, leg, or ankle.

I decided to get in the walking lane and start some laps. Levi was busy running around the track the whole time, stopping occasionally to check up on me. He spotted me walking and winked. "Your husband sure does take care of you." Someone said making me jump. I turned and one of the players was jog alongside me as I walked. I didn't know his name, so let's just say Johnny.

"Didn't mean to scare you there." He said. I nodded and told him it was fine.

"But, um, yeah. He does take care of me." I told him. He nodded. "I just wanted to say thank you." He said.

"For what?" I asked.

"For taking the time out to work with this team. I'm sure working with us is a task." He joked. I nodded. "It is but you get used to it. Trust me, I know. Working with Major League Baseball players ain't a walk in the park either. Especially my husband." I said.

"Your husband?" The player asked.

"Yeah, Levi plays for the San Fransisco Giants. My last team." I told Johnny. He nodded.

"That's cool. But I just wanted to slow up to tell you that." He said with a smile. I thanked him and kept walking. Levi was still running. He actually whizzed by me three times. I counted.

On his fourth time around and my second lap, I felt something move. "Woah." I said and held my stomach. I hear Levi coming up on so I put my hand out to stop him. "Baby, I just felt something move." I said. Levi rushed to me. "Are you ok?" He asked. I nodded.

"Yeah, but it felt weird. I think peanut just moved. Here, feel." I said and placed his hand on my stomach. The movement stopped. "Come on, move for daddy." I said to my stomach. I felt a kick. Levi's face was in shock. "He just moved!" Levi said excitedly. I grinned as he kept moving. He and I went to sit in the grass.

"This is amazing but it scared me. I didn't know what happened at first." I told Levi. He nodded with the smile still on his face. "Here, let's take a picture and document it." I said. Levi helped up my camera and we smiled. "It's going in the scrapbook. Baby's first kick." I said.

After helping me up from the ground and grabbing up my stuff we left. Levi and I left to get something to eat. "We should think of a name." I said as we ate. Levi nodded. "We should. How about Levi Jr?" He asked with a smirk.

"You thought." I said and took a sip of my drink.

"Well, how about Matthew? Chase? Chance? Luke? Daniel? Steven? Hunter? Grayson?" Levi asked. I gave him a blank look.

"The first three, maybe. But the last five were your brother's names." I said. He shrugged.

"I like Matthew. It sound nice. Or what about Ethan." I said. Levi thought over it.

"Either of those, as long as he has my middle name." Levi proposed. I thought it over.

Matthew Bradley? Ethan Bradley? They both sound pretty nice. "I really like Matthew, babe. Good job." I said and fist bumped him. I caressed my stomach. "Hello, there, Matthew Bradley Anderson." I said to my growing stomach. The baby made little movements after hearing my voice. I smiled at Levi.

After we ate, the ride home wasn't too bad. Levi was singing every song on the radio though. I laughed my butt off. "Why are you laughing?" Levi asked.

"I'm laughing because it's entertaining watching you sing. There's always time for a good laugh and you make me laugh daily." I told him. He smiled and shook his head.

"Nah, you do. Especially when you get up late at night and waddle to the bathroom." Levi said with a snort. I looked at him. "You find that funny?" I asked with a serious face. He nodded.

"Hilarious." He said. I shook my head. "And all this time, I thought you were asleep!" I said with a laugh. "Nah, I hear you when you get up so I listen closely to make sure nothing don't happen to you." He told me. I awed obnoxiously loud. Levi grimaced. "Lay off, momma whale." He said and I laughed.

"What happened to momma bear?" I asked as he pulled into the driveway. "You're still momma bear but what I just heard was nowhere near it. Come on, let's go inside." He said and switched the truck off.

-

"Levi." I called as I walked into the room from the bathroom. He sat up from the bed and looked at me. "Can I have a kiss please?" I asked with a baby face. He looked at me weird then chuckled. "You want a kiss?" He asked. I nodded and climbed onto the stool into the bed. I scooted closer and sat next to him. He leaned in and before his lips touched mine, he pulled out the actual candy. "Here's a kiss." He said with a smirk and tap my nose.

"Not what I meant, but you know I love chocolate." I said and opened the wrapper. "I know, so do I." He said and crashed his lips onto mine.

"Gosh I love you." I said and popped the candy into my mouth.

"I know." Levi said and pulled me closer.

Chapter 28

"Woah man, your child is a kicker!" I said as I got ready. Levi peeped his head into the bathroom. "He's active, like his dad." He said with a smirk. "Yeah, but this dude has got some serious kicks on him." I said as I finished applying lip balm. Levi shrugged. "I don't know what to say then." He told me.

"Maybe he's practicing to be a kicker for a football team one day. Or a soccer player- ooh most definitely a soccer player." I said as I felt another kick at the end. "No way, babe. We create baseball players. Those were his swings." Levi said as he guided me down the stairs. I find that funny because he and his brothers are talented at many sports, baseball being their best sport.

"If that's what you think." I said with a smile.

"That's what I know." He told me and gave me a kiss. I grabbed his truck keys and headed towards the door. "You still gonna get my car serviced today right?" I asked. He nodded. "Yep, and I'm gonna drop by for lunch. Be careful in my truck today, ok babe?" He said.

I rolled my eyes. "Ok, Levi." I said and opened the door. "I'm serious!" He yelled after me. I blew him a kiss and started the truck. He watched as I backed out of the driveway and headed off to work. Levi could be so protective sometimes.

-"Y'all re doing great today. Keep up the hard work and you'll be back on the field in no time." I said and dismissed the players for lunch. I made my way to the break room to rest my feet. I slowly lifted my feet into the chair across from me and took a deep death. I pulled out a fruit salad and started to eat. "It looks like a ballon was inflated in your stomach." A familiar voice said. I looked up from my phone and saw Mike. "Hello, Michael, why are you here?" I asked.

"What? Matthew can't see his favorite uncle?" He asked and leaned down to hug me. I started to say that Matthew wasn't born yet and couldn't see you but I heard another voice.

"No, that would be me. I'm his favorite uncle." Jake said as he walked into the room. He hugged me too.

"Nah, that's us. Well mostly me." I heard a familiar voice say. I looked and I saw Hunter, Steven, Daniel, Luke, and Grayson. I looked confused. They all gave me a hug. "Hey sis." Grayson said.

"Hey baby Anderson." I said with the confused look still etched on my face. "What are all y'all doing here?" I asked. They all started talking at once. "One at time please." I said with a hand held up.

"The family reunion." Grayson said. I looked at him confused.

"You don't know?" Jake asked. I shook my head. "I'm sure Levi told you at one point and time." Luke said. I shook my head again, becoming annoyed at the fact that Levi wasn't here right now. "Where is my husband?" I asked them, trying to get up. Hunter sat me back down. "Woah, no need to get up. We'll go get him." He said.

"Find your little brother please." I said. He nodded.

I pulled out my phone and started to play a game. "Luke, can you do me a favor please?" I asked with puppy dog eyes. He sighed. "What is it?" He asked.

"Can you please take my shoes off? My feet are killing me." I said. He nodded and bent down to take off the dreaded shoes. Thirty minutes later and still no Levi. "Ok, my break is up in five minutes, and it takes my two to get out of this chair. So, just follow me to the practice field where I'm set up and just wait with me there." I said.

They all followed once I was able to get up. The guys only didn't help because they were having too much fun watching me struggle to get up. When I walked back into the area, everyone looked at me weird. I would look at me weird too. Who shows up to work with seven guys? Five of them being my brother in laws and the other two my friends. The only one that was missing was my husband, wherever he was. I rolled my eyes at the thought and started back with my players.

After another two hour workout, I was finished. I'm not even sure how I finished up because the guys were making noise the whole time so I sent them out to an end zone with a football. I grabbed my backpack and Levi's keys. The guys and I made our way to the parking lot. I saw my car pull up and Levi hopped out quickly. I rolled my eyes and walked past him to his truck. "Looks like somebody's mad!" Grayson shouted after me. I chuckled.

"I'm not mad, just confused!" I shouted back then climbed into Levi's truck the best way my pregnant self could.

I drove home with Levi close behind. While driving, Levi passed me. I blew the horn at him while he sped past. "How are you gonna not show up for lunch, not tell me about a family reunion, and on top of that, speed past me on the way home?!" I yelled at my retreating vehicle.

Once I pulled into the driveway, I parked Levi's truck and switched it off. I hurried walked into the house. Levi was standing in the living room. He was about to say something but I stopped him. "Ok first, give me a hug. I haven't seen you all day. Second, a kiss." I told him and got both of those. "Third, what is this about a family reunion?" I asked. "Ok, so there's a family reunion at home for our families and since I have time off and you do too we should go." He explained. I nodded but looked confused.

"We talked about this a week ago, which I can see you forgot about." He said with crossed arms making his muscles flex. "We did?" I asked.

"Yes. In our room. We were eating pineapples and I told you about the family reunion. You said,'Oh sure! It'll be fun!' Then we decided to go. Our flight is in two hours." He said. I nodded slowly.

"Ok, I got that. Now tell me why your brothers and best friends are here." I said.

"I honestly do not know." He said. We turned to the guys who were on our couches watching tv. "Guys? Why are you here?" Levi asked them.

"I was told to make sure that each of my brothers make it home. You were the last stop. I flew to New York for Hunter, Atlanta for Steven, Florida for Daniel, and Arizona for Luke. Jake met us here along with Mike." Grayson explained.

"And who's idea was this?" Levi asked.

"Momma's. She wanted all her babies home, here words not mine." Grayson said. I was just sitting there processing the whole thing. "And are you sure I agreed to this thing?" I asked Levi. He nodded. "And don't think you're getting out it either, Chelsea. Your momma wants you home too." Grayson said.

"Man, I gotta start remembering stuff." I said.

"Tell me about it." Levi muttered.

-

"Come on, we're gonna be late if we don't leave now." Levi said.

"Matthew, tell your daddy not to rush me." I muttered as I picked up my backpack. I heard Levi chuckle. He guided me out the door to his truck. We pulled up at the airport a couple of minutes later. Once we were settled down on the plane, I got sleepy and decided to take a nap. I placed my head on Levi's shoulder and went to sleep. That didn't work for long because Matthew started to kick. I tapped Levi's shoulder.

"Can you please talk to Matthew? He's very playful at the moment and I'm trying to catch a nap." I said. He nodded and rubbed my stomach. "Hey, bud." I heard Levi say before I drifted off to sleep.

-"Wake up, baby." I heard Levi's voice. I slowly sat up and stretched. Soon, the plane landed and I was fully awake. When we were able to get off the plane, I rushed to the bathroom. "Kinda of rude Matt, don't you think?" I asked. Lately, I've made it a habit to talk to my son so he could get used to my voice. Levi and I think it's a good idea so we go along with it. To others I may seem crazy talking to my growing stomach.

"Levi, your child stepped on my bladder and I just had to go before I peed on myself." I said into the phone.

"Ok, well hurry up. The truck is out here and I put our stuff in already. I'll be waiting."

After hanging up and washing my hands, I found my way to the gate where Levi was waiting. He grabbed my hand and led me to the truck. I looked out over the scenery as we traveled home. "We're gonna stay at your parent's house so you can have some peace and quiet at night, ok?" Levi told me. I nodded and said ok. "You must've set that up?" I asked. He nodded.

"Yeah, I wanted us to have some peace and quietness which we both know we wont have at my parent's house. My brothers are staying there along with Jake and Mike so I'm sure there will be no type of relaxation of any kind." He said. I chuckled. "How is it that grown men can still act like kids?" I asked.

"I guess you can say that I'm the only grown up one?" Levi asked with a smile. I shook my head. "You have your ways but other than that, you are all grown up. You have a wife and a child on the way." I said with a smile.

"Well, when you put it like that." Levi said with a smirk and placed a hand on his chin. I shook my head and laughed. Levi was the only one out of his brothers married and to have a child. His brothers have girlfriends but I'm not sure if the guys are ready to settle down. Hunter is the oldest and he's thirty two. I believe that he and his girlfriend in New York are ready to settled down. The same goes for Luke, Daniel, and Steven.

Grayson was only twenty three and I still call him baby Anderson, so I'm not sure if he's still hanging on to that bachelor card or not. Once we pulled into Levi's parent's yard, the truck was surrounded with family members. Levi came around to help me out of the big truck. He ducked his head in before he helped me out. He ran a hand through his hair and smiled at me. "You ready?" He asked, referring to all the family members waiting for us. I shook my head.

He chuckled and gave me a kiss that lingered on my lips a little. I wrapped my arms around his neck and pulled him closer. "Can't I just stay?" I asked into his neck. He chuckled. "No ma'am, we gotta get out. C'mon." He said and helped me out. Levi closed the door and grabbed my hand.

We walked into the house to say hey to everyone. I found myself sitting in a chair with my feet propped up, eating barbecue. "Awe, my baby's having a baby!" I heard someone say. I looked up from the rib I was about to bite and saw my momma. "Hey, momma!" I said with a huge smile. We hugged and she sat beside me to talk. I saw Levi's mom and dad along with mine. Also his grandparents and mine too.

Everyone gushed at the fact that I was pregnant. The thing that bothered me the most was that people always wanted to rub on my stomach. Why? What is so entertaining about rubbing on a pregnant woman's stomach? I found it irritating and weird. I was sitting in the house under the air with some of the other ladies here. Today was the first day of the reunion and it was barbecue day if you couldn't tell. Tomorrow, we were going to the water park.

On the third day, we were all gonna drive down to Biloxi to go to the beach. "Levi takes good care of you right?" His mom asked. Everyone leaned in to listen to my answer. "Yes, he does and barely lets me do anything." I told them. After more interrogations about Levi, he walked in. He smiled and said hello to everyone. Levi fixed himself a plate and sat beside me.

The ladies were engulfed into their own conversations. Some were watching us, intently may I add. "How you holding up?" He asked me. I shrugged. "I don't know what's more irritating. People rubbing on my stomach or nosey aunts and cousins trying to peek into our business." I told him. He chuckled. "People tried to touch your stomach?" He asked. I nodded my head frantically.

"Yes! They'd either openly try to or try to sneak in a touch or two. Like this." I said and demonstrated how they rubbed my stomach on him. I placed my hand on his abdomen and started to rub around like everyone did earlier. He made a face. "I'm gonna have to get you out of here." He said and grabbed his trash. He threw it away and came back to help me out of the chair.

"Chelsea ain't feeling well, so I'm gonna take her to the house so she can lie down." Levi told our families. They nodded and shooed us off. Once we made it to my parent's house I collapsed onto the bed. "You are the best." I said to Levi. He flopped down right beside me. "I know."

Chapter 29

"Ok let's try a new game." Levi suggested.

"What's wrong?" I asked with a smirk. It was currently one in the morning. Levi and I decided that we should play a game to pass the time.

"Oh nothing, I just don't wanna continue to be beaten at Madden Mobile by my wife." He said with a playful smirk. I laughed. Right now, I was beating his butt in Madden Mobile and he was being a sore loser about it. "I love you." I said with a cheeky smile. "So. You're still beating me." He said. I laughed because this man was sitting here pouting right now. I crawled over to him the best I could and wrapped my arms around him.

"Come on, do it back." I said and came closer. Eventually he caved and wrapped his arms around me. "What am I gonna do with you?" He said.

"You could hold me and we could get some sleep before we wake up everyone in the house?" I suggested. He laughed. "Good idea." He said and kissed my forehead. He turned the lights out and got under the covers. I snuggled up to his naked torso and closed my eyes.

-Knock, knock, knock"Levi, someone is knocking." I mumbled. The knocking continued. I looked up and Levi was sound asleep. I decided not to wake up him up. He needed his rest. My poor husband has been working his tail off for the next season. I got up and walked to the door. I opened it and saw my cousin standing there. "If you don't mind, Raleigh Phillips, my husband and I are trying to sleep." I said with a playful attitude. She squealed out of excitement but quickly quieted down.

I stepped outside of the room and closed the door so we wouldn't wake up Levi. She hugged me. "Oh my gosh, Chelsea look at you!" She gushed. I smiled at her. We talked for a long time and decided to continue our conversation later. I turned to go back into the room. I reached for the door handle and opened it. I ran into something or someone, rather. I looked up and Levi was looking down at me. He wrapped his arms around me and pulled me into the room, closing the door quickly.

He pinned me to the bed. "You know I like waking up with you in my arms." He said. I sighed and traced his muscular arms. "You needed your rest. Someone was knocking and I didn't want them to wake you." I said. He sighed and leaned down to kiss me. "Let's go eat breakfast." He said and helped me up. He grabbed a shirt and threw it on.

I made my way downstairs with Levi not too far behind. We sat down and ate breakfast with the family. After eating, everyone went to get ready for the water park. I went up stairs to do my hygiene routine. Levi went outside to help load up coolers for lunch. I got out a blue two piece maternity swimsuit. I found Levi's black swim trunks and laid them on the bed. I pulled the swimsuit on and put one of Levi's old shirts on over it along with some athletic shorts. I left my hair down and started to walk around to find my sandals.

The door opens and Levi walked in. He went into the bathroom to get ready. I walked in and gave him his swim trunks. He pulled down his basketball shorts and his boxers to put the trunks on. He smirked at me while he did. "Here, you little weirdo." I said and left the bathroom leaving him laughing. Levi came out shirtless. He reached into his suitcase and pulled out a Costa shirt. I guess he knew what I was looking for because he pointed to the dresser. I saw my sandals sitting in front of it in plain sight.

I slipped them on and grabbed a bag with some sunscreen and towels. We walked downstairs to meet everyone. "There they are. You guys take a long time to get ready." My mom said.

"Chelsea couldn't find her shoes." Levi said with a smile. I rolled my eyes and kept walking. Everyone chuckled and we all got ready to leave. We got into the truck and everyone followed each other to the water park. When we got there, Levi and I found a spot for me to sit. "I want you to sit here so I can keep an eye on you." He said while taking his shirt off. He sat in front of me so I could put sunscreen on him which wouldn't help. He'd still be tan anyway.

"What am I, a kid? Last time I checked, Mr. Levi, I am twenty four years old." I said.

"Yeah, twenty four years old and pregnant. I want you to stay out of the sun ok?" He said. I said nothing. "What was that?" Levi asked and looked at me.

"I said ok." I told him. It really didn't matter to me. I just wanted some relaxation. "Ok, Mr. Husband, you're all set." I said. He got up and so did I along with him. He spread his arms out and I sprayed the sunscreen on his chest and abs along with his arms. I rubbed it in, trying my best to ignore the intense stare from him.

"My turn." I said and took off the shirt and athletic shorts. Levi rubbed the sunscreen for me just like I did for him. Soon, he left to join his brothers at the slides. It wasn't long until they were all at the wade pool, talking. I settled down and pulled out a book to read. While reading I could see Levi sneaking glances at me from the corner of my eye. I looked up and Levi was already looking at me.

"I want to get in." I said.

"No." he said. I rolled my eyes.

"Don't make me have to come sit on you. It's too hot and I don't want you out there just yet." He said. I sighed and turned my head. He returned to his conversation. I waited for a good fifteen minutes and decided to try again. I made sure to look Levi in the eye as I got up too. I made my way into the pool and sat down. Levi came and stood over me. "I swear you are the most stubborn woman I know." He muttered.

"Right back at 'cha" I muttered. He sighed and sat with me pressed against his body. "I guess I'm gonna be staying here for a while huh?" He asked. I rolled my eyes.

"Levi, I wanna have fun just like everyone else." I complained.

"Yeah but I don't want you to get hurt." He said.

"Get hurt?! Levi, it's a water park." I said, becoming annoyed at this. He sighed. "I just want you to be safe at all times." He said.

"Have you been reading one of those protective pregnancy books?" I asked. He turned his head. "You have haven't you?" I asked. He slowly nodded.

"Baby, I will be fine. Now let's go have some fun." I said and got from under him. I grabbed his hand and led him further into the wade pool. I made sure he stood right under the big bucket that was filling up. It would top over in a couple of seconds. Splash! The bucket tipped over and splashed water all over Levi as I stepped out of the way.

I couldn't help but laugh. Levi looked over to me and narrowed his eyes. "You strategically placed me there, didn't you?" He asked. I nodded as I kept laughing. He burst into laughter along with me. The rest of the day was fun and relaxing. It was very needed.

-

I had fun at the water park. Everything went smoothly, not counting the part where I had to stay put because of Levi. Currently, we all were sitting at a big picnic table outside the water park. We were actually at a park beside the water park.

I watched as the little kids played on the set. The sun was slowing setting and everyone was sat back relaxing. I took in a deep breath and inhaled the strong scent of pine in the air. Soon, it was time for me and Levi to leave. He and I were going to go to our house here back home. We didn't stay there only because it was in a different town. I got up and said goodbye to everyone.

"Be safe!" Someone yelled out.

"We will, thank you." Levi was with a smile. We hugged our parents and left. As Levi started the truck, I messed around with the radio. "Must you always touch the radio when we go somewhere?" Levi asked. I shrugged my shoulders and smiled. "You don't mind." I said and continued to mess with the radio. He chuckled.

"Just keeping you happy." He said.

"A happy wife is a happy life!" I said in a fake man voice. Levi laughed. "What was that?" He asked.

"Isn't that what men say? You know, a happy wife equals a happy life?" I asked while he was still laughing. After he sobered up he cleared it up for me. "Something like that. But please don't use that voice again." He said and reached over to grab my hand. I let out a chuckle and sat back as he drove. When we finally reached our home I rushed into the house.

I loved our home down here. It was big enough to raise a family in and was very homey. It sat on many acres of land that Levi's grandpa owned. I rushed to the door only find that it's lock. "Dang it, its locked." I muttered. I had to urinate really bad.

"Wouldn't want people stealing things from our house now would we, Chelsea?" I heard Levi say with a chuckle. I ignored his sarcasm and started to bounce. He unlocked he door and I rushed in. I found my way to the bathroom on the first floor and used it. After finishing my business and washing my hands, I made my way to the living room.

I turned the big tv on and decided to watch something on Netflix. I texted Levi.

Wanna Netflix and chill;)

On my way!

I laughed at how fast he responded back to my message. In no time I heard the pounding of his footsteps down the stairs. He was in a pair of sweatpants with his shirt off. Levi hopped on couch and placed an arm around me. I leaned into his side and pressed play. As we watched the movie, I could feel Levi's wandering hand.

His hand inched closer to my boob. I watched as his hand scooted closer and closer to my left boob. Right when he was about to touch it I said something. "Levi there is a child here." I said in a scolding manner. He pulled his hand back, startled.

"What? Where?" He asked. I gave him a really look. I looked down to my stomach and back to him. "Matthew? He's asleep." He said.

"Actually, your son is very much awake. You didn't notice because of that wandering hand of yours." I said with a laugh. "Is he really awake?" Levi asked and placed a hand on my stomach. It seemed that at the perfect time, Matthew decided to kick. I saw a smile form on Levi's face. "Would you look at that. Huh, he is awake." He said with a laugh.

"Why you trying to grope my boob anyway?" I asked. He looked at me then to my chest.

"Just look at them. Their huge!" He told me. I looked down. They actually were huge and were hurting at the moment. "Their hurting." I said to myself more than him.

"Want me to, uh, mass-"

"No, I think I need a nap." I said and started to get up. Levi grabbed my wrist and pulled me back down. "You think a nap is gonna solve all your problems?" He asked. I shrugged. "I don't know about all of them. But I can start with this one." I said with a smile.

He pulled me closer. "I don't want you to get up. I want you to stay right here." He said and kissed my forehead. And I did. I stayed right there, falling into a peaceful sleep.

Chapter 30

It was currently twelve and Levi was still sleep. Tomorrow, we were leaving to go back to San Fransisco. I finished up the light lunch I was making and headed upstairs to wake Levi. He had never slept this long since high school.

He mostly woke up at eleven. I opened the door and saw him sleeping. I shook him softly to wake him up so he could eat something. "Wake up Levi. Come on, you've already missed breakfast this morning." I said as I shook him. He slowly got up but as he did, he coughed badly. I recoiled just a little bit but then reached over to give him a tissue for his nose.

"Thank you, Chelsea." He said. Levi's voice was all nasally and hoarse.

"Oh my gosh, Levi you're sick." I said and quickly sat beside him to find out more. He shook his head. "Just a mere cold. I'll be fine." He said and sniffled again. "No, it's more than that. Listen at that horrible cough." I said with a worried expression.

"Im gonna take you to the doctor." I said and grabbed my phone to make an appointment. "No, I'm good." Levi said as I dialed the number. I ignored him and continued to dial the number. He groaned as I talked on the phone with the doctor. "Get dressed, we are going to the doctor." I said and left the room.

I ate a little bit of the lunch that I fixed and went back upstairs to see if Levi was ready. I went up there and found Levi sitting in one of our chairs looking out the bay window. I placed my hand on his shoulder and he looked up. "Ready?" I asked with a smile. He nodded and kissed my hand. "You look pretty." He said and twirled me around to look at me. I smiled. "Thank you!" I said and started to tell about the dress I had on.

It was actually a pre-wedding gift from his aunt. It was a maternity dress that stopped right at my toes. It was a pretty teal color and had a sparkly silver belt that went with it. I pair it with sandals and left my hair down. He smiled as I told him about it. "But enough about the dress. Let's get you to the doctor. Dr. Martin said that you have the first appointment." I said and he groaned.

"I don't wanna go." He said.

"Levi, you are sniffling, coughing, and your eyes are puffy like you've been crying." I said and grabbed his hand. "Now I know you haven't been crying. Unless it's something you wanna tell me?" I asked. He shook his head and tugged at his shirt. Levi had on a pair of jeans, a t shirt, and his boots. Levi grabbed his Mississippi State hat as we left our room. I led him to my car and we got ready to leave. As we were riding, Levi let his seat back and paced an arm over his eyes. I hated to see him like this.

Levi didn't get sick much, but when he did it was the worse thing for him. It would take him about a week to get over it. Once we arrived to the doctor's office, I checked him in and we were called back right away. "Anderson." The lady called. Levi and I got up and followed her back into a room. Dr. Martin came in and shook both of our hands. "Long time no see, Chelsea and Levi." He said with a bright smile.

His eyes zeroed in on my stomach. "A very long time. Congrats on the wedding and baby." He said. "Thank you." Levi said and kissed my hand. I smiled. Dr. Martin was an older guy, around forty-five. He's been around for a couple of years now. "Ok, Mr. Big shot, Chelsea tells me that your sinuses are acting up again huh?" He asked Levi. Levi just nodded.

"Yeah, I have a runny nose and my eyes are swollen. I have no idea where the cough is coming from though." He said. Dr. Martin looked down at his clipboard and signed something. "I prescribed a packet of medicine for your sinuses and something for that cough." He said with a smile. We thanked him and left for the pharmacy.

The wait wasn't too bad at the pharmacy although we saw a couple of people from high school there. They saw us and we all just started a conversation. The funny thing was that most of them weren't married. Most of the girls were single and here I am pregnant and married. I wouldn't change a thing.

I am married to the love of my life and am giving birth to my first child in a couple of months. That is a blessing that I am thankful for. "Nice seeing y'all." Levi said to our classmates as we left. His voice was very deep and raspy, sort of like his morning voice. It was absolutely sexy.

That was one thing I like about Levi when he was sick. But when he's sick, he likes to cuddle. Like a big panda bear. I already know that when we get home, he's gonna want me to lay in the bed with him. I wouldn't mind though. I stopped by our mailbox and collected our mail when we got home. I drove up the long driveway and parked my car in the garage next to Levi's truck.

After getting Levi to take his medicine and to eat a little food, we chilled for the rest of the evening. "Whew! Taking care of you is hard work." I exclaimed as I got into bed. Levi chuckled. "It's the same for you, don't worry. The only thing about you is that you're mean when you're sick." He said with a small laugh. I smiled and crawled into his arms. "But you love me anyway." I said. He laughed. "Yes I do." He said and kissed my forehead.

-LeviMan I hate being sick. I knew something was wrong when I first woke up this morning. Chelsea made it easier though. I don't know what I would do without her.

Earlier today, we were in the pharmacy and ran into some old friends. They all went to high school with us and we're good friends. Something one of the guys told me stuck with me after we left today. He said,"One day, in gonna find something like what you and Chelsea have. It is truly beautiful how much y'all love each other."

I smiled at his words and thanked him for his kind thoughts. I told him that when he finds the one that he'll know. I looked down to a sleeping Chelsea. Her stomach was getting bigger by the day, making it harder for me to wrap my arms around her. But I do it anyway.

She postponed our flight for two days just so she could take care of me. I was just hoping for speedy recovery but then again, time off with my wife in Mississippi is great. I feel that lately she has been working herself too hard. She's hardheaded though or a fireball like some people say.

The guys at work miss her being around. I honestly do too. I felt that I was at my best whenever she around. Our new head trainer is Mike and he is a good trainer. It just feels weird without Chelsea there. I'm just hoping that the 49ers treat her right.

I sat up as Chelsea started to move around. She turned and opened her eyes. "Oh I didn't mean to wake you up." She said.

"You're fine. I was awake anyway." I said.

"I only woke up because our son decided it was playtime." She said, making me laugh. I have a feeling that Matthew would be a sporty kid when he grows up. "I love it when you say that." I said with a smile. She looked up at me. "What?" She asked.

"Our son." I repeated.

"Well yeah. Who else's would he be?" She joked. I laughed. "I don't know. I'm glad that he's ours." I said and kissed her forehead.

-ChelseaA week and some months later.

"I am about ready to explode." I said.

"You look fine." Levi said.

"I can barely see my toes."

"You still look gorgeous." He said.

"Why did you do this to me?" I asked him.

"It takes two to make that happen, babe." He said with a smirk.

"My toes look fat." I complained even more.

"Their adorable though." He said.

"You are having too much fun with this. Look at me, I look horrible." I said on the verge of tears. He rushed to my side from his side of the room and pulled me into a hug. "You look beautiful. I'm pretty sure Matthew will have your good looks and my charm." Levi said with a wink. I laughed and he leaned in to kiss me. "Atta girl, keep up your positive attitude." He said.

"Uh, I still don't know." I groaned. Levi sighed and wrapped his arms around me. "You look absolutely beautiful." He said and kissed my cheek. I rolled my eyes. "You say that all the time." I told him.

"Well, what do I say? That you look bad?" He asked with a slight smile. I laughed and shook my head. "I appreciate your help, baby." I told him and leaned up to kiss him.

I looked at myself in the mirror. It has been three months now. I am now eight months and my doctor says I'm due at anytime. It was now March of the next year and I was excited to have Matthew.

Christmas and New Years went along smoothly with no problems. For me at least. Levi and I traveled back to Mississippi for the new year and while down there he started to mess around with fireworks. I could remember it clearly.

Flashback I crossed my feet and turned the tv on. As I did this, I heard a string of curse words from outside. I got up semi quickly and waddled to the window. I saw Levi in the front yard bent over some fireworks. I shook my head.

I grabbed my phone and dialed his number. "Hello?"

"Levi what are you doing?" I asked.

"Nothing much." He said. I watched from he window as he tied the fuses together. "Nothing much, huh? Levi why are you messing with fireworks?" I asked. He stopped working and looked around.

"I'm not working on fireworks." He said. I sighed. "Levi look up at the house." I said. I waited as he looked up. I made sure to wave my hand at him so he could see me. That wouldn't be hard to do anyway. I was huge.

"How long have you been standing there?" He asked.

"Ever since the first curse word." I said with a smile. He laughed. "Go sit down, I don't want you on your feet." He said.

"Just as long as you be careful. I love you too much to lose you to fireworks." I told him. He sent up a flying kiss. I caught it and placed it on my heart. "Love you too. Now, let me get back to this." He said and hung up.

I watched as he continued. Soon, it was time to light them up. He had me come onto our front porch and watch. I tugged at his jacket as we waited. "Yeah?" He asked.

"Is it time yet?" I asked. He chuckled and shook his head. Five minutes later we found ourselves saying happy new year and making out. I pulled away. "Are you gonna stand here and kiss me all night or light those fireworks?" I asked. He nodded and pulled out a lighter.

I watched as the fuse got shorter and shorter. Then I noticed where it was leading. It got closer and closer to my favorite porch swing in the front yard. "Levi that's getting awfully close to the-"

Boom!!!I gasped as the fireworks took place. They were beautiful but I was focused on my swing. I looked at Levi who was already looking at me. "Just fix it." I said and walked into the house.

End of flashback

"Are you ready?" Levi asked. I nodded. He had a game today so I was gonna go with him. I didn't have to train today anyway. Or for a while at least. The season was over. I looked down at my attire. Black tights and a huge jersey with our last name and Levi's number on it.

"You look cute with that jersey on babe." Levi said as he came into the room again. He was wearing a pair of sweats and a t shirt. Levi was all excited because I was able to come to his game. I was too. I missed coming to the field. After he grabbed up his stuff we left for the game. When we got there we were swarmed by paparazzi as we entered. I kissed Levi and made my way to my seat.

As I waited for the game to start, the press box staff was playing music through the speakers. One song in particular caught my attention. It was Some Type of Love by Charlie Puth. It was a really good song and it kind of reminded me of Levi.

We've been through a lot and through it we've stuck together. I love him and he loves me. And I think that the song summed that up perfectly.

Chapter 31

"Ok let's get this game started!" The announcer said into the microphone. I clapped and cheered along with the crowd as the players were called. "And we have Mr. Levi Anderson!" The announcer said after announcing some of the other players. "Go Levi!" I yelled as he ran out.

"Here supporting Levi today is his brother, Jake and his wife, Chelsea!" The announcer said. I looked around.

I spotted Jake making his way to me. I smiled brightly at him. He pointed to the big screen. I looked and saw myself up there. I waved to the camera man and sent a flying kiss. After the players were announced, the game started so I got comfortable. Jake came and sat beside me. "What are you doing here?" I asked.

"Oh just here to support the brother." He said with a smirk. I chuckled and watched as the pitcher threw his first pitch. "No seriously." I said.

"Oh, I opened another riding club here in San Fransisco." He said. I nodded. "Congrats, this makes five locations right?" I asked. He nodded. "Sure does and now I have an excuse to come see my nephew very now and then." He said. I smiled. Jake was a nice caring friend of Levi's. I loved their little bromance. It was quite entertaining.

Levi won't admit it but he loves him. They are basically brothers. Levi was up to bat next and was standing in the small practice circle. I just happened to be sitting right there. I pulled out my phone and started to take pictures of him.

-LeviIt was my turn to bat next. I stepped into the small circle and took some swings. I watched the pitcher's pattern. "Curveball, high, low, and rise." I heard someone mutter. I looked to my left and saw Chelsea sitting with Jake. She was also watching the pitcher. She looked up and smiled at me. Chelsea smirked and started to talk to Jake. From the look in her eye, I could tell she was talking about me.

"I bet Levi.....right now." I heard. I could hear bits and pieces of what she was saying. I shook my head and tried not to focus on her right now. "Levi is so...." she continued. Finally it was my turn to bat.

With two on base and one out, I stepped into the box. The pitcher loaded and I watched as the ball came towards me. It was a curveball that I almost swung at. I saved my self from hitting though. He loaded again and sent the ball in. Just before I could move away, the ball hit me on my arm. It was a walk. I shook my head.

This wasn't the way I wanted to make it on base but hey, I can't help the screw up of the pitcher. My next teammate came up to bat. He hit a double which got me to third with a slide. Only one more good hit would get me home. The next guy that came up was good for hitting home runs. Hopefully, that's what would happen.

It wasn't quite a home run though. It was a triple and a good one at that. As I ran into home I looked over at Chelsea who was cheering for me. I smiled to myself as I walked back to the dugout.

I got ready for the next inning and grabbed my glove.

-Chelsea

Inning after inning I watched the game. By the ninth inning I was tired. Hopefully Levi would want to just get something to go instead of cooking.

I sipped on my Gatorade as I waited for Levi to come out of the locker room. Soon I spotted his tall figure making his way to me. I smiled as he got closer. "Hey babe." He said and leaned down to kiss me. "Hey, you did great out there." I said with a huge smile.

"Thank you, baby. You know, I could hear everything you were saying right?" He asked with a small laugh. I shrugged and held onto his hand. Once we made it to his truck, Jake was there waiting along with Shaley and Mike.

I smiled at them. "Hey guys." I said.

"Hey, chickadee. You're getting bigger by the day." Shaley said as she hugged me. Well, it wasn't much of hug because my stomach took up most of the space. "Yeah I know. My doctor says that Matthew could be due any day now." I told her with a smile.

"I can't wait until he gets here so I can spoil him. That is, when Levi doesn't have a hold on him." She said with a laugh. I looked over to Levi and saw him chatting with Mike and Jake. We all left to go and eat. Levi and I went home early because I had a doctor visit tomorrow.

When Levi came to bed he seemed a little extra happy. I looked up from a new drill I was writing and frowned. "You seem happy." I said with a smile.

"Thank you for your observations baby." He said. I chuckled. "Hey, it's uncommon. After a game you usually come home, take a shower, and fall asleep in your recliner. Then I'd have to wake you up but tonight it's different. How come?" I asked.

"Well let's see. We won the game tonight and in a couple of more days our first son will be here. Why not be happy?" He asked with a smile as he got into the bed. I smiled. "I'm excited too." I said. As I said that, Matthew started to kick. I placed a hand on my stomach and smiled. Levi looked over to me from his phone and smiled.

He kissed me. "I love you, you know that?" I asked. He chuckled. "Yeah, I know that. I'd love me too." He said with a smile. I laughed. "Conceited much?" I asked. He shook his head.

"I'm just kidding, I love you too, baby." He said and kissed my nose.

-"Well looks like Mr. Matthew will be here in a few days." Dr. Brown said. I smiled at her.

"We are excited." I said with the smile still on my face. She laughed and nodded. "I can tell. Your husband hasn't stopped smiling yet." She said. I looked over at Levi and he was for sure cheesing like a Cheshire Cat. I laughed. "We're just excited for our first son." I said. She chuckled and nodded.

After leaving the appointment, Levi rode with me to work. "I have to go to the restroom first. Then we can go and talk to coach together." I said as we walked in. He nodded and took a seat in a nearby chair. After doing my business and washing my hands I left the restroom. "Ready?" Levi asked. I nodded and grabbed his outstretched hand.

I smiled to some of my coworkers as we made our way to the coach's office. I knocked on the door. When we walked in he smiled at us. Levi and I took a seat in the chairs. "So today will start your maternity leave. I want you to stay healthy and get some rest. Thank you for all that you've done." He said once the meeting was over. I smiled and shook his hand.

-It was currently seven and Levi was getting ready to leave. He was getting ready for his workout. Since he was gonna be staying with me some of these days he was gonna miss workouts with the team. So, now he goes everyday. "Why you wanna leave me?" I asked with pouted lips. He came out of the closet dressed in a pair of basketball shorts, a t shirt, hat, and his tennis shoes.

"I'll be back in two hours, baby." He said. I rolled my eyes. "You act like that isn't a whole one hundred twenty minutes." I said and he laughed.

"I will be back baby. I promise." He said and kissed me. I rejected his kiss but he didn't like that. Levi kept peppering kisses on my lips over and over. "You are funny, babe. But count on it, I will be here in two hours tops. I promise." He said. I sighed. "Ok." I said sadly.

"Come on, any other time, you would want me to leave out of your sight quickly. Now you're pouting." He said.

"Hormones?" I asked. He chuckled.

"Let's just go with hormones. I'll see you later baby." He said and kissed me one more time before leaving. Once he left I got settled down on our bed and turned a movie on. Right during the middle of my movie I felt a sharp pain. It went away instantly so I ignored it.

It wasn't until ten minutes later that I felt another one. Then another one ten minutes after that. Ok, please don't tell me what I think it is. I sat up and pulled back the covers.

I walked downstairs to find some juice and to take some pain pills that were prescribed to me. After drinking a little of the juice I opened the pill bottle. The door jingled with keys inside it. Levi walked in and sat his keys on the counter. "Hey baby." He said. I smiled to him.

Right when I was about to take the pill something wet hit the floor. I looked down and there was a puddle by my feet. Levi looked down from the puddle up to me. I looked also. "Now you're a grown woman, and I don't think that's urine." Levi said. I started to roll my eyes but I gasped as another pain emerged.

Then it hit me.

I was in labor.

Chapter 32

On this twentieth day of March at seven thirty pm, I went into labor. It seems that Matthew is wanting to take his precious time. Levi took me to the hospital and although we both seemed pretty calm, I know that we both were freaking out majorly. I feel that all the preparing we went through probably just shot right down the drain.

After I was checked in and given a room everything seemed to slow down. Dr. Brown walked in with a smile on her face. "Good evening, Mrs. Anderson. Ready for your first childbirth?" She asked. I smiled and nodded.

She prepped me and checked for any dilation. "Well, looks like you are not dilated enough yet to push. So, if you and Mr. Anderson would like to walk around a bit then feel free to." She said with a smile. I looked over at Levi and he gave me a smile with a nod. "Thank you." I said. She made sure my IV was situated and that everything was stable enough for me to leave the bed.

Levi grabbed my hand and led me out the door. I held his hand with one of mine and pulled the IV along with the other. "You know, it's almost been a year since we've gotten married, right?" Levi asked. I looked up at him and smiled.

"Yes, in a two months actually." I said with a smile. I knew that he was trying to keep me calm as we walked. I went along with it. It's amazing that we're are about to welcome our son into the world and soon be married for a year. When we had been married for six months I found out that I was pregnant. The doctor said that I was one month. Turns out, I was two and a half months instead of one.

I was very excited. "Levi, Matthew is gonna look like you." I said with a smile.

"Probably. But it doesn't matter, he's gonna be great." He said with a smile.

-Three walks around the hospital later, I was in great pain. I was dilated far enough and was almost ready to push. "Mrs. Anderson is getting an epidural right?" My doctor asked.

"Of course." Levi answered.

Soon, I was ready to push. "Ok, Mrs. Anderson. When I count to three, I want you to give a big push." She said. I nodded and stayed repeating my breathing exercises. "One....two....three." She counted. I pushed.

"He's starting to crown!" She reported. I smiled. I looked over to Levi and he grabbed my hand. "One...two...three!" My doctor counted again.

"Aaahh!" I reacted as I pushed again. I squeezed Levi's hand tighter. "You're doing great baby." He encouraged with a since as I squeezed his hand tighter.

"One...two...three!" Dr. Brown counted once again.

"Mrs. Anderson this is the quietest any if my patients have been. They are usually yelling at the father." She complimented. I laughed. "Why blame him when I know that I helped get us get here? He didn't do most of the work." I said.

She laughed. "Smart lady." She said.

"Ok last time. One....two...three!" She said. I pushed as hard as I could. "Daddy, wanna do the honors and cut the cord?" She asked him. He eagerly got up and went to cut his cord. Then I heard it. The beautiful sound of my beautiful baby boy's cry.

"Welcome to the world, Matthew Bradley Anderson." Levi said. Our doctor gave him to the nurses to get him cleaned up. As my eyes got heavy, a smile made its way to my face. Levi kissed my forehead. We finally welcomed our son into the world.

-"Is she still asleep?" I heard someone say. I slowly opened my eyes. Levi was sitting in a chair beside my bed with Matthew in his arms. "She's awake now." He said to whoever was at the door. The door opened and my momma walked in. I smiled. "Oh my gosh, look at him!" She squealed.

"Here, mommy, want to hold our son?" Levi asked. I nodded with a smile. I reached my arms out and he placed him into my arms. I gushed at how handsome our baby boy was. "Oh my gosh, Levi. He has your mouth shape." I whispered. Matthew started to stir.

"Hey, Matthew. It's mommy!" I whispered excitedly. He finally opened his eyes. They were a nice hazel color like his father's. I smiled at him. Mike, Shaley, and Jake came by to visit us. They all gushed at him. I laughed because Mike was acting like a big baby. "He's just so adorable!" I remember Mike saying.

"He's beautiful." I said to Levi. He smiled at me. "Just like his momma. Baby, I am so glad that I have you to call my wife and the mother of my child. Thank you for all that you do, I love you." He said. I smiled and leaned in to kiss him.

"I couldn't do it without you." I said back. He just grinned. Matthew made a small noise. We looked down to him and smiled. Finally our son was here and as beautiful as ever.

-

"Momma, I did not expect you to be here." I said to my momma. She sat in a rocking chair, holding Matthew. "I know. I was coming to surprise you. But then your husband called and said you were in labor." She said with a smile. I returned the smile and placed a gentle kiss on Matthew's head. After letting my momma hold him,

Levi placed him back into his crib. I sighed. "Let's take a nap!" I said excitedly. Levi and my mom looked at me then started to laugh.

I shrugged. I was pretty tired. I looked over to the crib where my son was sleeping. Then I looked to Levi who was also looking. My phone buzzed over and over with notifications. It was Facebook. I opened my phone and saw that Levi tagged me in a post. There was a picture of me sleeping after giving birth and a long paragraph.

People were commenting well wishes and congratulations. I smiled and did my best to try and thank them all. I felt as if everything was complete now. I had my family.

-Six months later

"Waaahhh!" Matthew screamed. I rushed to make his bottle and gave it to him. Not too long after that, he was out like a light. Matthew is now six months and is growing everyday. He looks like his father more and more but he's a momma's boy. It was five which meant that Levi was due home at any minute.

I didn't have to work today so Matthew and I stayed home and I did some cleaning. Levi and I decided that Matthew wasn't old enough to go to daycare yet. So, when we both have to work, I take Matthew to work with me. It doesn't cause a problem because he sleeps most of the time and I don't move and around as much also. He sits in one of those baby carriers and just chills out.

Whenever one of us has to work and the other doesn't, whoever isn't working watches Matthew. For the past few weeks, Levi and I both had to work. On our anniversary, Matthew was well over two months. I was still on maternity leave and Levi had just a small break. We didn't do much, but Levi promised me that we'd get a chance to celebrate sooner or later.

It really didn't matter to me because I was with my little family. But, Levi being Levi, he pulled some strings and got my mom to fly out here. She watched the baby while we had a night out in the city. It was very nice and ended with gifts from both Levi and I.

The door opened and I heard Levi walk in. I rolled the up the cord to the vacuum cleaner and sat it in the closet. I made my way to Levi and kissed him. "Hey, baby. Where's Mathew?" He asked. I pointed upstairs. Just when we were about to head to the kitchen, the cries of Matthew could be heard through the baby monitor. Levi jogged upstairs and got him.

I could hear him through the baby monitor. "Hey, little man. Daddy's gotcha. It's ok." I heard Levi mutter to him. Slowly, Levi made his way downstairs with Matthew. I smiled at them. "My boys." I said and placed a kiss on Matthew's head and Levi's cheek. He smiled. I looked down to Matthew and saw that his eyes were focused on us. The most wonderful feeling in the world is when you see your baby's angel face staring back at yours.

My heart swelled with happiness as I o served Matthew just as he observed me. -Levi I watched as Chelsea watched over Matthew. For the past few months it has been hard. Being a new parent was a challenge but it was worth every minute. Chelsea made it look easy though. As Matthew grew, Chelsea brought him to one of my games. It was a little too chilly for home so they left at the end of the sixth inning. I wished that they could've stayed but for the time that they were there, I loved it.

I set Matthew in his rocker and turned it on slowly. "So," Chelsea started,"I was thinking that you make dinner tonight instead of me." She said with a smile. I looked at her weirdly. "Me? You want me to cook? Babe, I can barely watch spaghetti on the stove for you and you want me to cook?" I asked. She nodded with a small smile.

"You can do it. I'll help guide you through it." She said. I sighed then slowly nodded. She led me to the kitchen after setting up the baby monitor for Matthew. "Ok, I want you to make spaghetti." She said with a smile. I frowned. "You would ask me to make spaghetti when I told you I'm not even good at watching it food you." I complained. She gave off a small laugh.

"I'll guide you through it, I promise." She assured me. I sighed and nodded. Chelsea clapped her hands together. "Let's do this." She said. Oh boy, here we go. -ChelseaLevi's spaghetti wasn't that bad. Just a tad over cooked but other than that, it was delicious. I sat Matthew down in his crib and got ready for bed. His sleeping schedule still hasn't been sorted out yet. I give about another month before he fixes that messed up sleeping schedule of his. I crawled into bed and snuggled up to Levi. He placed an arm around me while he watched Sports Center.

He changed the channel and E! News popped up on the tv. There was a picture of him. "And a big congrats to baseball star, Levi Anderson. He is now father of one little handsome six month old boy. His name is Matthew and look at how adorable he is." The reporter gushed. I looked up to Levi and laughed.

"Here he is from a couple of weeks ago sitting at a game wrapped in his mother's arms. Look at how cute he is." They said. A picture of Matthew and I from the game popped up. He was looking very adorable and I was looking quite hot if you ask me. "Yes, they are adorable. Levi and his wife, Chelsea celebrated their wedding anniversary not too long ago." The reporter went on. A picture of Levi's tweet from that night popped up. It was weird because Levi and I were rarely on tv. Especially me.

"I'm just loving this couple right here. Best wishes to Levi, Chelsea, and little Matthew." They finished up. Levi switched the tv off. I looked at him and laughed. "So who leaked the pictures?" I asked.

"My manager. He wanted publicity and he also thought that Matthew was adorable. His words not mine." Levi said with a small laugh. I sighed and smiled. "Well I though that Matthew did look adorable. And that I looked pretty hot in that picture, don't you think?" I asked with a wink. Levi smirked. "Sure do. No one is as hot as my wife." He said. I smiled and kissed him.

"Alright, let's get some sleep before Matthew wakes-"

"Waahh!"

Chapter 33

Four months laterDiapers, diapers, diapers, and more diapers. "We are freaking knee deep and diapers. How can someone so little poop and urinate so much?" I asked frustratedly to no one as I changed Matthew. He just giggled and played with his little toy in his hand. I smiled down to my growing boy and smiled.

Mathew was learning new things everyday. I made sure he was learning right along with any kid who would be in daycare. I sit down and count numbers with him everyday. He's starting to say little words such as mama and da. He doesn't get the whole word out but when he sees Levi, da is the only thing we hear. He has a love for his dad.

Speaking of Levi, he walked right into the house from outside. He was changing the oil and checking the air conditioners in our vehicles. "Da!" Matthew shouted.

"Hey, Matthew!" Levi said as he washed his hands. He went pick him up but Matthew was faster. He was a fast crawler. We all were getting ready to travel to Mississippi so our families could see Matthew. I had to leave to go run a fitness test for the players this week. I grabbed my keys, kissed Matthew's cheek, and gave Levi a kiss. "I'll be back in about two or three hours." I said as I walked to the garage.

"Ok, we'll be here. Maybe we'll go to the park or something." He said. I nodded with a smile. "Da!" Matthew said again. Levi chuckled. "Looks like he wants to spend time with his dad, so bye mommy." He joked. It rolled my eyes.

"Sounds like a good idea. Love you, see you later and be careful today please." I said and gave more kisses. "Babe, we got this. Go to work. We'll see you when you come home. Love you." He said, kissed me, and shooed me out the door.

Whenever I did make it home I found Levi sleeping on the couch. Matthew was asleep on his chest. I took a picture of that daddy and son moment. I shook Levi awake slowly and picked up Matthew. He opened his eyes and rubbed them. "Hey, you're back." Levi said with a smile and yawn. I nodded.

"Yeah, it didn't take as long as I expected. So for dinner, how about we go out to eat?" I asked. He shrugged and nodded. I took Matthew to his room and laid him down. I went to our room and changed clothes. I put on a pair of skinny jeans and a pretty maroon top. Levi came out of the closet dressed in jeans, his old college baseball t shirt, boots, and his ball cap. I fixed up Matthew's baby bag and fixed bottles just in case.

Levi stepped into Matthew's room to grab him. All of us were matching. Levi's shirt had maroon in it and Matthew's shirt was white with maroon writing. We looked cute. Matthew's car seat was already in Levi's truck so we went in it.

"Table for two and a baby please." Levi said to the hostess. She nodded and looked for a table. While we were waiting I had a chance to observe Levi. Compared to him, I was short. I looked up at him. He held Matthew in one of arms, which made his muscles show a lot more. He looked down to me and winked. "I see you staring at me from the corner of my eye. You like what you see?" He asked. I smirked.

"Yes, I do. Matthew is so adorable." I said. Levi's smirk dropped and I laughed. I looked at Matthew. He was asleep on Levi's shoulder. One thing about Matthew was that he had chubby cheeks like Levi when he was younger. He has long curly hair and his eyelashes are super long. He was the splitting image of his father at his young age.

"Your table is ready." The hostess told us. We followed her to our seat and sat down for a good dinner.-"You got everything?" Levi asked.

"Yeah, I just have to make a quick bottle for Matthew real fast." I said as I finished up putting my clothes on. "Ok, how about I make the bottle and you get Matthew to the truck? It won't take long plus that way I can lock up the house." Levi said. I nodded and finished up.

Once Levi got into the truck, we started towards the airport. When we got there, we were right on time for luggage check and boarding. Matthew's eyes wandered around the airport as his daddy carried him through. He was fairly quiet during the trip other than when we landed. It was sort of bumpy and poor Matthew couldn't stand it. I had to hold him to calm him down.

Once we we were able to get off the plane and get settled into our vehicle, he calmed down.

"It's ok, momma's gotcha." I murmured to him while Levi put in the luggage. I was excited to get home because some of my family just happened to be visiting and Levi's brothers are home too. The news spread that Luke and Steven proposed to their girlfriends. It was cute by the way Jake explained it. He wouldn't be there this time because of a problem that came up with one of his clubs.

"Y'all ready?" Levi asked as he got in the truck. I nodded and sat back for the ride. We went to our house. Everything was already set up for Matthew in his room here so all we had to do was put new bottles in the cabinet. Today, everyone was coming to our house for dinner. The best part was that I didn't have to cook.

My aunts, mom, and grandma were making dishes along with Levi's aunts, mom, and grandmother. They were all coming to see us and to spoil Matthew. Our family didn't want us to travel much with Matthew even if he was ten months. When we got to our house I set Matthew down on the floor and let him crawl around.

As usual, he did his exploring. It was funny because he stopped in front of the full body mirror in the foyer and stared at his reflection. He started to babble towards his reflection. I took a quick picture and went to open the door for Levi. Levi came in with our luggage and sat it by the door. It wasn't much, considering the fact that we had a whole wardrobe here at this house.

"So what's for dinner?" Levi asked as he walked into our room with Matthew. "I don't know. I'm not cooking." I said with a smile. He frowned. "How am I gonna eat?" He asked.

"Our families are coming, remember?" I asked. He nodded. "Oh yeah, I forgot about that. Everyone is gonna get a chance to see Matthew today." He said. I nodded. "Yep, and Matthew is gonna meet everyone. He probably won't remember most of if." I said. Levi chuckled. "Have some faith in him, babe. Tell her Matthew." Levi said to our son. Matthew made a noise.

It only came out as da but I guess that was his way of saying something. I laughed and started towards the door. "Mama!" Matthew called.

I turned and he was trying to get out of Levi's hold. He let him down and Matthew made his way to me quickly. I picked him up and kissed his cheek. As I was walking down the stairs, the doorbell rang. I opened it and smiled. "Hey!" I said to my momma. She came in and hugged me as much as she could, considering the fact that Matthew was in my hands. "Oh my gosh, look at him! He's grown so much, the video camera and pictures don't do him justice!" My mom said.

She took Matthew from my hands and walked towards the living room. My dad walked in and gave me a big hug. He made his way to the living room to see Matthew. Levi made his way downstairs and greeted everyone. He and I went to get the food that my mom brought from my dad's truck. His parents soon pulled up too. They made a beeline for the house to find Matthew. I laughed.

"Our parents are gonna spoil our son." Levi told me. I nodded. "Yeah, just wait until the rest of the family gets here. It's gonna be even worse." I said. He laughed and nodded.

-Dinner with our families was good. This was the second time that dinner was held at our house and it was fun. We all ate, sat around, then ended up dancing around. Everyone enjoyed playing with Matthew and didn't want to let him go. But when it was time for him to go to sleep, they had to. Reluctantly, may I add.

"Is that everything?" Levi asked when he came in from outside. I nodded as I wiped down the kitchen counters. "Yeah. Mathew just went to sleep about fifteen minutes ago and I just finished up the kitchen." I told him. He nodded as he looked into the refrigerator.

"Where's my pie?" He asked while looking inside the fridge.

"What pie?" I asked.

"You know, the chocolate pie you made me earlier?" He asked. I shrugged. "I don't know, maybe it got thrown out." I said and walked away quickly. The truth was the I took the pie upstairs to our room to eat some of it. It forgot to put it back so he wouldn't notice. Levi must've noticed my behavior because he was hot on my heels.

When we got to the room he grabbed me and pinned me to the bed. "You think you're slick don't you?" He asked with a smile. I shrugged and smiled back. "Kind of." I said. He laughed. "I'll share the pie with you and we can watch a movie." He said. I smiled.

"Of course. Two of my favorite things, eating pie and watching movies with my husband." I said. He smiled and kissed me.

I turned a movie on and he ran downstairs to get another spoon. We got comfortable on the bed and snuggled up to watch the movie. "We used to do this all the time." Levi said.

"Snuggle? We do that every night." I said. He shook his head. "No, watch movies and eat pie." He said.

"Oh that. That was back when we were dating." I said. He chuckled and nodded. "Yeah but now we're married. We should do that all the time." He said. I nodded.

"Let's work it into the schedule, babe." I said.

"Yeah, let's do that." He said. I looked up at him.

"You're going to the batting cages tomorrow morning right?" I asked.

"Eh, now that I think about it, I just might go in the early afternoon." He said and stretched a little bit.

"I want to take Matthew. For some reason he finds it fascinating when you're doing something baseball related." I said.

"Hey now, you make it sound like a bad thing." He joked. I laughed. "I don't know. He's quieter and more attentive." I said.

"Well bring him. He should see his daddy play the sport that made his mom fall in love with me." He said and poked my side. I rolled my eyes.

"I fell in love at my own will. Baseball was just a bonus with you." I said. He laughed.

"Well then softball was one for you then." He said.

"What about now?" I asked.

"Well, let's see. You've matured and is more knowledgeable, which I find sexy. You are the mother of my child and many more to come. And lastly, because you're not afraid to be who you are. You are the best wife any man could ask for. I'm just glad you're mine." He told me and placed a kiss on my head.

I awed and kissed his cheek. "What about me?" He asked.

"Besides from being a great athlete, Levi you are just full of life. I love how you're not afraid to say what you want and do what you want even if it ends badly. You're a great dad and anyone could see that. I couldn't have been blessed with a better husband like you." I said. He awed and wiped away fake tears.

He pulled me close and kissed me hard. Levi tugged at my hair and wrapped his body up with mine. "Ugh, and so extra." I said which made him laugh. "I love you too, babe." He said.

Chapter 34

Swing after swing, ball after ball. "Levi, we have been here for two whole hours. How long are you gonna bat?" I asked him and looked as his shirtless figure took another swing. He looked over to me with a raised eyebrow. "Don't raise that eyebrow at me." I said with a pointed finger. He sighed and dropped the bat. He came out the cage and sat beside me. Matthew pulled at Levi's arm and crawled his way into his lap.

"See? Matthew even wants to know." I said and kissed Mathew's cheek.

"Ok, I'll take a break. And to answer your question, thirty more minutes." He said. Matthew shook the noisemaker in his hand and babbled on about something. Levi started to play with him. My phone rang so I got up to take it. I looked down and it was my boss.

"Hello?" I answered.

"Hey, Mrs. Anderson. I know you're not in the state currently but I had to call to thank you for all of your hard work. Our injured players are doing way better than when they started."

"Oh thank you! I'm glad their doing better." I said and looked over to Levi and Matthew. Levi was trying to get Matthew to hold his bat. I smiled.

"It's all because of you, thank you." He said.

"No, thank you. It isn't all me. They have a sense of motivation." I said. Levi gave up with the bat and gave him a ball. Matthew's first move was to put it in his mouth but Levi stopped him. Soon he threw.

"Well like is said before, thank you! I'll see you when you're back!" He said.

"Ok, bye now." I said and hung up. I walked back to the bench. "We have a pitcher on our hands, Chelsea." Levi said with smile. I chuckled.

"I see that." I said with a smile. Mathew reached for the ball again. Levi gave it to him and placed him on the ground. Matthew could stand on his feet soundly but he wasn't to the point of walking yet. Or so I thought. Levi tapped my shoulder lightly. I looked up from the game I was playing and quietly gasped.

Matthew tottered slowly towards the ball he threw. Quickly, I videoed it. He picked up the ball and walked his way back to us. I smiled and cheered. "Oh my gosh, Matthew! You're walking now, bud!" I said to him excitedly. He just giggled. Levi chuckled. "Come on, let's go celebrate this little milestone." He said and grabbed up his stuff.

I picked up Matthew and grabbed my things. We made our way to the truck and I buckled Matt in. "Where we headed?" I asked as Levi got in.

"To the ice cream shop." He answered. I nodded and pulled my seatbelt on. Once we pulled up to the ice cream shop, Matthew was sound asleep. When Levi got out I noticed that he was still without a shirt. The view was good, believe me, but I could see the women from inside ogling at him. When he opened my door I grabbed his arm. "Sir, you don't have a shirt on. Haven't you heard of no shirt no service?" I asked. He chuckled.

"I'm gonna put a shirt on, baby. I know how jealous you get." He said with a wink. I rolled my eyes.

"Yeah, jealous." I said. He laughed and kissed my forehead.

"Come on let's go get some ice cream." He said and picked up a sleeping Matthew. He held him in one arm and held my hand also. We walked in and got scoops of ice cream. While eating the ice cream, Matthew woke up. I sat him in a high chair and gave him a small bowl with a spoon. Some of his ice cream made it to his mouth but most of it found its way to his shirt. But mostly the bib I put on him.

I looked over to Levi and he was on his second bowl of double scoop ice cream. "How are you gonna go from working out to pigging out on sweets like that?" I asked with a laugh.

"You know how much I like this kind of stuff." He said with a smile. I couldn't help but smile back at him. His phone rang and he took it out to see who it was. "Gotta take this, I'll be right back." He said and got up. I nodded as I wiped Matthew's mouth. Levi placed a kiss on my lips before he stepped outside.

While he was gone a young teenager came to my table. "Hi, is this your baby?" She asked. I nodded with a smile. "Yes, his name is Matthew." I told her. She smiled.

"I saw him when you guys walked in. I just wanted to say that he is so adorable." She said and walked away. "Thank you!" I called after her. "No problem!" She answered. As she walked out of the ice cream shop, Levi came back in. He sat down and placed his phone in his pocket. We finished up our ice cream and headed home.

"We need to talk." Levi said and led me to his office after I laid Matthew down for a nap.

"Ok, what is it?" I asked as I sat down on his couch.

"My manager called and wanted to know how you felt about doing an interview with me." He said.

"An interview?" I asked. He nodded.

"ESPN wants to do a special on me and my family. They want you and my parents to be apart of it. Your parents would even have a little part in it." He explained. I nodded as I took in the information.

"So what do you think? Because I told James that I wouldn't say anything to him about until I knew your decision." He said. I thought for a moment.

"This is big news, Levi." I said. He nodded.

"Yeah, big news. There's even talk about airing it on tv." He said.

"This sounds like a great opportunity. I'm in." I said with a smile. He smiled and gave me a kiss. "Let me call James so we can settle the plans." He said. I sat in the couch the whole time while Levi talked to his manager, James. The whole idea of an interview sounded wonderful.

Lately, Levi had been getting a lot of buzz because of how well the season has been going. He's a great athlete and it shows through his work. I figured that this interview would be a great deal for him. After he got off the phone he called his parents and mine. They agreed to it and were excited for the whole thing.

The doorbell rang. I got up to see who it was. I looked through the peep hole and it was covered. I rolled my eyes. "Grayson, it is very rude to come to someone's house and cover the peep hole." I said as I opened the door.

He tackled me with a hug. I invited him in along with Luke, Steven, Daniel, and Hunter. They all hugged me. "Where's Levi?" Hunter asked. "In his office." I said as I sat down on the couch.

"Where's Matthew?" Grayson asked quite loudly. I shushed him. "He's asleep." I said.

"Waaahh!" I heard from the baby monitor.

"Well he was asleep. Thanks a lot, uncle Grayson." I said as I got up. He apologized and walked with me to Matt's room. Matthew was standing up on the side of his crib. He smiled when he saw us. Grayson picked him up, making Matthew giggle. I smiled at the two. Matthew had taken a liking to Grayson over the last few days.

It was kind of the same for Levi's other brothers but Grayson was Matthew's favorite for now. "Hey, Matthew! Your favorite uncle is here!" Grayson said to him as we walked back downstairs. As we settled down on the couch, Levi's office door opened.

Levi looked confused once he saw his brothers sitting in our living room. "Da!" Matthew shouted. Levi smiled to him.

"Hey, Matthew." He said to him.

"Uh, Chelsea? Wanna tell me why my brothers are here right now?" He asked me.

"What? You don't love us no more?" Daniel asked, feigning hurt.

"Well I never!" Grayson shouted in a high pitched female voice, making us all laugh.

"Nah, I'm just surprised that's all." Levi said and took a seat in his recliner.

"Did you forget what today was?" Luke asked. Levi shrugged. I raised an eyebrow.

"Um, just taking a wild guess here babe, but it looks like their going hunting." I said to Levi. He looked from me to his brothers. I probably didn't notice before but they were all dressed out in camouflage and had paint on their faces. The attire simply didn't stick out to me because they wore it every other day. Levi was the only one who didn't wear it religiously.

He nodded. "Oh yeah, I forgot about that, babe." He said. I shrugged.

"Let me go get dressed." He said and made his way upstairs. The guys made themselves comfortable like they always did and started to watch some tv. "Chelsea! Have you seen my overalls!" Levi yelled from upstairs. I rolled my eyes.

"Let me go upstairs before this man ruins our closet." I muttered, making the guys laugh. I walked upstairs and went into our room. I was a little late on the mess up call. Levi had clothes strewn around everywhere. "Levi, you've only been up here for five minutes and look at our room." I fussed. He came out of the closet shirtless with only boxers on.

"I can't seem to find my hunting gear." He said. I knew exactly where that stuff was but I was angry with him at the moment. Our room was a complete utter mess. "Go like that for all I care. I don't mind." I said and brushed past him into the closet.

"Of course you wouldn't. You love to see me partially clothed." He said and wrapped his arms around my waist. I pushed him off. "No sir. Don't try and flirt, look at this mess you made." I said to him.

I reached up and grabbed a container that said Levi's hunting gear across the side. I shoved the container into his arms and walked out of the closet. I sat crossed legged on our bed.

I watched his muscles flex as he put on his clothes. "I'll clean it up when we get back." He said. I shook my head. "No, you clean it now. If you wait, it'll never get cleaned up." I said with an eye roll.

"I love it when you're authoritative." He said with a wink. I rolled my eyes.

"Stop trying to flirt your way out of stuff, Levi. Just please, please clean up your mess and go." I said and laid back on the bed. Five minutes later I felt weight on top of my body. Levi's face was inches from mine. He propped himself up on his elbows and stared into my eyes. "I'm finished cleaning up. Now before I go, I want a kiss from my lovely wife." He said with a smile. I leaned up and kissed his cheek.

"There's your kiss, now get off so I can go back downstairs." I said and tried to push him off. He wouldn't budge and I gave up after trying twice. "A real kiss, Chelsea Jane." He said. I sighed and was about to say something when his lips crashed onto mine. Our lips moved in sync as Levi pressed his body to mine.

This kiss went on until I felt someone's friend poking my thigh. Levi hopped off me and fixed his appearance in the mirror. I walked over to him. "You're gonna leave looking like that?" I asked with a raised eyebrow.

"Never, but you will be penalized for your actions later. That was so unfair." He said and made his way to the bathroom. When he came out, I gave him one more kiss. "The room is clean, I have found my clothes, and you gave me a kiss. Anything else you want to torture me with?" Levi asked. I shrugged.

"No sir, you are free to go." I said and hugged him.

We made our way downstairs. Grayson handed Matthew to me and they got ready to go. "See you later, Matthew." Levi said to him and kissed his head.

"Ok babe, see you later." He said to me and kissed me.

"Bye, Levi. Be careful." I said and closed the door. I walked upstairs to grab a jacket for both me and Matthew. I placed him in his playpen while I got his bag together. He and I were gonna go to Levi's parents house to meet the new fiancé's of Luke and Steven. I packed diapers, an extra outfit, and bottles along with toys.

Matthew's car seat was in Levi's truck so that's what we took. The drive to Levi's parents house wasn't that long. On the way there, Matthew fell asleep. When we pulled up, Levi's mom rushed out of the house. She scooped up Matthew and took him inside after hugging me. I made my way into the house and sat down Matthew's bag by the couch. I heard voices from the kitchen and went there.

"There she is. Girls, this is Chelsea. She's married to my fifth son, Levi." Brenda said. I smiled to them and took a seat.

"So you were the first to marry into the family, how exciting." One of them said. They were both really pretty. "Yes, that's true. Congrats to you both on the engagements and good luck." I said with a laugh. They laughed and thanked me.

"Well, this is Grace, Luke's fiancé." Brenda told me. I smiled and shook her hand. She had pretty long brown hair and was gorgeously tanned. The other girl was of mixed race and had pretty curly hair. Her eyes were a mix of green and honey gold. Her name was Dana.

"Oh wow, the guys did a really good job. You girls are beautiful." I said to them.

"Thank you, but your beauty shines through though." Grace said. I smiled and thanked her.

"Don't be modest, you are beautiful and so young." Dana said. Both of them were in their late twenties. The more we talked, the more we got along and the more I felt that these girls were right for Luke and Steven.

Chapter 35

"Oh my gosh, he's so cute!" Dana gushed as she played with Matthew. I laughed as she and Grace took turns making silly faces at him. He woke up from his nap fifteen minutes ago. It was around five in the afternoon and I'd been here for an hour. During that hour I busted my parents, helped prepare for dinner, and talked with Dana and Grace. They were really nice and caring.

"Guess what we got!" I heard someone shout as they walked in the house. It came from the back door.

"Fresh meat! Fresh meat!" I heard a familiar voice shout.

"Must you be loud when you come into the house, Grayson?" Brenda scolded her youngest son. We all laughed.

"He's still a youngster momma, can't blame him." Hunter said and sat some bags on groceries on the counter.

"Hey, I'm twenty three." Grayson argued.

"Yeah, but you act like a three year old." Luke said as he walked in.

"Hey, darling." He said to Grace and kissed her. Steven came in and gave Dana a hug. It was sweet watching the couples be loving to each other. You could see the love in their eyes as they interacted. Joe walked in and hugged his wife.

I looked around for Levi but didn't see him. "Levi shot a buck and is outside cleaning him, Chelsea." Grayson told me. I nodded and went outside to see him. I made my way to the shed and opened the door. Levi looked up and smiled when he saw me. He had his shirt off and was cleaning the buck. "Congrats, you still have skills I see." I told him. He smiled.

"Yeah, I wish you could've seen it." He said. I nodded. "Yeah, it would've been a sight to see." I said.

"I heard you met the new fiancé's." He said.

"Yep and apparently, I'm a legend. I was the first to marry into the Anderson family." I said with a laugh. He chuckled. "Well it is true. How lucky you are!" He excitedly as he finished up. I rolled my eyes.

"Real lucky." I said sarcastically and left the shed. I heard water running then footsteps as they followed me. "Hey!" Levi shouted after me. He soon caught up and wrapped his arms around my waist. "I saw that eye roll. You know you love me." He whispered in my ear.

"I know I love you too. Nothing has changed here, Levi." I said with a smile. He chucked and placed a kiss on my lips. "Ew, you guys are supposed to be a married couple and you're acting like y'all are dating." Grayson shouted from the porch.

"Back off! I can love on my wife all I want!" Levi shouted at his little brother. "It's hurting my eyes! And put a shirt on!" Grayson shouted as Levi hugged me even more. Levi leaned in and kissed me even more. Grayson screamed and ran into the house, making me laugh. Sometimes he did act like a three old. Levi grabbed my hand and led me into the house. Dana and Grace were in the kitchen with Levi's mom helping prepare the food.

"Levi. Son, why don't you have a shirt on?" Brenda asked him. He chuckled. "I was cleaning the buck I shot and didn't want to mess up my shirt. Plus, Chelsea don't mind it so hey why not?" He said with a smirk. We all laughed. I handed Levi his shirt.

"Dana and Grace, this is my goofy husband Levi." I said to them as he slipped his shirt on. They looked up and smiled.

"Nice to meet y'all future sisters." Levi said and hugged them.

"Where's Matthew?" Levi asked me. I pointed to the living room. He pulled me along with him. Matthew was sitting on the floor, playing with Grayson. "Oh how cute, the kids are playing together babe." Levi said, making us all laugh.

"You may laugh now, brothers but this is why I'm the favorite uncle." Grayson said to his older brothers. Levi and I took a seat on the love seat. I crossed my legs and he placed a hand on my thigh. He rubbed circles with the pad of his thumb.

"Come on, let's take a walk." Levi said and pulled me up. "But we just sat down." I whined. He rolled his eyes. I got up slowly and made my way to the door. "Chelsea and I are going for a walk. Could y'all watch Matthew for us?" Levi asked his brothers. "Sure, no need to ask." Hunter said.

"Fifty dollars an hour and a extra ten dollars if he poops." Grayson said as he stood in front of Levi. I laughed. Levi just turned around and started towards the door, shaking his head at his little brother. He grabbed my hand as we walked.

"Remember when we used to meet at our mailboxes when we were younger?" Levi asked.

I nodded. "Yeah, that was when I actually enjoyed playing with you." I said. He laughed. "Those were the good times. Still the good times now." He said and wrapped an arm around me. I nodded. "I'm glad I married you." I said to him honestly.

"This is the first time in hearing this in a while. Why is that?" He asked.

"Well, lets see. You make my life interesting. And let's face it, if I weren't married to you I'd probably be single living with five dogs." I said. He laughed. "I'm glad I have you, babe." He said.

"But in all seriousness, I'm glad I have you. I know that I can be difficult sometimes. You are a trooper for handling such a woman like me." I said. He nodded. "I am so grateful that God sent me you. We've been married for a year and already have one son. Plus you've been dealing with me since we were kids. There's no one else in the world that can take your place." He said. I smiled.

We walked for a couple of more minutes. "So." Levi started.

"So." I repeated.

"More children?" He asked.

"There's a possibility." I said with a smile.

"You know I have a lot of love to give right?" He asked me.

"You remind me, daily." I said.

"Let's get started on them." He suggested with wiggling eyebrows. I laughed. "That's in speculation." I said.

"No that's in the near future." He said with a smirk. I laughed and pushed him away. "You horn dog!" I shouted with laughter. He laughed along with me. "I warned you earlier at home. Don't think I forgot." He said with a smile. I nodded. "I know you didn't forget." I said.

"Good, because you wanna know why?" He whispered in my ear.

"You have a lot of love to give." I whispered back.

"You got that right." He said and kissed me.

-"Alright let's eat!" Joe shouted as we walked back into the house.

"Y'all were gone a long time." Luke said with a raised eyebrow.

"Yeah, two hours to be exact." Grayson said with an outstretched hand. Levi slapped his hand. "I'm not asking for a high five. Where's my money, big brother and big brother's wife?" Grayson asked.

"With those prices, it is possible that in the future, you won't be asked to babysit our children." I said to him. He shrugged. "It's worth a try. I'll still be the favorite uncle." He said with smile. I laughed.

"Hm, I don't know. Daniel may take that title away from you." I said and pointed to the couch. Daniel was sitting on the couch making Matthew giggle uncontrollably. "Yo! Danny boy! Back off, son!" Grayson shouted as he made his way to them. We laughed as he did.

After dinner everyone was out in the backyard sitting around the fire pit. Matthew was asleep so Levi and I were outside too. Whenever I did come outside Levi pulled me down into his lap. He started to whisper sweet nothings in my ear. It got ridiculous though because the sweet stuff turned into idiotic stuff.

"Why is the sky blue?"

"Your skin is so soft."

"Let's get a trampoline."

"You are so beautiful."

"You know, I'm glad you're tall." He whispered. I turned to him. "Why?" I asked.

"Because if you were short, how could I kiss you all the time? My neck would have a killer crook, no offense to the short women out there." He said with a smile. I laughed.

"Ok that was random and sweet." I said. He winked. "Let me demonstrate my point." He said and got us up. Levi led me into the backyard and started to dance with me. Quickly he placed a kiss on my cheek, forehead, and finally my lips. "You're so silly." I said with a laugh. "But you love it." He said and kissed me once more.

As you can see, the comments changed from idiotic to sweet. Grace and Dana were inside looking at our wedding pictures for inspiration. "Come on." I said and pulled Levi with me. He placed a hand on my waist as we walked inside. Grace and Dana were so into the book that we startled them when we sat down.

"You guys had a beautiful wedding." Grace said.

"Thank you." I told her. Her and Dana were looking at a picture of Levi acting silly.

"Hey, I remember that picture. That was the part when I had to crawl under your dress and get the thingy off your leg." Levi said with a smirk and sipped his beer. I laughed. "Yeah. You were a little too into that." I said, making Grace and Dana laugh.

"Your face was priceless." He said with a wink. I chuckled laid my head on his shoulder. "When are you guys leaving?" Dana asked.

"We leave tomorrow, right Levi?" I asked. He nodded. "I have a game in a week and the practices are starting up again." He said.

"Oh yeah, Luke did say that you play professional baseball." Grace said. Levi nodded with a smile.

"Yeah, San Francisco awaits. But we'll be back before the year is over." He told them. We all talked and talked as the evening stretched on.

Soon, Levi, Matthew, and I were back home getting ready for bed. Levi kept his promise and gave a whole lot of love that night. The next morning, we were all ready to go.

Chapter 36

"Hello, Chelsea how are you?" The reporter asked. I smiled.

"I'm fine, Sarah thanks for asking." I said.

"That's good. I'm gonna ask you a few questions involving both you and Levi so feel free to answer as many as you would like." She said. I nodded and got ready for the question.

"So when did you first meet Levi?" She asked.

"We met when my mom and I attended their housewarming party. Their parents just had a house built across the street from our house over the summer. After meeting, we sort of just stuck together." I explained.

"How long have you know him exactly?"

"Well, when we met, I was eleven and he was twelve. I've known my best friend for ten plus years." I told her.

"Your best friend of how many years?" She asked.

"Fourteen, almost fifteen to be exact." I answered with a smile.

"Wow, that's a long time. So the chemistry just sort of fell into place?" The interviewer asked.

"You can say that. It came naturally. I mean, being around the same person for over ten years something was bound to happen." I told her.

"So high school life. How was it and how was Levi as a person?" She asked.

"High school was just high school. Of course with Levi being an athlete, he had to stay ahead of the game. He was a complex character. It's not that he didn't like school, he would just rather be somewhere else. There were many times when I had to stop him from trying to leave early. We did homework together and helped each other with each of our sports. Levi always had a go getter attitude. Whether it was in the classroom or on the field." I said.

"And you played softball, correct?"

"Yes, I did. From high school into college." I answered.

"When it did come time for graduation, was your choice easy?"

"It wasn't easy and it wasn't hard. It was either go here or there. With Levi having a full ride scholarship to the school of his choice and me having the same thing, it was a personal choice. You know, whether I should follow him or go on my own path. Eventually I did go on my own path." I told her.

"Did this choice affect your relationship with him?"

"It did. We went years without talking and just being friendly. Keeping in mind that we weren't together also. There were jealous girlfriends and other situations. We didn't become close until a few years later. After college I became an athletic trainer and started working for a company. I was transferred to the San Francisco Giants, where Levi and I reconnected." I explained.

"And you're currently the athletic trainer for the 49ers in San Fransisco, correct? How's that working out?" She asked.

"Yes, I am their trainer. It is working out just fine. It's a little different not seeing Levi constantly day after day though." I said with a small laugh. She chuckled.

"I understand that you two tied the knot recently." She said. I nodded and flashed my ring.

"Yes, we got married a year ago."

"And you now have a son, correct?" She asked.

"Yes, Matthew. He turned one two months ago." I told her.

"And very adorable. Does it get difficult whenever Levi is gone for away games and such?"

"Sometimes it does. I have to remember that he's only a phone call away. It gets pretty tough especially with us being new parents and all. I kind of wish that he could stay behind but I know that his job calls for him to be there." I said.

"Now that you've come to witness one of his many triumphs, what do you think of Levi as a person now?" She asked.

"He's amazing and continues to amaze me everyday. When you've known someone over ten years and you've gotten a chance to watch them grow physically and mentally it pulls at your heart strings. Levi has grown into an intelligent man and is an amazing athlete. I feel that there is still more room to grow. You're never finished learning." I finished.

"Alright then, thank you so much for your time." She said.

"Well thank you for having me, Sarah." I said with a smile.

I got up and walked back to the little dressing room they had for Levi and I. I was dressed in a form fitting black dress with a semi-plunging neckline and black heels. My hair was curled to perfection and my make up was done nicely. I walked into the room and took my shoes off. Levi was sitting on the couch eating a sandwich.

"There you are, I've been looking for you." He said and took another bite.

"I just finished my interview." I told him.

"I finished up fifteen minutes ago." He said and bit another piece of the sandwich. I looked over to the other couch and saw Matthew sound asleep. He was matching with Levi and I for pictures later. "So you said some nice things about me, right?" He asked. I smiled.

"Nope." I said and popped the 'P'.

"But come on, it's my birthday." He said. I laughed. "I know. You're twenty six now and old." I said as I rested my head on his shoulder.

"I wouldn't talk if I was you, little miss thang. Your birthday is close." He said and poked my side.

"I was just kidding. You're young and good looking." I told him. He smiled and kiss my forehead. I turned the tv on and saw my parents on the screen. They were currently doing their interview.

"Wait, don't tell me you saw my interview." I said and sat up. He nodded.

"Yeah but not all of it. I loved the way you described our life." He said and kissed my forehead. I smiled and leaned into his chest. Matthew started to stir and slowly opened his eyes. He sat up and crawled his way off the couch.

He waddled his way to us and climbed into his daddy's lap.

"It was one part of your interview I liked. I'm your best friend, huh?" He asked with a smirk. I rolled my eyes.

"No."

"Awe come on, just admit it. You're my best friend too, babe." He said.

"Better not tell Jake that." I joked. He laughed.

"He should know by now that my woman is number one." He said. I smiled and gave him a kiss. It was meant to be a quick peck but he extended it. That left lipstick on his lips. "Oh how cute, you got lipstick on your lips." I said and laughed.

"Oh how cute, I smudged yours." He said with a wink and laughed back. I got up and fixed my lipstick. While I was wiping off the lipstick off Levi's lips, someone knocked on the door. I opened it and Levi's manager was standing there. "Hey, James!" I said with a smile.

"Hey there." He said with a warm smile. "Looking good as always, Chelsea." He continued with a smile.

"Watch it." Levi said and got up. James chuckled.

"Chill out, Levi, I'm just here to tell you that it's time for the pictures." He said and left. I checked my makeup once again. Levi grabbed Matthew and my hand. He led us to the photoshoot down the hall. "There's that gorgeous family!" The photographer exclaimed. I smiled at her. She had us sit down and try out different poses.

The shoot didn't take long, but after it I knew that I was ready to get out of those shoes. As we were walking back to the dressing room to change and gather our stuff I hopped out of the shoes. "That's a new record, babe. You usually take them off way earlier than that." Levi said with a laugh. I rolled my eyes and started to change.

I changed into a pair of skinny jeans, a cute blouse, and flats. I changed Matthew's clothes and Levi changed into some athletic wear. When I turned around to look at him he was wearing gym shorts, a t shirt, and his Columbia hat backwards. In addition to his apparel was his glasses. They made him look very attractive.

"Whew! I haven't seen those things since middle school." I said, referring to the glasses.

"Oh hush, you saw them last night. You love these glasses." He said. I nodded and kissed his cheek.

After picking up lunch, we headed home. I had to help Levi pack for his away game. The team had a game in New York. "Come on, baby, you gotta help me pack." Levi said and started to shake me. I was currently laying face down on the bed throwing a fit. "I don't want you to leave!" I shouted into the pillow.

Levi sat beside me on the bed and started to rub my back. "I'll be back before you know it." He whispered in my ear. "Yeah ok, but who am I gonna cuddle with at night?" I asked as I sat up. "I'm sure Matthew wouldn't mind extra kisses from his mom." He said and pulled me into his chest.

"No, he thinks he's a big boy now. Watch." I told him and called Matthew into our room. Matt shuffled into our room with his toy truck. "Give momma a kiss." I said and opened my arms. He shook his head with a smile, looking like his dad. "Big boy! No kiss momma!" He said. It was muffled but that was the gist of what he said. Levi laughed.

"That's not funny. He's looks and acts a lot like you." I said to him. Matthew ran back to his room. He just chuckled and kissed my forehead. "So you're not gonna help me pack?" He asked. I glared at him.

"Too soon?" He asked.

-"Smile for me!"

"I will smile when I see you in person." I said. Levi and I were currently face timing on my computer. He was in his hotel room.

"Stop being a big baby."

"I'm not a big baby. I just miss you a lot."

"Try not to think about it as much. Close your eyes and lay back." He said. I sighed and did as he said.

"Now, imagine me there. Kissing you and hugging you. Remember I got a lot of love to give. I'll be home in a day." He said. As he said this a smile came to my face. A beep noise sounded from my computer. I opened my eyes and Levi was gone. "This guy just hung up on me." I muttered. I heard shuffling on the stairs.

"Who's there?" I called. There wasn't an answer but the noise got louder. I ran to the closet quickly and grabbed a bat. I stood in front of the door ready for the intruder. Gladly Matthew was with Mike and Shaley. The bedroom door opened and Levi walked in. I'm glad I saw it was him because I almost hit him. "Whoa, babe it's just me." He said.

"What are you doing here?!" I asked. He smiled and opened his arms. I jumped into his arms. "We got back today. I've been downstairs in the guest bedroom the whole time. Funnily enough, it resembles a hotel room." He said. I laughed. Levi placed a kiss on my lips. "Gosh I've missed you." I said.

"I missed you too. Any news for me?" He asked. I smiled. "There actually is." I said.

"Ok, well tell me." He said with a smile. I bit my lip and slowly smiled.

"So how do you feel about welcoming baby Anderson number two into the world pretty soon? Oh, and the producer sent us a copy of the interview also." I said. His face was a face of complete shock. I smiled. "You mean, you're pregnant?!" He asked excitedly. "Was that all you heard?" I joked. Levi picked me up and twirled me around.

"So, how do you feel?" I asked. He set me down and looked me in the eyes. "Absolutely wonderful. I love you so much." He said.

-••• Nine months and beautiful baby girl later •••

"Anna-Jane Anderson, what a beautiful baby girl." I said to her as she slept. Levi named her and gave her my middle name just like Matthew had his. My middle name was just a hyphen of her first name. I smiled down to my sleeping girl. Levi was in the arm chair with Matthew who was sound asleep. He smiled at me and AJ.

-I walked into our home and sat my keys down on the counter. The players did a good fitness test today, it went fairly quick. I walked upstairs and kissed Matthew's head. He was playing with his toys. Levi and AJ were in our room taking a nap. I went downstairs to start dinner.

Soon, Levi woke up but Anna was still asleep. Later on that night after dinner Levi and I, along with our two kids, watched a Disney movie. I placed a kiss on Matthew and Anna's head. I loved our little family very much. "You make me, undeniably happy." Levi whispered right before he fell asleep.

Chapter 37

Waking up with little people around me has become ordinary. Kids grow fast. Matthew is already three and Anna-Jane is getting ready to turn two. The pair were a challenge to handle. With two kids, it feels like I'm forty years old but in reality I'm only twenty eight. Levi and the kids were currently out getting ice cream while I stayed home to clean and get the house ready for our families.

My parents, Levi's parents, his brothers, and both of our aunts and uncles were coming to visit today. They all were in San Fransisco to visit this week. We decided to have a big dinner at our house. I'm not sure how everyone was gonna fit but we'd make it work. I have to put it on my mental to do list to talk to Levi about moving into a bigger house.

The door opened and Levi walked in with our two sleeping children. "They played themselves to sleep, babe." He said with a chuckle. I smiled and kissed their heads. Levi started to head upstairs to lay Matthew down. I took Anna-Jane and walked upstairs to put her in the room she and Matthew shared. They weren't old enough to have separate rooms yet. Plus, the house only consisted of three bedrooms, one of which is a guest room.

When I came back downstairs, Levi was getting himself a beer out of the fridge. "You know, our house is starting to feel small." I said as I took out ingredients to start a salad. This was my contribution to the dinner tonight. "Yeah, I was thinking the same thing. That's why I bookmarked a couple of homes last night. I showed you." He said. I frowned. "You did?" I asked.

He nodded. "Yeah, it was around one in the morning and AJ had just went to sleep. I showed you and you'd said that the houses look great." He explained. I frowned. "I don't remember." I said. He shrugged.

"Maybe you were just too tired to fully pay attention. But that's alright because I'm gonna show you again anyway." He said. I nodded and continued to chop the veggies. I was glad that we were considering a new house. There was a feeling deep down inside that said that we weren't threw producing children. And for that very reason, we needed more space.

Somehow we both knew that Anna-Jane would not be our last child. After I finished up the salad, Levi and I sat down in his office to figure out the housing options. There were many wonderful choices. The house that we lived in now was made for a small family with just one child or two. But with two kids, the house still seemed cramped. So, we need the space. At our home in Mississippi, there was room for six to seven kids and two guests.

That was Levi's idea. When the house was first built, Levi insisted that the house be spacious for a big family. At first I didn't believe him but now I'm starting to now. There would only be a matter of time before baby number three came scrolling into our lives. An hour later, the doorbell rang and our home was filled with noisy relatives in each corner of the main floor.

Everyone seemed to be enjoying themselves very much. Matthew and Anna-Jane were running around with their cousins who were the children of Steven and Dana. Grace and Luke were settled on the couch. Grace fed their twins. Grayson's daughter, Bella, was sitting with Anna-Jane on the floor.

Grayson had a daughter with his beautiful girlfriend of many years, Sadie. She was black and was very gorgeous. Sadie went to the same college as Grayson and had been putting up with the man child for some time now even if he was a lawyer. In a few weeks, they would make it to one of their official years of being together although they've messed around for more than that. The chemistry was there. Little to her knowledge, Grayson was gonna propose to her tonight.

Daniel and Hunter sat with their wives as their kids ran around with Matthew. I smiled as I looked at my family. "Chelsea, AJ is starting to look more like you everyday." Raleigh told me. I smiled and thanked her.

"Yeah but she's a little diva like her dad." I said and she laughed. "No, I think she gets that from her uncle Grayson." Levi said and pointed towards the girls. Grayson was playing with Bella and AJ. Anna-Jane watched as her uncle made silly faces. Bella just giggled at her dad.

Soon, everyone was gone and it was quiet time around the Anderson residence. "Houses, houses, houses." Levi said as he walked into the living room. I groaned. "Can we not think about houses right now?" I asked. He sighed and put his laptop down on the other couch. "Ok, what you wanna talk about?" He asked as he sat beside me.

"Let's talk about how fast our kids are growing up." I said with a fake emotional tear. He chuckled and pulled me in close. "Yeah, they're growing fast." He said. We watched as Matt and AJ sat on the floor watching a cartoon movie.

"Anna-Jane reminds me of Grayson and I when we were kids. He and I would always watch movies together, just us two." Levi said. I smiled. "That's probably why he's always finding his way to visit us and to talk to you." I said. He chuckled. "That's probably true." Levi said.

AJ yawned and got up from the floor. She crawled into her daddy's lap and started to shut her eyes. "Ugh, such a daddy's girl." I said. Levi chuckled.

"But nothing compared to that momma's boy right there." He said and pointed as Matthew jumped his way into my lap. "Sleepy." He mumbled. I let out a small laugh. Soon both the kids were asleep. Levi and I made our way back downstairs to watch a movie. "I've been thinking." Levi started. I looked at him.

"About?" I asked.

"Well I know we've been talking about houses a lot lately." He said.

"Yeah?" I said, motioning for him to continue.

"But I wanna stray away from that for a minute. You ready?" He asked.

"Lay it on me." I said sat up to listen.

"I bought a warehouse recently and-"

"You what?!" I asked.

"I bought a warehouse recently and I've been thinking about turning it into something. I want an opinion on it from my lovely wife." He said.

I frowned. "Why am I just now hearing about this?" I asked. He shrugged. "You've been busy with work and the charity softball games lately." He said. I sighed and nodded.

"You're right but if you want my opinion, I think you should turn it into a sports academy." I said. He frowned. "Sports academy?" He asked. I nodded. "You know, like Mr. Simon's place when we were younger." I reminded. He nodded with a smile. "That sounds great." He said.

Mr. Simon was a man who owned a sports academy in the neighboring town. He had workers who helped younger kids, teenagers, and adults with their various sports. Softball and baseball was their main specialty but there were other experts for other sports like football and soccer. "We could name it the Anderson Sports Academy." Levi said. I nodded.

"Sounds good. Now you gotta get with people to get it going." I told him. He nodded. "Yeah I will. But I have one condition about the whole thing." He said.

"What is it?" I asked.

"You are going to run it." He said. I was shocked. I mean it was his idea. "Are you sure?" I asked.

"Yes, positive. I don't know anyone better that can do this." He told me. I smiled and hugged him. "You're the best." I said.

"I know." Levi said. I rolled my eyes. -Levi walked out of the bathroom and straight to the closet to get dressed. "I wish you didn't have an all day practice." I said as I got ready.

"I know. I was looking forward to watching you pull a muscle." He said with a smirk. I narrowed my eyes at him. "You think I've lost my touch in softball?" I asked. He shrugged. "You said it not me." He said with a smile. I threw a pillow at him, which he dodged.

I was getting ready to go to a charity softball game with the other wives of the baseball team. We would play two games that day just like a tournament. I walked over to Levi and tucked the tag in from his shirt. "That's been happening a lot lately." He said with a chuckle.

I nodded with a smile. "Yeah, you're just so uncoordinated." I said. He gave me a playful glare. After finishing up getting ready, Levi helped me get the kids up and ready to go. They were gonna be with me all day during the games.

"Bye daddy!" The kids shouted as Levi headed for the door.

"Bye kids, be good for mommy!" He said and stopped to give me a kiss.

"Behave today, ok?" He whispered before kissing my forehead. I grabbed his arm and pulled him closer. "I'll try." I said to him. He chuckled and kissed me once again.

"Who's ready for some softball games?" I asked Matt and AJ. They screamed and started to do their happy dances. I laughed and got them into the car.

-"Way to go!" I yelled as my team members ran into the dugout. Our team was currently winning.

After finishing up shaking hands with the other team I looked to the fence. To my surprise, I saw Levi standing looking handsome. If anyone would've saw him, they would think that he was a mean person because of the facial expression he wore but that wasn't the case. I'm guessing Matthew and Anna-Jane saw him because soon he held them both in his arms. I walked to the fence and tapped his shoulder. He looked down at me and smiled.

"Hey babe." He said.

"Hey. I thought you had an all day practice?" I asked. He smiled. "I lied." He told me with a wink. "Oh well, you're here now. Gimmie kiss." I said with a smile. He grinned and placed one on me. After joining him and the kids on the other side of the fence, we walked to the concession stand to grab some snacks.

We sat down in the stands and gave Matt and AJ their food. "So I got the paperwork settled for the warehouse." Levi said. I smiled. "Really? That's great, babe." I told him. He nodded, the smile still present on his face.

"And I've also checked on our house situation." He said. I nodded. "I found a house that would be great for our growing family. It's big enough for us and six kids. Two of which would have to share." He explained. I nodded, taking in the information.

"I hope you know that I plan on expanding our little family more." He whispered in my ear. I smiled. "Oh I already know." I told him and kissed his cheek.

"Because-"

"Yeah, yeah, you have a lot of love to give. Blah, blah, blah." I said with a smile.

"You are something else." He said with a laugh and pulled me closer.

Epilogue

"This is it." I said. This house was simply beautiful and it was big enough for our accommodations. Levi wrapped his arms around my waist. "You sure this is the one?" He asked. I nodded. "Yeah, I love it. The neighborhood is nice, it has a nice backyard for the kids to play in, and the school system seems fair." I told him.

"Look at you, sounding like a mom." He said with a laugh. I shrugged. "Didn't I give birth to two kids?" I asked. He nodded with laugh and kissed my cheek. "Come on, let's go get the realtor." He said and grabbed my hand.

-"Why did I decided to come and help?" Grayson asked to basically no one. I laughed and patted his back. I walked to the kitchen where Sadie was. We were setting up the kitchen, getting it ready for dinner later. "Sadie, your fiancé is being a big baby again." I told her. She just shook her head.

"That's always." She said with a smile. Grayson peeped his head around the corner. "You weren't saying that last night when I-"

"Grayson!" Levi yelled from the living room.

"Saved by the big brother." Sadie muttered. I laughed and patted her back. We soon finished the kitchen and started with Matt and AJ's room. When we finished their room we got dinner ready.

"Thanks for flying out here Sadie and Grayson." I said. They shrugged it off and said that it was no big deal. The kids were gonna stay with Mike and Shaley tonight while we finished up the house. Everything was set up and in place, waiting for them to come home in the morning.

"It was no big deal. Besides, Bella was ready to see her grandparents." Sadie said. I smiled at that. Their daughter was just a total sweetheart. She was very mature for her young age compared to her father. He's still as playful as ever, even as a lawyer. "Yeah, plus this is like a vacation for us. We won't get many considering the fact that we are trying to plan a wedding." Grayson explained. I nodded.

"My brother is finally getting married." Levi said and faked a tear. Sadie chuckled.

"Baby Anderson is moving on up in the world." I said, making Sadie laugh. Grayson playfully glared at me. "Yes, we are getting married. I don't need constant reminders from the two of you." He said. Soon, Sadie and Grayson got ready to leave. After they left Levi and I crashed into the bed. After all, it had been a long day.

-"Mommy!" AJ and Matthew screamed as they ran into the house. Anna-Jane stopped to hug my legs before she ran off to play. "Where daddy?" Matthew asked.

"Daddy went to his practice. He's coming back." I explained to him. He nodded and headed to explore his new room. I took AJ's hand and led her to the living room. We took a seat on the couch and decided to watch a little tv. The door slammed and Levi walked in. "Daddy!" AJ shouted.

"Hey baby girl." He said and kissed her forehead. Matt ran downstairs and hugged his dad's legs. I just patiently waited my turn until our kids finished loving on their dad. I laughed when the two toddlers were able to knock him down. After they finished hugging him they ran off to go and play. I let a small laugh and walked to where he was laying on the ground. I held out my hand.

"Need some help?" I asked. He smiled and grabbed my hand.

"Thanks." He said and pulled me down to him. I laughed as he did. He moved some hair out of my face and just stared at me. "What?" I asked.

"I forgot what I was gonna say but I love you." He said with a laugh. I laughed too. "I love you too, Levi." I said.

-•Six years, two more kids, and one on the way later•

"Matthew!" I yelled from the car window.

"Yeah mom?!" He answered.

"Your fly is unzipped." I whisper shouted. His face turned red with embarrassment. My nine year old rushed to the truck with a look of total look of frustration. "Yes, Matthew?" I asked. He looked up at me and gave me a really look like his father always did. I let out a little chuckle. Once Mathew got the zipper up, he left.

"Bye honey, love you." I said.

"Bye mom, love you too." He said and walked towards his team.

"I'm getting old." I muttered as I drove off. I went to pick up AJ from her friend's house. After picking her up, we went to the academy. The sports academy finally became a reality and became my full time job. No more training professional athletes for me. I'm training the future ones, which brings me so much joy.

"Is daddy at the academy?" AJ asked.

"Not at the moment. He's at his own practice then he's gonna pick up Trevor and Colten." I told her. She just nodded. I felt kicks from my growing baby inside me. I was seven months and was ready to welcome our fourth son into the world. It seemed that little Kade was ready too. He is a very active child.

I pulled up to the academy and got out. I opened AJ's door and she hopped out too. She ran straight inside and to my office. When I finally got there, she had gotten herself a snack from the mini fridge. I put more juices in the fridge seeing that Levi would be here with the boys in thirty minutes.

I opened up my computer and checked on my appointments and classes today. "Hey mommy!" Trevor said as he pushed the door open.

Trevor jumped onto the couch and sat next to his sister. "Where is your brother, Trev?" I asked.

"With daddy." He said. I nodded. Trevor was the next child after Anna-Jane. He wasn't as active as his other brothers but was very smart for his age. At age six, he read everyday and enjoyed it. But with his siblings, you'd have to tie them down to make them read. The door opened again and Levi walked in with Colten. "Had a little goldfish accident today." Levi said with smile as he took a seat beside me.

"Hey, big boy!" I said to Colten.

"Momma!" He called.

In my office there was a big mat where the kids usually played at. They all took a seat down there and waited as I handed out a snack to each of them. To anyone who didn't know us, they'd think that four would be a hassle. It really isn't. I owe that all to Levi. He's a great help with our kids and they love him very much.

Many years ago, if you would've told me that Levi would be my husband and that we'd have four kids along with another one on the way, I would've laughed in your face. But that's not the case now.

Now, I have a wonderful and beautiful family. I walked to the fridge and grabbed some water.

"Did you forget all about me?" Levi whispered in my ear as I opened my bottle of water. A slow crept its way onto my face. He rubbed circles on my stomach and kissed my neck. "Never." I told him and turned around.

"Oh my lord look at them." I said and pointed to the kids. Anna-Jane and Trevor were wrestling at the moment. "Our girl is one tough cookie, huh?" Levi asked with a smirk. I laughed and nodded. When we looked back at them they seemed to have gotten over the issue they had and started to play together again.

I looked at the clock and it was around time for Matthew to arrive. His friend's mom was gonna drop him off. I was right because the door opened and he walked in. "Hey mom and dad." He said and joined his siblings in the floor.

"Look at them." Levi said as he hugged me from behind. I smiled snd sighed. "Our wonderful children. Most of the time wonderful." I said, muttering the last part.

"Thank you." Levi said. I looked up at him.

"For what?" I asked.

"For sticking by my side for all these years. For becoming my wife, the mother of my kids, my best friend, and many other things. Just thank you. I love you, Chelsea Jane." He said. I smiled back at him. "I love you too, Levi." I said.